upon an *April* night

KRISTA NOORMAN

BOOKS by KRISTA NOORMAN

The Truth About Drew
Goodbye, Magnolia
Hello, Forever
Until Then
18 Hours To Us
Another June with You
Bittersweet
Not the Billionaire
Lawfully Secure
Upon an April Night

Copyright ©2020 Krista Noorman

All rights reserved. No portion of this book may be reproduced, stored in a retrieval system, or transmitted in any form or by any means – electronic, mechanical, photocopy, recording, scanning, or other – except for brief quotations in critical reviews or articles, without the prior written permission of the author.

This novel is a work of fiction. Names, characters, places, and incidents are either products of the author's imagination or used fictitiously. All characters are fictional, and any similarity to people living or dead is purely coincidental.

Scriptures taken from the Holy Bible, New International Version®, NIV®. Copyright © 1973, 1978, 1984, 2011 by Biblica, Inc.™ Used by permission of Zondervan. All rights reserved worldwide. www.zondervan.com. The "NIV" and "New International Version" are trademarks registered in the United States Patent and Trademark Office by Biblica, Inc.™

Cover photo ©Freepic.diller/Freepik

ISBN: 9781657752252

*Create in me a pure heart, O God,
and renew a steadfast spirit within me.*

Psalm 51:10 NIV

Chapter 1

April 2011

Torture. That's what this was. For the past hour, Duncan McGregor had been frozen in place on Jamie's couch, pretending to watch a movie as he tried not to think about the fact that her smooth, bare legs rested across his lap.

His gaze kept landing on a triptych of images displayed on her living room wall, all close-ups of flowers. The one focused on overlapping petals of a pink rose caught his eye the most. But staring at photographs or the television did nothing to distract him from the beautiful girl at his side.

He could still recall the day four years ago when Jamie Linde had walked into their home with his sister, Shannon. The girls had met at a gathering of Grand Rapids wedding photographers and had become fast friends. Duncan had never been so instantly attracted to someone before. She was the cutest thing he'd ever seen with her short, cropped brown hair, streaked with magenta highlights, and an even shorter skirt. She was fun and spunky, the kind of girl who was sweet on the outside but wouldn't bat an eyelash at a dirty joke and had probably told her fair share of them. Jamie certainly was unexpected, and it was the first time in years he'd been so drawn to a girl, which made being around her tricky.

Because a year before they met, he'd made some big changes in his life and his relationship with God. He'd been headed down the wrong path after high school, especially when it came to getting physical with girls.

It was Nana who told him, "Duncan, you are better than this, and God's got better for you. You know what's right, so do it."

This was days after he'd been caught by his father with a girl in his bedroom, doing things he shouldn't have been doing. It wasn't the first time his bad behavior had gotten him into trouble, but it *was* the first time his grandmother had told him in her honest, straightforward way to quit screwing around and be a better man.

Jesus took hold of his heart after that. His eyes were opened to the error of his ways, and he repented, becoming fully devoted to God. He saw girls differently, treated them with the respect they deserved, and stayed out of the bedroom. He was on the lookout for the one God had for him—a good Christian girl that his parents and grandparents would approve of.

And that was definitely not Jamie.

But they were friends. They hung out occasionally, mostly with Shannon, and they flirted. Often. But he knew his attraction to her could easily undo his resolve, so he never went there with her. He never crossed any lines.

Tonight, however, he was having a hard time keeping his hands to himself, because he was dying to know if her legs were as soft as the rose petals in that photograph on her wall.

He rubbed a hand over the back of his neck, gripping his auburn hair in frustration.

"That looks fun," Jamie suddenly said, pulling him out of his thoughts.

He turned his attention back to *27 Dresses* just as the main characters started kissing.

When he looked over at her, her tongue darted out to wet her lips as she stared at the screen.

"We should do that," she said.

His brain short-circuited for a second. *Did she really just say that?*

She turned her eyes on him. "I dare you to kiss me like that."

He swallowed hard, his heart racing in his chest. He'd never wanted anything more in his life. "Quit joking around," he managed.

"What makes you think I'm joking?" Her lips curved up a little, and the look in her eyes let him know she was serious.

His hand moved to her leg then, his thumb caressing the velvety skin of her calf. Softer than a rose petal. He knew it. He shouldn't have touched her, but it was too late. He had started something, and the wall he'd built between his present and his past was threatening to fall.

She pulled her legs from atop his, and in one swift motion, she was on his lap, one knee on either side of him. Her arms slid around his neck, and she leaned closer until their lips were a breath apart.

His fingers clenched into fists, wanting to touch her, but fighting it with everything he had. He remained still, and she seemed to sense it, leaning back to look at him.

Their gazes locked, and he saw confusion in her warm brown eyes.

Jamie chewed on her bottom lip, and her cheeks colored to a pretty shade of pink as she looked away. "I'm such an idiot. I so misread this situation." She began to move from his lap, but a longing deep within to keep her close had his hands sliding around her back, locking her body snugly against his.

Her lips parted as her eyes met his.

He swallowed hard, just as surprised as she was.

And then he did it. He touched his lips to hers. The kiss was soft and tentative at first before turning slow and passionate, like he'd imagined it would be with her. Her lips were heaven as she returned his kisses with just the right amount of pressure. And it was good. So good. Maybe the best kiss of his life.

But they hadn't stopped there. Breaths quickened, hands traveled, and the kiss deepened, giving way to crazy longing and lust, which had completely clouded his brain. And when she unwound herself from his arms and stood, holding her hand out, he took it and followed her to the bedroom.

Chapter 2

Two weeks later

Getting to know Denver was like a new adventure every day as Duncan became acquainted with the beauty of the location, local businesses and eateries, and the people who called this city their home. His freelance design job at Masalis Sporting Goods was going well so far. He always found it easier to create branding for a company when he was among the products and people, which was why he often traveled rather than working from his home in Michigan.

As he sat at the desk they had given him to work from and stared at his computer screen, his mind wandered back to that morning at Jamie's apartment. Even thinking about it now, his heart rate increased, remembering what he'd experienced with her.

They hadn't really talked much afterward. She told him about upcoming weddings she was photographing. He told her about this trip. She asked if he would call her when he got there. He simply nodded, kissed her forehead, and held her until they fell asleep.

She had looked so peaceful in the dim morning light of her bedroom, lying there on her side, her arm draped across his stomach. Her shoulder-length chestnut hair was spread out across her pillow, the magenta highlights standing out against the crisp white pillowcase.

His attempt to slowly slide out from under her arm had only made her snuggle up to him, and it took all of his willpower to continue maneuvering out of her bed and away from the warmth of her.

When he was dressed, he paused beside the bed, glancing down at the beautiful woman lying before him. His stomach was tied up in knots as guilt overcame him. She wasn't his wife, and he'd made a decision years before that he would not have sex again until he was married. In his reckless youth, he'd been careless with girls' feelings. But he was a grown man now, and he hadn't meant to be careless with Jamie. He knew she cared about him, and he cared about her. But there wasn't a future there. There couldn't be.

Jamie wasn't the kind of girl you marry. She was a free spirit, a party girl, not serious enough for him. She was not a religious person, and he would not be in a relationship with someone who didn't believe the way he did.

He was finding it impossible to focus on the graphics on his screen as he thought back to the moment he gave in and kissed her. Just after his lips had touched hers for the first time—soft and sweet and oh-so-intoxicating—a small voice in his head had told him to stop, but he'd turned a deaf ear to it. He had ignored what he knew was right for temporary pleasure.

He raked his fingers through his hair and groaned aloud.

"Hey, Duncan." A voice jerked him back to reality. "Everything going okay?"

He turned to face the owner of the company, Kyle Masalis. "It's coming along." He nodded toward his computer screen.

Kyle rested his fingertips against his beard-covered chin as he observed Duncan's designs and gave a nod. "Looking good."

"I'll have new logo concepts ready for you to look at soon."

"That's great, but I actually stopped by to ask if you'd like to join my family for church on Sunday."

Duncan perked up. "Really? That would be great."

"I'll text you the time and place."

"Sounds perfect."

Kyle patted him on the back before walking away. He turned back suddenly. "Oh, and you're invited to lunch at our place too."

"Thank you."

Kyle nodded and wandered away.

Duncan smiled to himself. God had brought him to this place at the perfect time. He needed to be away from Michigan right now, away from Jamie, to reset and work on his relationship with God. And what better place than at church. He'd been wanting to find one to attend while he was in Denver and had thought about venturing out last week, but he'd skipped it in favor of a morning hike instead.

He wished he could say that hike had been spiritual and transformational, but his mind had mostly been on Jamie. She had texted him a few times, asking how Denver was, but he hadn't replied. It was a jerk move, but he didn't want to lead her on. He fully expected to get chewed out by Shannon when he got home. He was sure Jamie had told her everything by now. Just another reason to stay in Denver as long as possible.

On Sunday, Duncan drove to a quaint Bible church on the outskirts of Denver and met up with Kyle and his lovely wife, Melissa, and their six-year-old twin daughters, Jenna and Aubrey. Kyle proceeded to introduce him to person after person from the church, people whose names he would definitely have to hear more than once to remember.

A tall, slender woman approached with cascading espresso brown hair and a killer smile. She walked straight to Melissa and hugged her, then Kyle, then each of the girls.

"Good morning, family." Her voice was as smooth as silk. "And stranger I don't know."

"Duncan, this is my sister, Dréa," Kyle said.

Duncan almost couldn't find his words. "Nice to meet you, Dréa." He held his hand out to her.

She reached out and gave it a firm shake. "You too."

"Duncan's here from Michigan to freshen up the company's brand."

"About time."

Kyle frowned at her.

Dréa leaned closer to Duncan and lowered her voice, but not so low that her brother couldn't hear. "I've been telling him to get a new look for years."

The scent of lavender overtook him. "Well, I'll do my best."

The sound of the worship band floated through the open doors, and Kyle ushered them into the sanctuary.

Duncan sat next to Kyle, and Dréa took a seat beside him.

"Do you want to sit by your brother?" he asked.

"This is fine, thanks."

They stood and sang choruses along with the worship band, and Duncan couldn't help but notice that Dréa had the voice of an angel, at least what he imagined an angel would sound like.

The pastor's sermon was about forgetting what is past and going all in for God, which he needed to hear. Guilt and shame were eating him up, and he needed to put what happened with Jamie behind him and be all in again. There was no changing the past. All he could do was move forward.

And moving forward with the right kind of girl was what went through his mind as he glanced over at Dréa's left hand and saw no sign of a wedding ring.

At Kyle's place, Duncan and Dréa gravitated toward each other, and she kept him company while Kyle grilled burgers in the back yard, Melissa prepared the rest of the meal in the kitchen, and the girls played on the swing set.

"Did you like our church?" she asked.

"I really did. Everyone I met was so welcoming. It felt like a place I could call home while I'm here."

She smiled. "I'm happy to hear that. How long will you be here?"

"I'm not sure yet, but a project like this can take a couple of months. Sometimes longer."

"I see."

"So, you know what I do for a living. How about you? What do you do?"

"I'm a DJ," she replied.

"A DJ, on the radio?"

"Yep."

"Well, you have the voice for it, that's for sure."

One of her eyebrows raised. "You like my voice?"

"Who wouldn't?"

She turned her head away a little. Had he made her blush?

"How long have you been a DJ?" he asked.

"Five years. I started there straight out of college. Did you always know you wanted to be a graphic designer?"

"I wouldn't say that, but I've always liked art, and I'm a bit of a computer nerd, so I guess you could say my interests merged."

She gave him another megawatt smile. "I like that."

The girls suddenly whizzed by in fits of laughter as Jenna chased Aubrey in a lively game of tag. Birds chirped in the tree in the corner of the yard, the food on the grill sizzled, and the scent of burgers wafted their way.

"So, Duncan from Michigan, what else do you like to do?"

"I like being outdoors. I went hiking at St. Mary's Lake last Sunday. It's beautiful there."

"You should hike the Sky Pond Trail sometime. Breathtaking views. That is if you're up for a longer hike."

"I'm game."

"How about I take you there next Saturday."

His mouth dropped open, a little taken aback, but in a good way.

She chuckled at his expression. "Was that too forward?"

"Not at all. I'd love that." He grinned.

"Great." She looked pleased with herself. "It's a couple hours from here, so we'll want to leave early. Can I get your number? I'll text you my address."

"Sure." He rattled off the numbers, and she entered them into her phone.

The girls ran across in front of them again, burping and giggling.

"Girls!" Kyle cried. "We have a guest."

Duncan and Dréa laughed at the girls' antics. Her laughter, like her voice, enveloped him like a warm blanket, soothing and comforting. He could listen to her all day.

"Sorry, Duncan." Kyle shook his head as he removed the burgers from the grill and walked into the house.

"No problem." The phone in Duncan's back pocket vibrated, and he pulled it out.

"There. Now you have my number." Dréa winked at him. "I'm going to see if Melissa needs any help."

He nodded and looked at the phone. Besides the text from Dréa, there was another he had missed.

`I won't bother you anymore, Duncan. Just know I'm thinking about you, and I hope you're happy in Denver.`

His heart sank.

Jamie.

Chapter 3

Seven weeks later

Jamie's hands trembled as she set the pregnancy test on the edge of the sink and eyed it. She couldn't believe this was happening. Last night while helping Shannon photograph a wedding rehearsal, she had gotten sick, but she'd assumed it was food poisoning from the rehearsal dinner. It never crossed her mind that *this* might be the actual reason she lost her meal until today when she'd photographed a wedding. She'd felt queasy all morning and thought it was residual effects from the food poisoning, but one of the bridesmaids was pregnant, and it occurred to her that she hadn't started her period. In fact, she couldn't remember the date of her last period. Early April? Before she and Duncan …

A wave of nausea hit her, and she took a deep breath in and let it out slowly.

Oh, man, is this morning sickness?

Unable to stay in the bathroom with the test staring her down, she moved toward the door, glancing back at the last minute to give it the evil eye. "You better be negative."

She moved to the living room couch and plopped down. It wasn't uncommon for her to be late during the busy wedding photography season. She was often a week or two off when she was constantly working and overly stressed. But she couldn't remember if she'd had a period in May, which was the reason she'd bought the test.

After a few minutes, she glanced at her phone. Enough time had passed that the result was inevitably waiting. She stood and headed toward the bathroom, but stopped halfway, terrified of what she'd find.

"I can't be pregnant."

She knew that wasn't true. It was entirely possible. She had missed taking one of her birth control pills before she and Duncan had slept together, but she'd taken it as soon as she remembered, to get her back on track. Everything was fine. This had to be her mind and body playing tricks on her.

Jamie moved into the bathroom. She closed her eyes and took a deep breath then looked down at the test. The air rushed out of her lungs as she retreated a couple of steps and sank onto the edge of her tub.

Positive.

Tears filled her eyes, a few sliding down her cheeks, but she quickly batted them away and left the bathroom. The closest thing to the door was a pile of photography magazines on the end table, and her hand flew in that direction, sending them scattering across the floor. She moved through her living room, knocking over a small lamp, kicking a basket of neglected knitting supplies, clearing a few framed pictures from the top of a bookshelf with a whack.

How could she have let this happen? Why hadn't she stopped things when he said he didn't have protection?

What made this news worse was the silent treatment Duncan had given her since that night. He had told her he'd call when he arrived in Denver, but he never did. She'd sent him texts and left him messages with no replies.

His silence broke her heart.

But even though he'd blown her off, he had still been foremost in her mind. All she wanted was to talk, to see where they stood, to know how he felt about that night.

For the past two months, she'd been anxiously awaiting his return so they could finally have that conversation. Last night, he had unexpectedly shown up.

Jamie stood in the foyer of the church, waiting for Shannon to arrive for the wedding rehearsal they were supposed to be photographing. The bridal party had already spent thirty minutes going over the order of the ceremony and were about to do a walkthrough, and Jamie was beginning to worry. They were Shannon's clients. She had only agreed to assist. Where was she?

The door to the church opened then, and Shannon walked in.

"Where have you been?" Jamie cried.

"Something came up. I'll tell you about it later, okay?"

Jamie shrugged. "All right." Her eyes suddenly leapt over her friend's shoulder. "Duncan!" She was sure her grin lit up the room as she maneuvered around Shannon to get to him.

"Hey, you." He opened his arms and hugged her, but it felt stiff and forced.

"This town has been boring without you," Jamie told him, settling into his hug, wanting to stay in his arms all night.

He gave her a tight squeeze before abruptly letting go. "You missed me, huh?"

She gave him a hopeful smile. "Didn't you miss me?"

He didn't reply, and there was a weird tension in the air between them.

After helping Shannon with her things, he kissed his sister goodbye and gave Jamie a simple touch on the arm and a little smile as he walked past on his way out the door.

That's it? Jamie's heart sank.

"What did I miss?" Shannon asked.

She shook off her sadness. "They've gone over the order of the ceremony and are getting ready to walk through it."

"I meant between you and my brother."

Jamie tucked a hair behind her ear. "I don't know what you mean."

Shannon rolled her eyes as if to say 'Yeah, right.'

It was one of the most confusing moments of Jamie's life. She hadn't expected them to suddenly be a couple when he returned, but she thought there'd be more than an awkward hug and a few pleasantries. He'd acted like he barely knew her, as if nothing had happened between them at all.

She shook away the disappointing memory and sank onto her couch, surveying the damage she had caused in the aftermath of the test result.

Pregnant? What am I going to do?

She leaned her head back, her eyelids falling closed. What would Duncan say when she told him? How would he react? Could they have a baby together? It seemed improbable, especially after the way he acted last night.

She let her mind wander, remembering the feel of his lips on hers on this very couch and what came after that kiss. Her stomach clenched, and she jumped up and raced to the bathroom, emptying what little dinner she'd eaten into the toilet.

This can't be happening.

After brushing her teeth, she picked up the mess in the living room, placing all the broken things into a garbage bag, and returned to the couch. She didn't move for a long time, thinking about what she should do next. The thought of having a baby terrified her, but the thought of having Duncan's baby sent a thrill through her.

Shannon had invited her to Sunday family dinner tomorrow, so she needed to decide how she was going to break the news to Duncan. She went to her closet and found her cutest floral dress, laying it over the chair in the corner of her room. She'd go to dinner, looking as cute as could be, and after the meal, she'd find a time to ask him to talk.

He would be shocked. She knew that. But Duncan was a good guy, and she was certain he wouldn't abandon her in this.

She lay back on her bed and attempted to sleep, but it didn't come. Her hand rested on her belly. She imagined Duncan carrying a little boy with auburn waves and brown eyes around on his shoulders. He would be the world's sexiest dad. And as much as having a baby scared her, she felt she could face anything with Duncan by her side. They could do this.

The last word that crossed her mind before she finally drifted off was ... *together.*

Chapter 4

Dréa was getting along splendidly with Duncan's entire family. He hadn't been sure of how they would react to him unexpectedly bringing a girl home with him from Denver—he'd never brought anyone home before—but she fit in so well, it was like she was already one of them. And he was sure they could tell he was serious about her.

The house was filling up with family for this Sunday dinner, and he knew it was probably because of his special guest. Leo and Paolo, cousins on Mama's side of the family, had let themselves in an hour before. They had been fixtures in the house since Duncan and his sisters were young, and they knew by now, they didn't need to knock.

Great Aunt Pauline—or Paulie, as she was lovingly called—arrived only fifteen minutes before and was already chatting with Dréa like they were old friends. But that was how Nana's younger sister was. Kind and loving, getting along with everyone.

A knock on the door had Duncan racing to the foyer, hoping it was Shannon. He'd been hinting to his sister that he'd brought a surprise back from Denver, and he could not wait to finally introduce them. He'd kept the secret when he gave her a ride to a wedding rehearsal on Friday evening. All Saturday, she was off photographing a wedding. So today was the day his sister would finally meet Dréa.

Shannon's opinion meant a great deal to him. She was his best friend, and he needed her approval. But he had no doubt Shannon would love Dréa instantly, just as he had.

Duncan opened the door, but instead of his sister, he found Uncle Gene—Papa's older brother, Aunt Joanna, and their son, Maxwell. "Hey, I didn't know you guys were coming."

Aunt Joanna wrapped Duncan up in a hug. "Welcome home, sweetie."

"Thanks, Aunt Jo."

Gene patted him on the back. "Good to see you. How was Denver?"

Duncan's face lit up. "It was great. I really loved it." He stepped aside and motioned for them to enter. "Come on in. Everyone's either in the kitchen or the back yard."

Uncle Gene and Aunt Jo headed into the house.

Maxwell stepped through the doorway and opened his arms to his cousin. "How the heck are you, man?" Anyone who saw the two of them together would know they were family, with their auburn hair, long narrow noses, oval faces, and smooth jawlines. Both were tall with similar builds, but Maxwell had a couple of inches on Duncan.

"Can't complain." Duncan gave his cousin—five years his senior—a hug and slap on the back before looking at him curiously. "You shaved your beard off."

Maxwell chuckled as he rubbed his bare chin with his fingers. "I did it for a girl, and then she dumped me."

"No." A look of horror crossed Duncan's face. "Max, that beard was so epic. If I could grow one as thick and magnificent as yours was, I totally would, but whenever I try, all I get is fuzz."

The two of them laughed loudly.

"What are you guys laughing about?" Dréa asked as she wandered up to them.

"Beards." Duncan wrapped an arm around behind her waist.

She eyed him. "Beards, huh? Well, I hope you don't plan on growing one. I can't stand guys with beards."

Duncan's eyebrow raised. "Are you serious?"

She nodded resolutely.

"So, if I grew a beard, you'd leave me?"

"In a heartbeat." She winked and held a hand out to Max. "Hi, I'm Dréa."

"Well, hello." Max shook her hand and tilted his head toward Duncan. "You didn't tell me you had a lady friend here."

"I figured Mama already spread the word and that's why everyone showed up today."

Max chuckled. "I knew nothing." He looked back at the beauty beside Duncan. "I'm Duncan's cousin, Max. It's nice to meet you."

"You too, Max. I'm still trying to figure out who's who around here. How are you related?"

"Our dads are brothers."

"Okay, so on the McGregor side," she said. "There are so many people to remember. Both of my parents were only children, so big families are new to me."

"We're not all that. Constantly talking and laughing, not to mention the hugs. I don't know how any of us put up with each other," Max teased.

Dréa pointed a finger at him. "You're a funny one. I can already tell."

"I've been known to crack a joke or two."

Duncan snorted. "Sometimes they're even funny."

"Now who's the comedian," Max said.

Dréa laughed then tilted her head toward the kitchen. "I'm gonna see if they need any help." She leaned in and planted a soft kiss on Duncan's lips before departing.

Max shook his head as she walked away. "It must be serious for you to bring her home. Am I right?"

Duncan shrugged his shoulders and feigned innocence.

Max playfully punched Duncan's arm. "I'm happy for you. About time you found someone nice."

He knew Max meant nothing but the best, but the words *someone nice* didn't sit right with him. It was what he had been waiting for—someone nice to spend his life with—and he'd found the nicest girl on the planet. So why did Max's words bring with them a sudden urge to run in the opposite direction?

Max went to join everyone in the back yard, where several tables were set up as one long table so they could dine outside, and Duncan wandered into the kitchen to check on the ladies.

Nana and Mama were preparing the meal, and Dréa was assisting. She looked adorable walking around the kitchen in Mama's oven mitts.

"You will love Mama's spaghetti sauce. It's heavenly." He inhaled the scent, and his mouth watered.

Mama waved him off. "Oh, you."

"It smells delicious, Mrs. McGregor," Dréa said.

"Please call me Samantha."

Dréa smiled at her.

"We're here!" Duncan heard Shannon's voice coming from the front door.

Mama set down the wooden spoon she'd been using to stir the sauce and moved toward her daughter's voice.

Duncan grinned at Dréa, excited to see his sister. He quickly moved into the foyer and spotted Shannon hugging their mother. "Who's we?" he asked as his gaze moved past Shannon and fell on Jamie.

He swallowed hard at the unexpected reaction his body had to her. Her burgundy floral dress brought out the streaks of magenta in her hair. It was a little longer than he remembered and hung just below her smooth pale shoulders. The color on her lips matched the dress, and the memory of kissing her suddenly hit him so hard, he swore he could still feel the softness of her lips and the warmth of her breath mingling with his.

"I didn't know you were coming," he managed just as Dréa came up behind him and slid her oven-mitt-covered hands around his waist.

"Hello," Dréa greeted them.

His arms came to rest on hers, and the look of devastation on Jamie's face hit him right in the gut. "Shannon, Jamie ..." He couldn't stop his voice from catching on Jamie's name. "This is Dréa."

Shannon held her hand up in a little wave. "Hi, I'm Duncan's sister, Shannon. And this is my friend, Jamie."

"The photographers, right?" Dréa asked.

"Right."

Jamie said nothing.

"It's nice to meet you both. Duncan's told me so much about you."

"Dréa," Nana called from the kitchen. "Can you come help me?"

"Coming, Nana," she replied and headed to the kitchen with Mama on her heels.

"Nana?" Jamie blurted, looking like she might burst into tears.

Duncan hated that it was because of him. His eyes flitted from Jamie's to Shannon's and back and forth again. "I told you I brought a surprise."

"That's not the surprise I thought you were talking about," Shannon said. "I thought you brought me a sweatshirt or a coffee mug or something."

Duncan looked at Jamie then. His heart broke at the pain so clearly displayed. "I'm sorry, Jame. I didn't know you were coming. I just …" He didn't know what else to say, so he awkwardly turned and walked back into the kitchen, but not before hearing Jamie's words to Shannon.

"I think I lost my appetite."

Having Jamie there was unexpected and unsettling. Every time he glanced at her, she was either watching him or looking anywhere but at him and Dréa. He tried to keep his focus on the lovely woman beside him, but he couldn't shake his unease. Especially as the meal ended and Dréa reached under the table to squeeze his hand, giving him the signal that it was time.

Duncan blew out a breath and stood slowly, glancing around the table with uncertainty. He looked from face to face, his gaze skipping over Jamie. If he looked into her eyes right now, he wouldn't be able to go through with this.

"Uh, I have something …" He paused with palms sweating. "I have an announcement to make." His eyes locked with his sister's briefly, and she looked about as nervous as he did. "Dréa and I are engaged."

Everything was a blur after that. Mama and Nana gasped and covered their mouths. Dréa said something about how hard it was to keep the ring a secret the whole time she'd been there. The ladies of the family moved around the table to hug and congratulate them.

It was meant to be a happy moment, so why did he feel anything but?

Out of the corner of his eye, he saw Jamie stand and take off across the yard. *Crap!*

Shannon looked over at him and gave him a look of disapproval before taking off after her.

A sudden urgency overcame him, and he withdrew from Nana's hug and raced after Shannon, entering the house behind her.

"Shan."

Her long, dark hair flipped away from her face as she looked back at him.

"Can you please tell her I'm sorry she found out like this."

Shannon stared at him for a heartbeat. "What is the deal with you two?"

His heart leapt into his throat. "Nothing."

"Then why does it matter if she found out at all?"

"I don't know. I just ... I know I've hurt her, and that kills me."

Laughter and chatter was coming from the yard, and he knew he should be outside with his fiancée.

"Who is this girl you're marrying?" Shannon asked. "You just met her."

"I know ... but sometimes you just know."

"And with her, you know?"

He nodded.

Shannon's eyebrow lifted. "Then why are you so worried about Jamie?"

"Just please make sure she's okay." He gave her a pointed look and motioned toward the front door, afraid Jamie was already gone. "Please."

Shannon rolled her eyes and walked out the door.

Duncan lowered his head, breathing slowly in and out. He turned toward the yard and stopped in the doorway, leaning against the frame, watching everyone congratulate and welcome Dréa into the family.

She really was a lovely woman—kind, intelligent, witty, gorgeous, and strong in her faith. He had never questioned whether his family would approve. She was exactly the kind of woman they wanted for him, exactly the kind of woman he needed in his life.

From the outside, six weeks probably seemed fast. But he'd known within the first few dates that she was a keeper. And after the way he'd failed himself and God with Jamie, he knew he needed someone like Dréa.

He pushed thoughts of Jamie's hurt expression to the back of his mind and walked across the yard to enjoy this time with the woman he was going to spend the rest of his life with.

Chapter 5

Her sobs could not be contained. Jamie lay on the couch, shoulders shaking, as she let it all out.

Engaged? He's engaged? How did this happen?

Only two months ago, she'd been in his arms, and now he was marrying someone else. She couldn't believe it.

A knock at her door came, and she already knew who it was before she even answered. The knocking continued as she wiped at her cheeks and shuffled slowly to the door, finding Shannon's friendly face on the other side.

"Oh, Jamie." Shannon gave her a warm embrace, and the tears began again.

Jamie thought she had no sobs left, but she was wrong. She felt embarrassed for the loud sounds coming from her mouth, but she was incapable of controlling her emotions.

When she was finally calm, she let go of her friend. "You didn't have to come here, Shannon," she murmured. "You should be celebrating your ... brother's engagement." She could barely get those last two words out before more tears slid down her cheeks.

"He's an idiot," Shannon declared. "A total idiot."

"We already knew that much," Jamie managed, trying to summon some of her usual spunk. She walked to the couch and climbed under a blanket.

Shannon glanced around at the piles of tissues and took a seat on the opposite end of the couch, turning with legs crossed to face Jamie. "Can you please explain something to me?"

"What?" Jamie sniffled.

"What is it between you and my brother?" Shannon asked. "I mean, you two have always been flirty, but lately, it seemed like there was more happening with you two. Am I wrong?"

"You're not wrong." Jamie swallowed hard and stared down at her hands. "Something happened. Before he left for Denver."

"What happened?"

Jamie struggled to get the words out. What would Shannon think of her? Would she be angry? What would she say when she found out the whole truth? Despite her worries, she needed to tell her friend.

"We slept together," she admitted.

Shannon's mouth fell open. "Excuse me? You slept together? As in ... you had sex with my brother?"

Jamie nodded, feeling so ashamed. "Remember that night we were hanging out here, watching movies?"

Shannon nodded.

"You left early, but he stayed. We were flirting, as usual, and I dared him to kiss me. I never thought he'd actually do it. But once we started, we couldn't stop. We didn't want to stop." Tears burned her eyes and spilled over again. "It was the best night of my life," she whimpered. "I really thought this was it, that we were finally gonna make a go of it after all our flirting, but then he left for Denver."

"And what happened?" Shannon asked.

"He didn't call me. I thought he would. He said he would. He left before I even woke up, and the first time I saw him since was two days ago when he dropped you off at the church."

"I can't believe him!" Shannon looked appalled. "I'm so angry right now. I want to give him a piece of my mind and let his new fiancée know exactly what kind of guy he is."

"You don't mean that. He's your brother, and you love him. Even if he did something like this."

Shannon grew quiet, probably mulling over what Jamie had said.

"It's not like I haven't had guys use me before." Jamie lowered her head and more tears fell and plopped onto her lap. "I just never thought Duncan would be one of them."

Shannon reached over and laid her hand on Jamie's.

"And I would normally be able to shake it off and move on if it wasn't for ..." Jamie's shoulders shook with more sobs, and she buried her face in the pillow. How could she tell Shannon this?

As she tried to gather the strength to break the news, she felt Shannon scoot closer and rub a comforting hand over her back. She turned her head and rested it on the pillow, looking up at her best friend.

"I'm pregnant."

"You're pregnant?" Shannon's throat moved as she swallowed hard.

Jamie answered with a slow, sad nod. "I thought I was late from the stress of the wedding season or something, but then I remembered throwing up after the rehearsal dinner, so I took a test last night."

"And it was positive?"

"Yeah, I kind of freaked out and smashed some things." Jamie pointed to the trash bag. "And then I thought, it's Duncan. We could do this. We could raise a baby together. So, I planned to tell him after lunch today." The emotions hit her hard again, and her chin quivered as she fought them. "I don't know what to do now. I don't know if I should keep it."

Jamie felt Shannon sit up a little straighter. "It's not the baby's fault you and Duncan got carried away. That's my brother's baby, Jamie. Please, don't do anything without telling him."

"But he's getting married now. If I tell him, I'll mess up his whole life, and he'll resent me for it. And even if he were to leave her for me, it would be because of the baby, and I don't want him that way. I want him because he wants to be with me, and he obviously didn't or he would've called after that night."

"You'll never know unless you talk to him."

Jamie didn't know if she should. "It would be easier for everyone if I made it go away."

Shannon looked suddenly peaked. Jamie was about to ask if she was all right when she spoke again.

"Of course, it would be easier on Duncan if you terminated the pregnancy and never told him. But what about you? Could you go back to your life and pretend it never happened?"

That thought broke Jamie's heart. "I don't know. This isn't how I thought things would go down with me and Duncan. And honestly, if he and I were a couple, I'd want this baby. But I don't want to be a single mom. I know that."

Tears filled Shannon's eyes and slipped down her cheeks, and Jamie sat up to look at her. "Are you mad at me?"

Shannon wiped at her wet cheeks. "In our family, we believe every life counts, that God has a purpose for each person, including the babies not yet born, no matter how they came to be conceived. This baby is innocent, and it's our blood. A part of our family."

The McGregor family. She loved them all so much, and the thought that the baby would connect her to them warmed her heart. "You have no idea how long I've wanted to be part of your family."

"You *have* to tell him, Jame. You don't know what might happen when you do. Because no matter who this girl is he brought home, he cares about you. I know it. You should've seen his face when you left. He was so worried about you. He made me promise to check on you and make sure you were okay."

"Really?"

"Really."

Hope bloomed but was quickly pushed aside. She'd seen Duncan and Dréa together. The perfect couple. He would never leave Dréa for her. Jamie shook her head. "No, I can't hold onto false hope. How would I do this on my own? I don't have any family here. I can't afford a nanny or daycare. Not to mention the cost of actually having the baby. Doctor appointments. Food. Diapers."

"Our family would help. You know we would."

Could she do this with their help? Should she count on them for that? Could she keep the baby?

"I don't know what to do." Jamie covered her face and cried more.

"I'm here for you," Shannon assured her. "You're my best friend, and I want you to be happy. But Duncan is my brother, and if you don't tell him, I can't promise that I won't."

Jamie's eyes widened as she looked at her friend. "What? Shannon, come on."

"He has the right to know."

Jamie scrambled up from the couch and stared at her in disbelief. "Please don't do that. Not yet anyway."

"Are you going to tell him?"

"Yes."

"Before or after?" There was an edge to Shannon's voice, and Jamie wasn't sure if it was anger, but it sure sounded like it.

Truthfully, this whole situation felt impossible, and having an abortion seemed like the easier option.

"You're going to do it, aren't you?" Shannon asked.

"I don't think I have any other choice."

"You do have choices. Don't do anything rash." Shannon looked almost panicked.

"I can do whatever I want. It's my body."

"That's true. And I can sit here and tell you what I hope you'll do and the way I hope things will turn out, but there are no guarantees. I don't know how Duncan will react when he finds out ... and he will find out. Whether it's from you or me."

Jamie's face scrunched up in disapproval.

"If you end this pregnancy and he finds out after the fact, he might never forgive you."

Jamie stared down at the floor.

"But here's another option for you to consider." Shannon took a deep breath in and let it out. "Adoption."

"I don't know." Jamie hadn't had time to think about other options.

"I want to adopt the baby," Shannon blurted.

Jamie's eyes widened again. "Wait, what?"

"The reason I broke up with Micah all those years ago was because I found out I can't have kids. He wanted a big family. It was a dream of ours. So I let him go so he could have that with someone else."

Her heart shattered for her friend. "Oh, Shannon."

"It breaks my heart that you're going through this right now, Jamie." Tears filled Shannon's eyes again. "I'm so sorry my brother was so careless with you and your feelings. But if you don't want it, and if he doesn't want it, I will be this baby's mom. I want children. I always have. And if I can raise a baby that's biologically part of our family, I would be so honored to do that. You can be part of its life and so can Duncan."

Jamie was speechless. "I don't know what to say."

"Please, think about it, okay?"

"I will."

"And please talk to Duncan."

She simply nodded in reply.

Shannon said nothing else. She hugged her, said she loved her, and went on her way.

Jamie stared at the closed door for a while after Shannon left. Her mind jumped from one option to another and back again, and she became more confused than before. The walls felt as if they were closing in on her, and she couldn't handle any of it. She wanted out of there. She needed time away to think. And she knew exactly where she needed to go. She had no weddings to photograph until mid-July. She could do this.

Gathering her camera equipment, she opened her case and fished out the memory cards she'd used to help Shannon photograph the wedding rehearsal on Friday. She walked into the kitchen and pulled an envelope, paper, and a pen from the drawer and wrote Shannon a note.

I'm sorry I have to leave like this. I need time to decide.
Please, don't tell Duncan.
- J

She tucked the note and memory cards into the envelope, scribbled Shannon's name on the outside, and laid it on the end of the counter. If she didn't call Shannon in the next day or two, Jamie knew she'd be on her doorstep, and hopefully she'd use the emergency spare key to let herself in and find the envelope.

Shannon would probably freak out and see it as running away, but Jamie couldn't stay in the same town as Duncan and Dréa. And if she was going to terminate this pregnancy, she couldn't do it there, after everything Shannon had said to her. At least if she did it elsewhere, it wouldn't feel like Shannon was breathing down her neck.

It was her choice. But was it the right one?

Chapter 6

Though the family had been asking question after question for an hour, Dréa took it all in stride, calmly answering and showing a genuine interest in their lives too. But Duncan felt the opposite, and he couldn't seem to shake it.

"Tell us how you met," Mama said.

"And about the engagement," Nana added. Deep wrinkles formed around her eyes as she smiled.

Dréa's face lit up. "My brother introduced us, at church. We got along right away, and I asked him out that same day." She glanced over at Duncan.

"You asked him out?" Nana asked. "How progressive of you."

"I've never been shy about going after what I want," she replied. "Anyway, we started spending a lot of time together, and one of our favorite things to do was go hiking. Last week, he took me back to the very first trail we ever hiked together. We were standing in the most beautiful place, next to this gorgeous lake, blue skies, sunshine. It was perfect. And next thing I know, he's down on one knee, holding a ring, asking me to marry him."

The ladies all gave a collective sigh.

"What do you do for a living, Dréa?" Papa asked.

Out of the corner of his eye, Duncan spotted Shannon walking across the yard. He watched her stop behind Papa and lay her hands on his shoulders.

"I'm an on-air radio personality," Dréa explained. "I'm on a morning show with another DJ on a Christian music channel."

"Like Delilah?" Nana asked.

They all laughed.

"Not really," Dréa answered. "I don't have my own show or the kind of following she has. Maybe someday."

Duncan could feel Shannon's stare, and when he finally made eye contact with her, she tilted her head toward the house. He patted Dréa on the knee as he stood and followed Shannon into the house.

In the kitchen, Duncan reached into the cookie tin and snatched one of Nana's chocolate chip cookies, taking a big bite.

"You slept with her?"

Shannon's question caught him by surprise, and his throat suddenly closed up as a chunk of cookie became lodged there. He coughed a few times, and Shannon barely patted his back to help before it broke free and allowed him to breathe again.

"How could you do that and then get engaged to someone else in two months' time?"

He gave one more cough as his head fell forward in shame. "She told you."

"Of course she told me. She's heartbroken, Duncan. How did you think she would feel?"

His eyes shot to the back door, afraid someone would hear. "Keep your voice down."

"You didn't tell your fiancée?"

Duncan scowled at her.

"How could you, Duncan? Really, shame on you."

He felt nauseated. His sister's opinion of him meant everything.

"I never thought you'd be that guy—hooking up and sneaking out before the sun comes up."

Nausea turned to shock. "Is that what she said?" He shook his head adamantly. "I had to catch my plane."

"No, she didn't say you snuck out. I put the pieces together."

"That's not what happened at all. I stayed with her as long as I could. I didn't want to leave her." He couldn't believe he'd said those words, but he realized he meant them. He hadn't wanted to leave her. Despite the guilt he had felt, a part of him had wanted to skip out on the Denver job altogether and stay with her, but he'd known that would be immature and irresponsible. He never wanted to be that guy again, so he'd left and caught his flight as a grown man should.

"Why didn't you call her from Denver then? If you really care about her, why blow her off?"

His shoulders drooped. "Once I walked out of the apartment, I felt so guilty. I wasn't going to do that again until I got married, but I was always so attracted to her." He glanced toward the door again and kept his voice low. "She's such a cute, feisty little thing, and the second I kissed her, I knew I was lost. I was so strong for so long, but I lost the battle. And I was ashamed. I felt like I took advantage of her. She wasn't mine to have, but I had her anyway. And I didn't know how to tell her that without hurting her. What girl wants to hear afterward that the guy feels anything but happy and content and ... and in love, and I couldn't tell her those things."

"And walking away without any explanation was the answer?"

Duncan didn't know what the answer was. He hadn't then, and he didn't now. But he knew he'd handled it all wrong. He ran his hands over his face and pushed his hair back from his forehead. "I don't know."

"I've spent ten years second-guessing my decision to break up with Micah, wondering how different life would be now if I'd told him the truth from the start. Don't make the same mistake I made. Tell her the truth, Duncan. She deserves to hear it."

Duncan's heart broke for Shannon. She'd ended her relationship with Micah and kept the truth of her infertility and her Polycystic Ovary Syndrome from him for years. He knew it was her biggest regret and that she didn't want him to have any regrets in his own life.

"I can't look into those big brown eyes of hers and tell her that. I can't be near her and not want her still."

Shannon's mouth fell open at his admission. "Duncan, you can't marry Dréa if this is the way you feel."

"We can't base a relationship on physical attraction. And that's what it would be. I like Jamie. I always have. But when it comes right down to it, we don't know that much about each other. It's always been a pretty surface relationship. We goof around and flirt. We don't have deep conversations. I don't know anything about her family. I don't know how she became a photographer. Heck, I don't even know her middle name, and I knew all those kinds of things about Dréa after the first date."

"So get to know her."

Honestly, he wished he had known more about Jamie before they slept together. He felt like the stereotypical guy with one thing on his mind. Not that knowing about her parents or what her favorite color was would have made it right.

Shannon stared at him.

"My desire for her isn't a good enough foundation for a relationship. We may be sexually compatible—"

Shannon's hand flew up to stop him. "Too much information."

"But we have nothing else in common," he continued. "We don't share the same beliefs. It would never work." He knew Jamie didn't go to church and wasn't a Christian. "It was a mistake."

The look on his sister's face said it all. She was disappointed in him, and that broke his heart.

"Please, go talk to her," she said. "She deserves that much."

Duncan groaned, knowing Shannon was right.

A knock on the door interrupted them. He went to answer it and was surprised to see Micah, Shannon's ex, holding a bouquet of wildflowers.

"Hey, Micah. Long time no see."

Micah nodded. "It has been a long time. I hear you've been on a job in Denver."

"I have. Just got home on Friday."

"Welcome home." He didn't look like he was in the mood for small talk. "Is Shannon here?"

"Yeah, man. Come on in."

They walked into the kitchen to find Shannon about to take a bite of a chocolate chip cookie.

"I hope these are still your favorite," Micah said as he walked over and handed her the flowers.

She dropped the cookie onto the counter and took the flowers.

Duncan was happy for his sister and hoped maybe she and Micah were finding their way back to each other after all these years. Her glare pierced through him, and he gave her a weak grin and walked to the back yard, leaving them alone.

He took his seat beside Dréa again, and she intertwined her fingers with his as she continued to chat with everyone. Duncan's mind was not on what she was saying, though. He knew Shannon was right. He needed to be a stand-up guy and do the right thing. He needed to talk to Jamie, even though he really didn't want to.

It had been excruciating seeing her Friday and then having her at the house today. All the feelings and emotions he'd pushed aside when he left for Denver came rushing back the moment she was standing in front of him again. All he had wanted was to stare into her eyes, to feel her arms wrapped around him. He nearly groaned aloud at his train of thought but caught himself.

If he was going to talk to Jamie, it would have to be in a public place—a park or the church, maybe. There was no way he could walk into her apartment again. He wasn't sure he trusted himself to be alone with her.

When the conversation died down and the number of people in the yard dwindled, Dréa squeezed Duncan's hand.

"Hey, are you okay?" she asked.

"Mhmm."

Her eyebrows scrunched together. "I wish I could read you better. It's one of the downsides of a short courtship."

A little laugh escaped him. "Courtship, huh? Are we in a Jane Austen novel?"

"Don't mock." She poked his chest with her finger. "And who wouldn't want to live in a Jane Austen novel?"

"Every guy on the planet." He winked.

The concern on her face was not yet gone. "Are you sure you're all right?"

"Yeah, I'm just tired. It's been a busy day with lots of people around."

"I thought you'd be used to that. It sounds like this is how it's always been around here."

"Sometimes, but I got used to the wide-open spaces in Colorado."

"So, are you saying you'll consider moving when we get married?"

His eyes met hers. As much as he enjoyed Denver and loved her family, he wasn't sure how he felt about relocating permanently.

"I know we haven't made a decision yet, but like I said before, your work is freelance. You can do it from anywhere. I have a job in Denver, one that I love."

"I know."

"I don't want to take you far away from your family. They're all so wonderful. But please, can we talk about it seriously? Because it's a big decision."

Duncan took her face in his hands. "I know it is."

"And you don't even own a place here. You're still living at your parents'."

His hands dropped into his lap. "Because I'm gone so much. It's worked out fine so far." He didn't mean for his tone to sound defensive, but it seemed like a dig against his current living arrangement.

"I'm only saying that it's easier for you to relocate. You don't have a lease or a mortgage to worry about. Just consider it."

"I *will*. Can we talk about this later?"

She nodded, and he kissed her softly on the cheek then sat back.

Silence hung in the air between them. The warm glow of the evening sun was hitting the tops of the trees as a soft breeze rustled the leaves.

"Duncan."

He loved the way his name sounded coming from her lips.

"Something's bothering you. I can tell that much."

"I've got a lot on my mind right now."

"Can I help?"

He stood and kissed the top of her head. "I wish you could."

Chapter 7

The house stood quiet and dark before Jamie. If only she hadn't been in such a hurry to leave her apartment, she might have remembered the key to her parents' house. Knocking or ringing the doorbell at two o'clock in the morning probably wasn't the best idea since her parents had no doubt been asleep since eight. Maybe she should've waited until morning to drive the ten hours home to Hershey, Pennsylvania, but she needed to get out of Grand Rapids as fast as possible.

Jamie glanced back at her car then over at the lattice attached to the side of the porch. She'd climbed that more times than she could count to sneak out of the house when she was in high school. She walked across the lawn to get a closer look. Maybe it wasn't as sturdy as it had once been. Maybe it wasn't the best idea to climb up a rickety lattice in her … condition. Even if she *was* considering no longer being in that condition anymore, she didn't want to end up with a broken leg or worse.

She cautiously placed one foot on the old wood and grabbed hold, pulling herself up. She paused long enough to jiggle it back and forth to test its sturdiness. She was still close to the ground, so if it broke and she fell, she wouldn't have too far to go. But it didn't give, so she continued onward and upward, gritting her teeth with every foot gained. She'd never felt more relieved than the second both of her knees were firmly planted on the porch roof.

As she began to crawl across the shingles, the sound of an approaching car gave her pause. To any passersby, she would surely look like an intruder, so she lay flat on her stomach, hoping she wouldn't be spotted. Her heart beat rapidly as the car slowed, and she was only able to breathe again when it drove past and turned down another street.

Letting out a sigh of relief, she continued on toward her old bedroom window. Her parents knew by now about her sneaking in and out, but she had never told them the lock was broken or that she knew just the right way to jiggle the window to get it to release. She only hoped Dad hadn't figured that out and repaired it after she moved out.

Please be broken. Please be broken.

Jiggling it without making noise used to be her specialty, but it seemed louder than she remembered. Or maybe she'd just lost her touch. She cringed with each thump and creak it made until it finally gave way as it always had.

She let out a sigh and lifted the window fully open, scooting forward to stick one foot through onto her …

What the?

Her foot normally would've found her bed by now, but instead, there was nothing but air. She stretched her leg farther, trying to touch something with her toe. Finally, she put her other leg through, ducked her body under the window, and dropped into the room. But rather than landing on a solid surface, she bounced, completely throwing off her balance, and tumbled face-first onto the floor.

The light suddenly flipped on, and she looked up at her father standing over her, holding a baseball bat.

"What is it, Harvey? Is it a burglar?" her mother cried.

"I'll protect you, Sylvia!" Dad replied.

"It's me!" Jamie grunted as she lay there, holding the side of her head that had hit the floor. A sudden fear shot through her body, wondering if her fall had harmed the baby, but she pushed that thought to the back of her mind.

"Jamie?" Dad lowered the ball bat. "What are you doing here in the middle of the night?"

Her mother scurried into the room. "Are you all right?"

Jamie pushed herself up to sitting and glanced at her mom, grey hair up in rollers, then at her dad, who somehow looked balder than he had last time she was home, even though his head had been smooth as a cue ball for years. They looked much older than their sixties, but they'd always felt ancient to her since they had waited until they were forty to have her.

As she stood, she looked around the bedroom that was once hers. It wasn't much of a bedroom in its current state. In place of her bed were an exercise bike and the mini-trampoline that had landed her on the floor. A treadmill sat where her dresser used to be, and a small rack of weights was positioned next to her closet. "I see you've opened a gym."

"We're trying to stay healthy," Dad replied. "We work out every day now."

"I'm getting rid of my muffin top once and for all." Her mother smoothed her pajama top down over her belly.

Jamie chuckled. She didn't know her mother knew what a muffin top was.

"And we want to live long enough to know our grandkids," Mom added.

Jamie's laughter immediately silenced. If only they knew.

The sound of coffee percolating in the kitchen roused Jamie from sleep. She rolled over and yanked the colorful afghan from its usual place on the back of the couch, trying to block the noise so she could get more sleep. The kitchen soon filled with the sounds of shuffling feet, banging cupboards, and popping toast, and it was no use.

She sat up and stretched before moving to sit on one of the stools at the countertop bar. She watched her mother's morning rituals. Growing up, Mom had always been up at dawn, preparing breakfast—toast, eggs, and coffee for Dad before he left for work, toast and tea for Jamie before school. And she was still at it, though Dad was now retired. Jamie couldn't contain her smile when a plate of toast and cup of tea with a little milk and sugar were placed before her.

The comforts of home were exactly what she needed right now.

The aroma of Dad's eggs wafted her direction, causing a sudden wave of nausea. She took a couple of bites of her toast and a sip of tea, hoping it would settle the queasiness, but the scent of the eggs was overwhelming. She abruptly dropped the mug on the counter with a clink and bolted across the house to the bathroom.

This was so inconvenient. How could she possibly photograph the weddings she had scheduled in July? She'd be rushing to the bathroom, or worse, tossing her cookies in the middle of the ceremony. How humiliating and unprofessional that would be. Another reason to end this now.

When she cleaned up and returned to the kitchen, her mother stood still as a statue, staring across the room at her.

"What?"

"How far along are you?"

"I don't know what you mean." She picked up her partially eaten toast and nibbled.

Mom walked across the room and stood on the other side of the bar until she made eye contact. "Jamie Eloise, you be straight with me."

When her mother gave her *the look* and used her middle name, she knew she couldn't lie.

"A couple months."

"And the father?"

Jamie returned the toast to her plate. "He doesn't know yet."

"Is that why you're here? Running away?"

She shrugged her shoulders. Of course, it was.

"That never helps, you know."

She knew.

"What are you going to do?" There was no judgment in Mom's voice, which was one of the reasons she knew coming home would be a good idea. Her parents had never judged her for her decisions—even when she was a troublemaker in high school. They were patient with her, probably because they were older when she was born and had more life experience under their belts. They were good parents, giving her the freedom to figure out who she was with the right amount of discipline to keep her from going crazy with her independence.

"I don't know yet."

"Do you want to talk to someone?" Mom asked.

"Like who?"

"Our pastor?"

Jamie's face screwed up. "Since when do you go to church?"

"Since earlier this year when we decided we needed it."

"Is this some kind of late-life crisis?"

"Hey, your dad and I have a lot of life left to live."

"I know you do. It's just a lot of change with the church and the gym taking over my room and all."

"There's nothing wrong with wanting to better ourselves. Maybe you should try it."

Mom's words surprised her, and now she wasn't sure she should reveal her plans.

"I wonder what you'll have." Mom got a far off look. "Oh, can you imagine a little girl running around in the back yard? We'll have to get a swing set. Remember the one we used to have for you?" She giggled, clearly giddy at the thought of a grandchild.

"I remember."

"And that newborn baby smell. You will never forget that. It stays with you forever."

Jamie pushed the teacup and plate of unfinished toast across the counter.

"How are you feeling?"

"Not good," Jamie snapped.

"The first trimester is always the worst. It will get better in a month or so. The second was a breeze when I had you." She clasped her hands together. "Oh, and wait until you feel the baby move for the first time. It's the funniest fluttering sensation."

"Mom, stop."

"I know it's scary right now, but you can do this. I'm here for you if you have any questions or need someone to go to appointments with you."

"That won't be necessary."

Mom's brow furrowed. "Why not?"

"I'm not keeping it."

Chapter 8

"I wish I didn't have to go. This has been such a wonderful trip." Dréa wrapped her arms around Duncan's waist, and he rested his chin on her shoulder.

"I'm glad you came home with me."

"Your family is so wonderful. I love them all."

He pulled back but kept his arms around her. "And they love you."

"I wish you were coming back with me. I've never been in a long-distance relationship before, and I don't like the idea of being apart." Her bottom lip stuck out in a little pout.

"It won't be forever. You'll be back in a few weeks for the Fourth of July."

She leaned in and pressed a soft kiss to his lips. "That's too long."

He pulled her close again and hugged her tight. "We'll talk and text every day. It will fly by."

"If you say so."

When she pulled away this time, he was surprised to see tears. He'd not seen Dréa cry since they'd been dating, and it was a vulnerability he hadn't expected. She came across as so confident. He had no idea she'd be this sensitive about temporarily parting ways.

"I love you," she smiled sweetly at him.

"I know," he said with a laugh.

She eyed him warily.

"It's a line from *Star Wars*." He searched her face. "When Leia tells Han she loves him, he says 'I know' and then he's hauled away and frozen in carbonite."

"I've never seen *Star Wars*."

His eyes widened. "Whoa! What?"

"I'm not really into movies like that."

"Movies like what? Like one of the greatest movie series ever?"

She shook her head, clearly not taking him seriously.

"We can't get married until you watch it with me."

"Right."

"I can't marry someone who's never seen *Star Wars*." He was only half teasing, but she laughed him off.

"You're a funny guy, Duncan McGregor."

She placed one more kiss on his lips. "I have to get to my gate soon or I'll miss my flight."

"Okay." He reluctantly let her go, and she moved toward the security checkpoint.

"Dréa," he called.

She looked back over her shoulder.

"I love you too." The words felt foreign to him. He'd never said them to anyone other than his family, and he'd only recently started saying them to his future wife.

Her face lit up, and she turned and lay her bag on the conveyor belt.

He waited until she made it through the line and had her bag and shoes before leaving the airport for his car.

He felt uneasy as he drove home. So much had changed over the past couple of months, and a part of him wanted to go back to how he felt before—comfortable and happy, for the most part. He still felt that way when it came to his work. Working for himself was satisfying and allowed him a lot of freedom. But as far as his personal life, he hadn't felt this unsettled since he was in high school, since before he'd surrendered his life to Christ and gotten on the right path. And that confused him because getting engaged to a wonderful Christian woman like Dréa was supposed to make him feel *more* settled, not less. So why did the opposite feel true?

He was sure some of it had to do with the conversation they'd had about living in Denver. He didn't like the idea, because he knew how much he'd miss being close to family, but what she said made sense. His job could be done from anywhere. Hers couldn't. And she loved her job. He understood that. He knew compromise was part of marriage, of merging your life with another person's. He just thought once they got engaged, he'd be more excited about the changes to come.

These were normal fears about getting married. Everybody had them, right?

He shook off his thoughts and drove home. Mama, Nana, and Aunt Pauline were in the kitchen, and their discussion quieted the second he entered the room.

"What's going on?" he asked, eyeing them one at a time.

They giggled like schoolgirls, and Mama closed the notebook in front of her. "Niente."

"Why do I not believe you?" He knew there was no dragging it out of them, so he went to the refrigerator in search of food.

"Leftovers are on the top shelf." Mama stood and walked to the cupboard, twisting her long black hair up into a bun before retrieving a plate for him and laying it on the counter.

Duncan moved to her side with a container of lasagna. "I can do it, Mama."

She wrapped her arms around his waist and squeezed him tight. "I know."

He hugged her back and kissed her cheek.

"Are you feeling it?" she asked.

"Feeling what?"

"Dréa's absence."

"Oh ... yeah."

"I remember when your father and I were young and in love and he went on a trip out west for two weeks with some friends. The second he stepped on that plane, I could feel the distance between us. It was an ache in my heart I knew nobody else could fill. That's how I knew how deeply I loved him. He told me later that when he watched me walk away that day, it was the same for him."

"That's sweet, Mama."

"It will be difficult for a time, but then you'll be married and together every day."

"I know. I'm okay."

Mama took over, heating the food for him, and he stood there silently, listening to Nana and her sister talk about their annual Fourth of July party.

But he wasn't paying attention to what they were saying. His mind was on Mama's words. If he hadn't already been confused after he left the airport, he certainly was now. Because he didn't feel the way his mother had described. He wasn't aching for Dréa. Was he supposed to be? Was that truly the sign of love? And if so, why wasn't he feeling it? Why wasn't he miserable with her gone?

Maybe he just dealt with separation differently than his parents had. Maybe it wasn't the same for everyone.

When his food was ready, he walked out of the house into the back yard and sat down at the table that was still set up from Sunday's gathering. His gaze fell on the chair where Jamie had been seated that day, and he felt a tightness in his chest, remembering the look on her face when she saw him with Dréa. He could almost feel how much it hurt her, and that ache was still with him even now.

He poked at the lasagna, not having much of an appetite after all.

Maybe he should go talk to her. Apologize. Should they talk about what happened between them? He hated how he'd left things. It wasn't right the way he'd blown her off.

He shook his head. Going over there wasn't a good idea. He was afraid to be alone with her. Afraid of messing up again. Terrified that he wouldn't be able to stop himself.

An image of the two of them in her bed popped into his mind, and he bowed his head and buried his fingers in his hair, elbows resting on the table.

What is wrong with me? I've got this beautiful woman who has agreed to marry me—a woman I believe God brought into my life—and I can't get Jamie out of my head. I'm a disgusting man. I hate myself. I hate what I did to Jamie. I hate that I'm betraying Dréa by thinking about another woman. And I hate that I haven't been honest with her about what happened with Jamie.

A hand on his shoulder startled him, and he looked back to find Nana standing over him.

"Let's talk."

There was something about Nana's kind eyes that had always made it easy to confide in her. Even when he'd been a messed up teenaged boy, he'd felt safe and accepted by her no matter what.

Thirty minutes of spilling his guts to his grandmother was like free therapy. He told her everything, including what happened with Jamie. Shannon was the only other person who knew, but Nana was the best secret-keeper around, and he knew she would give him great advice, just as she had the time he got caught messing around with that girl in his bedroom.

"I guess you were wrong all those years ago. I'm not a better guy after all." Duncan hung his head as he brought up the words Nana had said to him back then.

Nana laid her wrinkled hand over his. "When you were younger, you made careless decisions because you had no direction and no real relationship with God. We're all human, Duncan, and we all mess up."

"Not you," he replied.

"Even me."

"I don't believe that."

"I've made my fair share of mistakes. I was selfish when I was a young girl. I wanted what I wanted, and I went after it. I even stole my sister's boyfriend."

Duncan's eyes widened. "You didn't."

"I did."

"Was it Papi?"

She shook her head. "His name was Roy." Her voice broke on his name and tears suddenly filled her eyes.

"Nana." He took her hand and squeezed.

"I loved your grandfather. He was the love of my life. But Roy was my first love, and you never really get over that."

"What happened? Why didn't you end up with Roy?"

Tears slipped down her cheeks, and she let go and patted his hand, then waved off his question. "That's all ancient history. My point is we all make mistakes. Sometimes big ones. What's most important is what we do after."

Duncan nodded.

"And I have faith that you'll seek God's guidance for what to do next."

If only she knew he hadn't been talking to God about any of this.

"You are a good man, Duncan. I believe that."

He only hoped he could live up to Nana's faith in him.

Chapter 9

After Jamie's announcement yesterday, Mom had been giving her the silent treatment. She hadn't lectured or tried to change her mind, but the quiet way she walked through the house, preparing meals, cleaning, and watching television, spoke volumes.

As much as Jamie knew her mother wanted an adorable, sweet-smelling baby to love and play with, there were too many reasons why now was not the right time for her to be having a child. First being her business. She was busy most weekends photographing weddings and during the week editing the photos, often late into the night. Where would she find time to care for a child? And how would she afford to pay someone to watch the baby while she worked? Her business was doing well, but not well enough for that added expense, not to mention all the other expenses that go along with having and taking care of a baby.

Jamie sat on the front porch, watching the cars drive by, feeling confused and lost. Her phone buzzed from an incoming call.

Shannon.

For the first time, Jamie didn't want to talk to her best friend. Shannon had made it very clear where she stood, and that she wouldn't support abortion. But knowing Shannon couldn't have children did give Jamie pause. She wished it hadn't taken her pregnancy for her best friend to confide in her about her situation. It was a difficult and private matter, she understood that, but how heartbreaking that Shannon had gone through it all alone.

Jamie hadn't seriously considered Shannon's offer to adopt the baby, because it felt strange to her, having her and Duncan's child raised by its aunt. How could she be around that baby and watch it grow up with someone else? And how could she go through the entire pregnancy only to give the baby away when it was over? The delivery scared her nearly as much as raising the baby herself. She wasn't sure she could do it or even wanted to.

The buzzing of her phone stopped, followed by another buzz a few seconds later, signaling a voicemail. She was afraid to listen at first, but curiosity got the better of her.

"Jamie! You are not going to believe who just called me. Vern! The owner of the building. Our building! Apparently, the sale fell through with the other buyer, but someone else has stepped up to buy the building, and Vern said they want to offer us the space for our studio after all. Can you believe it? Call me when you get this. He says he'll meet us there in an hour."

A surge of happiness rushed through her. It had been such a disappointment when Vern had decided to sell the building rather than rent them the space for their new studio. Shannon had taken it hard, so her extreme enthusiasm over this turn of events was not surprising.

Jamie's finger hovered over her phone. Part of her wanted to call immediately and share in the excitement, but she couldn't. Besides, she wasn't in Grand Rapids right now, anyway, so there was no way she could meet with Vern. She would let Shannon handle it. She trusted her to make good business decisions for both of them.

After thirty minutes had passed, her phone buzzed again. This time with a text from Shannon.

Please don't do anything you'll regret. Duncan has the right to know before you make any huge decisions. It's his baby too. And I was serious. If neither of you wants it, I'll raise it as my own.

Jamie stared at the text, realizing Shannon must've stopped by her apartment and found the note she'd left with the memory cards. Her heart ached and tears burned her eyes. This was exactly the reason she had left town. She couldn't make this decision with Shannon around. She couldn't think straight knowing how Shannon felt. Rather than writing her best friend back, she closed her phone and buried her face in her hands as the tears fell.

The front door creaked, and Jamie quickly wiped her face as her mother sat down in the wicker chair next to hers.

"Please talk to me, sweetie."

Jamie sniffled.

"I've always been your sounding board for all the decisions you've made in your life. Why can't I be that for you now?"

"I want you to, Mom."

"Then tell me what you're thinking. I promise I'll only listen."

Jamie told her everything. From her night with Duncan, her feelings for him, his sudden engagement, to Shannon's offer to adopt. She let it all spill out as tears wet her cheeks.

Her mom quietly listened, taking it all in.

"I just don't think I can be a mom right now. It's not the right time." Jamie brushed away another round of tears. "That's why I came home. So you would tell me what to do."

Mom took her hand and squeezed. "I love you, and I'd love to think you came home because you wanted my advice on the situation, but that's not why you came here, is it?"

Jamie looked at her curiously.

"You left because you feel guilty."

Nerves churned her stomach. "That's crazy. Why would I feel guilty?"

Mom looked down her nose at Jamie. "You're my daughter, and I know you. You left because of what Shannon said to you."

"I didn't ... I just ..."

"You couldn't go through with ending the pregnancy in the same town as the baby's father and aunt, especially after she said she'd adopt the baby."

There was never any use in hiding the truth from her mother. She always figured it out with her amazing mom powers.

Yet another reason the idea of motherhood freaked her out. She just knew she'd be a horrible mother, never able to live up to the attentive, encouraging, supportive stay-at-home mom she'd been blessed with. Jamie was a young entrepreneur, busy all the time with her photography business. Her full focus could never be on a child, not like the child would need anyway.

"You're right, Mom."

"I love you, and I will support you, whatever you decide," Mom said.

"You have no idea how much—"

"But I don't agree with it."

Jamie looked over at her. "I thought you supported a woman's right to choose."

Mom shrugged her shoulders. "I'm seeing things through different eyes these days. And it feels different when it's my baby having a baby."

"Mom." Jamie's heart ached again.

"And I don't think you should do it without telling Duncan."

Jamie's mouth fell open a little.

"If you care about him like you say you do, if you want him to stay in your life, keeping this from him is the wrong decision. Even if he's angry with your choice, not telling him at all is worse." Mom patted her on the knee and stood. "And that's all I'm going to say about that."

Jamie watched as her mother disappeared into the house, the screen door closing with a bang. There were plenty of times growing up that she'd hated her mother's blunt honesty and wished for one of those moms who put a cherry on top of every situation. Instead of "Everything will work out for the best" or "Don't worry, be happy," she got the hard truth.

Someone said something bad about you at school? That's life. Kids can be mean sometimes. Not everybody's going to like you.

Didn't make the team like you wanted? Sorry, them's the breaks.

The boy you like asked another girl to the dance? You can't win 'em all.

But she knew Mom's tough love was what she needed right now. She couldn't see the situation clearly, because she was too close to it. And thinking about Mom's advice had all kinds of questions running through her mind.

How would Duncan react if he learned I was pregnant? What if Shannon already told him? She wouldn't do that, would she? Maybe she would now that she realized I left town.

What if I ended the pregnancy and went home and he was there, waiting to talk about the baby, thinking I was still pregnant? What would I tell him then? Would he hate me?

Or what if ... what if I kept it and went home to tell him, and he said he and Dréa would raise it together?

That thought made her sick to the stomach, so much that she jumped up and hurled over the edge of the porch into the hedges.

She groaned as she wiped her mouth and wandered around the house to turn on the spigot and hose down the mess she'd made. As she tugged the hose around the front of the house, aimed, and squeezed the handle, the weight of a hand on her shoulder startled her. She abruptly spun around, still gripping the sprayer, accidentally soaking her childhood best friend, Pam.

"Oh my gosh!" Jamie fumbled to let go of the hose, tossing it away from them as if it had morphed into a snake. "Pammy!" She threw her arms around her wet friend.

"*Pammy*? Really? How old are we?" Pam squeezed her tight. Her curly brown hair tickled Jamie's cheek.

"I'll always call you Pammy. What are you doing here?" Jamie asked as they let go.

"Your mom called mine. Lamar and I just moved a few streets over from here."

"You did? That's amazing." Jamie couldn't help but hug her again, despite her soaked shirt. It was so good to see a friendly face, and she knew Pam would be on her side.

"What were you doing with the hose?" Pam asked when Jamie finally let go again.

"Watering the bushes." She laughed, which quickly turned to tears.

"Oh, girl, are you okay?"

"No," she whimpered as Pam put an arm around her and corralled her back to the porch chairs.

Pam disappeared inside the house and returned with two glasses of water and a towel to dry them off. "Here."

"Thank you." Jamie grabbed the glass and took a sip.

"You're welcome." Pam wiped herself down and took a seat, angling her body to look at Jamie as she handed her the towel. "Talk to me, James."

Jamie wiped at her shirt, smiling at the nickname only Pam had ever called her. She had missed her friend and hated how much time had passed since they'd last spoken.

"You've never been one to cry, so I know there's something big going on with you." Pam narrowed her eyes. "Spill it."

"I'm pregnant." Jamie stuck her lower lip out.

"Unexpected, I take it."

"Very." She took another sip of water.

"What are you gonna do?" Pam asked.

"I thought getting out of town, coming home, would give me space to make my decision without certain people in my life judging me, but then I got home and Mom was all upset about the possibility of losing her grandbaby."

"This isn't about what they want, it's about what you want."

"I know." Jamie dropped her head back against the chair. "Do you think I should tell the father I'm not keeping it?"

"Are you in a relationship?"

Jamie huffed. "I wish."

"Is there a possibility that you might be in the future?"

She shook her head, still feeling a pain in her chest over his engagement.

"Then why does it matter if he knows?"

"His sister is my best friend, so I'm pretty sure she'll tell him if I don't."

Pam sucked air in through her teeth. "That's tricky."

"I know. I mean, what if I get rid of it and don't tell him. It would always be this secret I'm keeping from him. And if Shannon tells him anyway, I risk him hating me forever."

"Maybe he would see it as you doing him a favor."

"I don't think so. Their family is very conservative."

"Pro-lifers?"

"The biggest." Jamie thought back to her conversation with Shannon, and her heart ached for her friend. "Shannon said she would adopt the baby if I didn't want to keep it."

"Wow, really?"

Jamie nodded. "She told me she can't have kids, but she would raise ours."

"What did you say?"

"That I'd think about it. What else could I say? I felt so bad for her. She lost her first love because of the no babies thing, and part of me just wants to give this to her. She's my best friend, and I love her."

"Then maybe you should."

"But when I really think about that as an option, it seems crazy. I don't think I could be around her and the baby, knowing its mine and Duncan's."

"I get that." Pam shook her head and lay a hand over Jamie's. "Whatever you want to do, I'm here for you. No judgment. I'll even drive you to the clinic if you want to go."

"Really?"

"Absolutely, I will."

"Thanks. The more I think about it, the more I want it to be over. I just can't be a mom right now. Duncan is engaged to be married, and I'll ruin his happy little future if I keep it."

"Oh goodness, this *is* a complicated situation you've gotten yourself into, isn't it?"

"That's an understatement."

Chapter 10

Duncan rubbed the center of his forehead, closed his laptop, then took a sip of iced tea. He leaned back in the kitchen chair and looked out the window into the back yard. Mama and Nana were planting flowers together along the privacy fence. Well, Mama was planting while Nana handed her things. She was spry for ninety-six years old, but not so much that she could kneel to work in the flower beds.

He stood and left his laptop on the table, filled two glasses of water, and wandered out into the yard. "Can I help with anything?"

"I think we're about done for the day," Mama replied as she pressed dirt into the hole where she'd planted some marigolds.

"It looks beautiful out here," he told the ladies.

They both beamed as they admired their handiwork.

"I have to humbly agree," Nana said.

Mama put her hands on her hips and nodded her head once in approval. "Me too. Next, we're going to help Paulie get the yard ready for your …" She glanced at Duncan then away. "For the Fourth."

Duncan raised an eyebrow at her. "For my what? What were you going to say?"

"Nothing," she replied as she snatched one of the glasses of water from his hand and took a sip.

"What are you two up to?" He eyed them. "You've been sneaky lately."

"Oh, fine." Mama set the glass on the gardening cart and clasped her hands together happily. "We're having an engagement party along with the family picnic on the Fourth."

"Samantha!" Nana cried.

Duncan laughed at how little he'd had to push to get Mama to cave. "Was it supposed to be a surprise? Because you are horrible at pulling those off."

"I don't know what you mean." She feigned innocence, but couldn't keep from smiling.

"Every surprise birthday party you've ever had for any of us was spoiled ahead of time."

"Lies!"

"Whatever you say, Mama." He kissed the top of her head before offering the other glass to his grandmother. "Here you go, Nana."

"Thank you, sweet boy." Nana patted his arm as she took the glass and swigged.

Duncan's cell phone rang. It was quarter after three, and Dréa was coming off her shift at the radio station. Long-distance relationships were no fun, but they'd been making it work with their daily phone calls.

"Hi, beautiful," Duncan greeted her as he returned to the house.

"I miss you, Duncan. I can't stand that we won't see each other until next month." Normally, Dréa waited until the end of their phone calls to say this, but not today. "This long-distance thing isn't working for me. I don't like it. Now that we're engaged, I don't want to be apart anymore. We need to pick a date that's soon and start our life together. I'm almost thirty, and my biological clock is ticking, and—"

"Dré, take a breath." He chuckled.

She sighed. "I'm sorry. I've just had a lot of time to think about all these things while we've been apart."

"We've only been apart for a week. And you're two years away from turning thirty. We have plenty of time for babies." Truthfully, the idea of having a kid right now scared the daylights out of him.

"Let's get married in Vegas," she declared.

He laughed. "Yeah, right."

"I'm serious. Let's elope."

He suddenly felt as if he needed to loosen the collar of a dress shirt, even though he was wearing a T-shirt. "What's the rush?"

"I don't want to wait. I want you here with me in Denver. I want to wake up in my husband's arms every morning, start and end each day together. Not a twenty-minute phone call once a day."

Her comment about having him in Denver irritated him. They hadn't come to a decision on that yet. He had always imagined settling down in his hometown, raising kids here. East Grand Rapids had been a wonderful place to grow up, and he wanted the same for his kids. But the couple of times he'd tried to share his feelings with her, it was like she tuned him out, like the decision was already made. It was as if her way was the only way.

He loved and admired her strength and determination, but he feared there wasn't room for compromise where this subject was concerned. And he wondered if she was the same about other areas of her life.

"Are you still there?" she asked.

"I don't want to elope. My family already has an engagement party planned for us at the Fourth of July party, and I know Mama and my sisters will want to help plan the wedding. Sophia can help you find a dress, and Shannon can take our engagement pictures and help us find a wedding photographer."

Dréa was quiet.

"Come on. I want to see you walk down the aisle to me, all beautiful in your wedding dress."

"I do want to wear a pretty dress and walk down the aisle to you," she admitted.

"I know being apart sucks right now, but we can get through this, okay? It's not forever. Just for now."

"I love you," she said.

"I love you too."

"Thank you for talking me down from the ledge."

"You're welcome."

"When I come to Michigan for the party, can we pick a date?"

"Yes."

That seemed to please her, and the rest of the conversation was filled with what happened in Dréa's day—mostly light-hearted stories about people who called in to the radio show with summer vacations gone awry.

Duncan mostly listened while she talked, still feeling unsettled about the Denver situation, and that remained with him long after they hung up.

Chapter 11

"Pam's taking me to the clinic today," Jamie announced at the breakfast table on Friday morning. "I made an appointment."

Her mom stopped pouring the milk into her glass and stared at her for a few beats. "All right. Do you want me to come along?"

Jamie could tell her mother wanted to be supportive, despite her true feelings. "It's okay, Mom. You don't have to come."

"I want to be there for you." Her mother wasn't one to cry often, but she struggled to disguise her watery eyes. "No matter how right you believe this decision is for you, the aftermath may be worse than you expect."

"I'll be fine. This is what I want. I've thought about it so much. It's best for everyone."

"For the baby?" Mom glanced out the window as she said it.

A knock on the door caught their attention. "That's Pam. I'll be back in a little while."

As Jamie moved toward the door, she heard her mother's footsteps closing the space between them. When she turned back, Mom held her arms open, and Jamie received the tightest embrace her mother had ever given her.

Thirty seconds ticked by with Mom still holding on.

"Mom," Jamie whispered.

"I love you."

"I know, Mom. I love you too."

Mom leaned back enough to look Jamie in the eyes. "I just don't want you to regret this decision. What if Duncan wants to raise the baby with you, Jamie? You haven't even told him. It doesn't seem right, him not knowing."

"Mom."

"And your dear friend who can't have a baby. You could give her that."

Jamie stepped away. "I've decided," she replied firmly. She turned and walked away quickly because if she stayed and listened to her mother's words any longer, she might let hope in about her and Duncan.

Been there, done that. She thought something special had happened between them, that they might have a future, and look how that had ended up.

She closed the door behind her and followed Pam along the sidewalk to her car.

When they were buckled in, Pam turned to her. "Are you sure this is what you want to do?"

Her brow furrowed. "Have you and my mom been talking?"

Pam shook her head. "I'm your friend, and I'm just thinking of you and your happiness, so I had to ask once more before we go."

"This is what I want."

"Okay then." Pam started her car and drove toward the women's clinic.

Jamie stared out the window for the whole drive, her stomach fluttering more and more the closer they got to downtown Harrisburg. She'd done some research on the clinic and read about the abortion pill. It seemed like the best, least intrusive way to go, and she hated the idea of a surgical procedure. She just wanted to end all this worry once and for all.

When they arrived, her heart was in her throat, and her hands were shaking.

Pam reached over and took hold of them. She said nothing, simply squeezed.

Jamie got out of the car and stared across the parking lot at the river. She took a deep breath in and let it out, trying to relax. Back in Grand Rapids, sitting downtown along the Grand River always made her calm, but today, the rushing Susquehanna River had the opposite effect.

"Ready?" Pam asked.

She nodded once, and they walked to the clinic.

Once inside, Jamie made her way to the receptionist. "Hello ... Hi, I'm ... My name is Jamie, and I have an appointment."

"Hello, Jamie." The receptionist reached for a clipboard and pen. "We need you to fill out these medical history forms."

Jamie took the clipboard, and they found two seats. She tried to steady her hand as she filled out the paperwork, but her handwriting came out shaky.

Pam lay a hand on her arm. "You'll be fine."

"I know."

Jamie finished and returned the form to the desk.

"Someone will be with you shortly," the receptionist told her.

"Thank you." She returned to her seat to wait. Her knees felt as if they were actually knocking. She hadn't expected to be this nervous.

Several minutes later, when Jamie was sufficiently nerved up, a woman came through a door at the corner of the room. "Jamie Linde."

Jamie walked toward the woman. "Can my friend come with me?"

"Your friend will need to wait here, but you can come back out in between stages if you want."

Jamie was disappointed and wondered what stages there were. She looked over at Pam, who gave her a thumbs-up. "I'll be here the whole time."

"Hello, Jamie." The woman led her down the hall to an exam room. "I'm the sonographer here at the clinic, and I'll be doing your vaginal ultrasound today to determine how far along you are." She handed Jamie a disposable paper sheet. "You'll need to undress from the waist down, and you can cover up with this."

"Okay. Thank you." When the sonographer left, Jamie undressed quickly and hopped up onto the exam table to wait. Now that she was here, her nerves were beginning to settle. A little. This wasn't as bad as she thought it would be. She could do this. Exam, pill, problem solved.

The sonographer returned, helped Jamie into the proper position on the table, and began the ultrasound.

Jamie's heart beat rapidly, not from nerves this time, but from the thought of seeing the little one hanging out in her uterus. *Relax. Deep breaths.*

"You don't have to look if you don't want to," the woman said as if she could sense Jamie's hesitancy. "Many women don't look."

"Okay. I ... I think I want to."

"All right."

Jamie turned her attention to the screen, and there it was. A little round head and tiny body. There was no doubt what she was seeing. There were even little arms and legs. Tears threatened as Jamie stared at its shape.

When the sonographer had finished, a nurse entered and did a blood test and checked her temperature, blood pressure, and heart rate. Then she dressed and was taken to a white-walled room with a small steel desk to one side, where she took a seat opposite the nurse.

"So based on your ultrasound and the rough date you gave us for the first day of your last period, you're eleven weeks along, which is past the ten-week cutoff for the medical abortion."

"What does that mean?" Jamie was still thinking about the image she'd seen on the screen of the baby inside her and wasn't sure she'd heard correctly.

"We can do an in-clinic abortion instead that will take no more than fifteen minutes. Much quicker than the pill."

"Wait, what? No, I wanted the pill." Jamie was in a sudden panic.

"We don't administer the abortion pill after ten weeks. I'm sorry. A surgical abortion is your only option today."

Her only option? This wasn't how it was supposed to go. She was going to take the pill and go home and lie there until it was over.

"The procedure is quite simple. The doctor will use a suction tool to clear your uterus. It's very safe. You may have some cramping afterward, and you should take it easy for the rest of the day, but you should be able to go back to your regular activities by tomorrow." When Jamie didn't respond, she continued. "If you'd like to discuss other options, we can go over those together now."

Jamie shook her head. "No. I ... I've decided."

"All right, well, I'm going to leave you to watch a short video that will go over the procedure so you're aware of everything that will happen."

Jamie stared at the screen as a drawing of a woman's uterus showed a suction tube removing everything from within. Like a little vacuum cleaner, sucking the baby out of there. That's what would happen to the tiny baby she'd just seen minutes before during her ultrasound.

Shannon's voice edged its way into Jamie's thoughts.

Could you go back to your life and pretend it never happened? ... In our family, we believe every life counts, that God has a purpose for each person, including the babies not yet born, no matter how they came to be conceived. This baby is innocent, and it's our blood. A part of our family.

She thought about the nurse telling her that surgical abortion was her only option, and Shannon's words rang loud and clear.

You do have choices ... Please don't do anything you'll regret. Duncan has the right to know before you make any huge decisions. It's his baby too.

Mom's words hit her next.

If you care about him like you say you do, if you want him to stay in your life, keeping this from him is the wrong decision.

Jamie trembled. Could she do this? Did she even want to?

The nurse returned then. "If you're finished, you can return to the waiting room, and I'll come get you when we're ready for you."

Jamie shook her head back and forth. "I'm sorry. I don't know if I can do this."

"If you'd like to speak with the doctor, he can answer any questions you have and go over the procedure with you as well."

Tears burned her eyes. "I can't. I can't do it."

"Would you like to discuss other options?"

Jamie brushed away the tears as she shook her head.

"I understand," the nurse replied, and proceeded to lead her to the waiting room.

Pam gave Jamie a look of concern. "Is it over?"

Jamie walked right past her and out the front doors.

"Jamie?" Pam followed close behind.

"I was too late to take the pill, and they wanted to do it surgically.

I just couldn't do it. I saw the—" She broke down, and Pam put an arm around her as she led her to the car.

Jamie squinted through her tear-blurred vision at a figure leaning against the front bumper. "Mom?"

"I know you told me not to come, but I couldn't stay home."

Jamie didn't say anything, she just went to her mother's open arms and wept.

"I couldn't do it, Mom."

"It's okay, sweetie."

She cried and cried until the tears subsided and the shoulder of her mom's shirt was wet through.

"Can I take you home?" Mom asked.

Jamie nodded weakly, hugged Pam, and headed home with her mother.

She stared out the window at the passing landscape, all the while thinking about the tiny little peanut inside her—part her and part Duncan. And for the first time since the day she found out she was pregnant, she let herself wonder if it was a boy or a girl. She thought about the vision she'd had of a baby with Duncan's features.

She shook her head. Where were her thoughts taking her? She may have changed her mind about the clinic, but her situation hadn't changed. She was still pregnant and confused and unsure of what to do. And Duncan was still marrying another woman.

The thought of telling him terrified her. How would he react? Would he be supportive? Would he be angry? Would he see her and their child as the one mistake that tarnished his perfect future? Her heart ached when she thought of a life without him in it. Especially if she had this baby.

She thought she knew what kind of guy Duncan was, but now she wasn't so sure. She never thought he'd be the kind of guy to blow her off after a one night stand, but that certainly seemed to be the case. And as much as she wanted to believe he'd help her raise this baby, she couldn't be certain, and she didn't want to do it alone.

By the time Mom pulled into the driveway, the tears were close to the surface again. She walked into the house, feeling defeated and emotionally exhausted, and collapsed on the couch. Sleep began to overtake her, and she felt her mom drape the afghan over her as she drifted into a deep sleep.

Chapter 12

A week had passed since Jamie's clinic appointment, and she felt no closer to a decision. She waffled back and forth, doubting her ability to be a single mom, fearing the outcome if she kept the baby and went back to Michigan to announce it to the McGregor family. Some days she thought about going back to the clinic and taking care of it.

At the breakfast table, she sniffled and wiped away tears as she took a bite of toast.

"Baby girl, you need to talk to someone. You need to get some help. Every day, you're in tears, and I don't know how to help you. I want to give you advice, but you know how I feel about this, and I don't want you to think I'm trying to tell you what to do. You need to talk to somebody outside of the situation."

Jamie grunted. "Like a therapist? I don't want to talk to a shrink."

"A friend of mine from church works at a family center. They have nice ladies on hand to talk with you about how you're feeling and answer questions. They'll go over options with you. No pressure. They are there to help you make the right decision for you."

"I don't know." The last thing she wanted was to go to an unfamiliar place and talk to a stranger about her situation. But maybe Mom was right. She was no closer to a decision than she had been last week, and the stress probably wasn't healthy.

"Will you at least think about it?" Mom asked.

Jamie took a drink of orange juice and pushed her plate away. She wasn't quite sure what she was getting herself into, but she heard herself say, "I'll go."

Mom's eyes widened. "You will?"

"Yeah. I don't know what to do. I need help making this decision, and I'm willing to try anything at this point."

Jamie followed her mother through the door of Faith Family Center. The space was bright with comfy chairs the color of dark chocolate and pillows in warm autumn tones set in a quaint waiting area. On the wall were framed inspirational quotes and Bible verses printed across picturesque scenery—fields, oceans, blue skies. The coziness filled her with a calm and replaced the uncertainty she had felt about coming there in the first place.

Almost as soon as they entered, they were greeted by a bubbly middle-aged woman, holding a baby on her hip. "Sylvia!"

"Hi, Gloria." Jamie's mom replied. "How are you?"

"Doing well."

"Who's this little cutie?" Mom reached out and shook the baby's chubby little hand.

"This is Carter. His mama is here going through some parenting classes, so we're keeping an eye on him." Gloria looked over at Jamie. "You must be Jamie. Your mom said you were in town for a visit."

"Nice to meet you." Jamie didn't know where to start or what to say, but Gloria spoke before she had a chance.

"Can I show you two around the place? We've just finished some remodeling, and I love giving people the grand tour."

"Sure. I've been wanting to see all your progress." Mom reached over and squeezed Jamie's hand as Gloria led them down a short hallway and around a corner into another welcoming space. A little room to one side had a half door and a large window to see inside. It was overflowing with toys and books, and a teenaged girl sat on the floor, playing with two toddlers. She noticed them through the window and came over to take Carter from Gloria.

Across from the playroom was a space set up like a store with racks of children's clothing and shelves filled with diapers and wipes and other baby supplies. "Many wonderful people from the community donate the things you see here. We're very blessed."

Mom and Gloria chit-chatted as they moved to another section of the building, which looked more like a doctor's office with a reception desk, waiting area, and separate room with an exam table and equipment. Jamie thought about her visit to the clinic. She hesitated in the doorway as her mother followed her friend.

"This is the newly remodeled area of the center," Gloria gushed.

"Very nice," Mom said.

"We offer free pregnancy tests and have a woman who comes and gives free ultrasounds when needed."

Jamie remained in the doorway and forced herself to speak. "What would you say to someone who is pregnant but doesn't know whether or not to keep the baby?"

"We would talk with them about what they're thinking, how they're feeling, and give them information about all of their options."

"*All* of their options?"

"Yes. We're here to provide a safe place to talk, and we also want to educate, so everyone who comes through our doors is fully informed about their options before they make a decision."

Jamie swallowed hard and glanced at her mom, whose eyes were full of understanding. "Is there somebody here I could talk to?" she managed. "I ... I'm pregnant, and I don't know what to do."

Gloria looked over at Mom then back at Jamie with so much kindness in her eyes. "Of course there is."

Jamie sat and talked with Gloria for over an hour. She let each of her fears and insecurities and hopes and dreams spill out of her heart in that room. Gloria was the perfect listening ear, and as she had said, she laid out all of the options available to her—keeping the baby, giving it up for adoption, even abortion, which Jamie had already learned about at the clinic.

"No matter what you decide, you will not be alone," Gloria told her.

Of all her fears about this pregnancy, *this* was the greatest. That no matter what choice she made, she would end up all alone. That if she kept the baby, she'd have to do it herself while Duncan was off living his happy life. And that if she didn't keep it, everyone in her life would judge her and turn away from her.

"God will never leave you," Gloria assured her. "He loves you and that baby of yours. He cares about what you're going through and wants a relationship with you. You can talk to Him about all of this anytime, and He will listen. All you have to do is pray."

She'd never been much of a religious person. Her life so far was evidence of that. But she did believe there was a God, and hearing that He actually paid attention to her and her life was a revelation. She'd always thought of Him as this high and mighty being, up in Heaven, looking down. But talking to Him, asking Him what to do ... well, she wasn't sure where to start with that. How did one even pray?

Seeing the change in her parents since she'd been home had opened her eyes to the way faith could change someone. Not that her parents were bad people before, but they were joyful now. It was hard to miss. And they were quick to tell anyone that going to church and living their life for God was the reason.

She felt a strong urge to know more, to learn what it was that had changed her parents.

"You've given me a lot to think about," Jamie told Gloria.

"You are always welcome here. Anytime you need to talk or if you need help, we're available."

"I appreciate that." She gathered the brochures Gloria had given her and stood.

"Remember, God loves you, Jamie, and He loves that little baby of yours."

Jamie thanked Gloria with a hug and rejoined her mother.

When they got into the car, Jamie took hold of her mom's hand and squeezed. "Thanks for bringing me here, Mom."

"Have you made a decision?"

"I'm getting closer. But I need a little more time."

"Of course."

Jamie let go of Mom's hand and smiled. She watched the familiar landscape as they drove home. Her gaze fell to her hand, realizing she'd been rubbing it back and forth over her belly. She glanced over at Mom, who hadn't noticed, or if she had, she wasn't letting on.

When they arrived home, she lay down for a nap. Pregnancy took so much out of her, and she felt like she was constantly tired. She had so many thoughts floating around in her mind as she closed in on a decision, but she was too exhausted to dwell on that for long.

A loud bang woke her with a start. She came out of sleep in a fog and sat up, listening to the now quiet house. *It must have been a dream.*

But as she was about to lie back down, she heard it again and jumped up from the couch.

"Mom?" She headed toward the back of the house, where she thought the sound was coming from. "Dad?"

"We're up here, honey," Mom called from upstairs.

Jamie took the steps quickly and found her parents moving the workout equipment from her former bedroom. "What are you guys doing?"

"We're making room for you and the baby," Mom replied.

"But—"

"We want you to know this is still your room. Even if … it's only for you. But if you have the baby, you can stay here with us anytime. We'll help you get started, and you'll have a place here whenever you need it."

Tears stung as she watched her dad shimmy the elliptical trainer across the floor.

"We love you, and we're sorry if taking over your room made you feel like this isn't your home anymore," he said.

Her throat felt thick with emotion. "I don't know what to say."

"You don't have to say anything."

"I'm not mad at you guys for wanting to get in shape and using my room to do it. I was surprised, that's all. And I haven't lived at home for a long time. It's your house."

"It's *our* home." Mom lay her hand over Jamie's belly. "All of us."

The dam broke then, and Jamie collapsed into her mother's arms.

"Oh, sweetie." Mom rubbed her back and comforted her, and Dad came to stand with them and lay a hand on her shoulder.

"It's a baby," Jamie whimpered. "I saw it on the screen at the clinic. It had a little round head and a body and arms and legs. And I just couldn't do it. I couldn't go through with it."

"It's okay, Jamie."

"I don't want to end my pregnancy." The words came from a place of truth and lifted a weight she hadn't known she'd been carrying. She let go of her mother and rubbed the wetness from her face with the sleeve of her shirt.

"So, what does this mean?"

"It means I need to tell Duncan."

Chapter 13

The past ten days at her parents' house had been just what Jamie needed as she worked up the courage to return home and spill the beans to Duncan. Mom and Dad were supportive and encouraging, doting on her, taking her out, spoiling her. They also got her in to see their family doctor at the last minute, who did an in-office ultrasound to confirm what Jamie already knew and started her on prenatal vitamins.

More and more, she could see the profound change in her parents and the way they lived. She often found them reading their Bibles—sometimes together, sometimes separate. Mom walked on her treadmill to Christian music. There was no longer alcohol in the house. And there was a new kind of joy that showed from the inside out, which made her exceedingly curious.

This curiosity was what brought her to the third-row center pew at a little Baptist church in Hershey, flanked by her parents. She had been introduced around when they arrived and had watched their interactions with church friends with great interest. There was genuine caring among them, and her heart warmed to see her parents so happy.

As Jamie people-watched and waited for the service to start, she felt a tap on her shoulder and turned to see a familiar face.

"Hi, Jamie," Gloria said. "It's so nice to see you here."

"Thank you. I'm happy to be here."

"How are you feeling?"

Jamie glanced around, feeling a little self-conscious. "Fine."

"We've been praying for you this week."

"We?"

"Your mom and I are in a women's prayer group, and you've been at the top of our list."

"Thank you. I appreciate it." Her throat tightened as she glanced at her mom. And why were her eyes suddenly stinging with tears?

"Your mom tells me you made a decision."

Jamie nodded. "I did."

"I'm happy to hear it."

She didn't voice her decision, and Gloria didn't ask, but she was sure her mom had already shared the news. "Thank you for all your help, Gloria."

Gloria lay a hand on her shoulder. "You're welcome."

The pianist began to play, and Jamie turned to face the stage as a man took to the pulpit and led the congregation in a hymn. She thought about her reaction to the ladies praying for her and how much it meant to her. As far as she knew, nobody had ever prayed for her before, and it felt big and important.

She paid close attention to the songs that were sung and the words of the pastor's sermon. It wasn't what she expected. His stories were real and relatable, shared from his own experiences or those of people in his life.

"When I was twenty years old, I didn't know what I was doing with my life. I had dropped out of college, was working a dead-end job, hanging out with the wrong people, getting into trouble. I didn't come from a church background. I was lost, and I didn't know it."

Jamie's heart stuttered at his words. *Lost? Was she lost?* Most days lately, that's exactly how she felt.

"But someone reached out to me. A kind neighbor lady, who had known me since I was a boy, asked me to help her install a new mailbox. What she didn't know was that only days before, my friends and I had driven by and smashed her mailbox with a bat. It was childish and immature, but that's where I was at that time in my life.

"I did the work for her, and she thanked me and paid me twenty bucks. I took it and went home, but I was overcome with guilt, so much that I went back to her later that day, and I said, 'Miss Freida, I can't accept this money. I'm sorry. I'm the one who did it. I smashed your mailbox.' She looked at me with such kindness and said, 'I know you did.' I was in shock. I couldn't believe she knew and yet she didn't seem angry or turn me in to the cops. I asked her why she paid me if she knew I was the one who did it. 'I would've paid anyone who did the job for me,' she told me, 'You came back and fixed what you broke. That's all that matters to me.' I was in shock that someone could let me off the hook so easily. That I could make such a big mistake and be forgiven for it, no questions asked.

"I stopped by to visit Miss Freida more often after that. She was a great source of encouragement and eventually invited me to her church. And it was there that I came to realize why she was able to forgive me without a second thought. Because God had forgiven her the same way. No questions asked."

Jamie barely listened to the rest of the sermon, because that story was stuck in her mind. She thought about it long after they had gone home and eaten lunch. She mulled it over while she packed her bags for the trip back to Grand Rapids the next day. And finally, she went to her parents, who were in the kitchen preparing dinner.

"Hey, can I talk to you guys about something?" She sat on a barstool.

"Sure, honey," Mom said over her shoulder.

"I liked the pastor's story today, and I've been thinking a lot about it."

They both looked at her.

"I don't really understand it all, and I thought maybe you guys could tell me your story."

"How we started going to church is different than Pastor," Mom said. "We weren't invited there by anyone. We both just felt like something was missing in our life, and we were in a place where we wanted to improve ourselves. It was kind of on a whim that we went to church that day. We thought we'd give it a try. And we immediately loved the people and felt welcomed, like we were a part of something special."

Dad spoke next. "Not long after, Pastor spoke about how to know beyond a doubt that you're going to Heaven, and we didn't know if we were, but we wanted to. So, we both made decisions that day to accept Jesus into our hearts, and it was the best choice we ever made."

Jamie leaned forward and rested her forearms on the countertop. "I can tell it's been life-changing for you both."

"It really has," Mom replied.

Jamie felt an ache deep in her heart, a longing to know the kind of joy her parents had found. "I think I want what you have. I want to know Jesus too."

"You do?" Mom instantly teared up.

"Gloria told me God loves me and my baby and that with Him, I will never be alone, and I haven't been able to get that out of my mind since."

"He does love you and the baby. He knew you before you were formed, and the same with that sweet baby you're carrying. He cares more than you could ever fathom. He sent his own Son to this Earth to die on the cross for our sins. That's how much He loves us."

Jamie felt a warmth come over her. "What do I need to do?"

"Just ask him to forgive you for the sins of your past, to make you new, and to come into your heart and life and be your Savior."

Nerves skittered through her body. "I don't know what to say."

Mom and Dad rounded the bar and each took one of her hands.

"We'll help you," Mom said.

And as her parents helped her pray, Jamie knew her life was changed forever.

Chapter 14

Aunt Pauline's back yard was filled with family and friends for the Fourth of July picnic at her home on Reeds Lake. With its expansive lawn, angling subtly down to the lake, there was plenty of room to accommodate their large family for these annual reunion gatherings. Nana and Paulie were the last of the five Bachman sisters, so every year the family was able to gather was special to them. Especially tonight, since they had gone all out for Duncan's engagement.

"Your family sure knows how to throw a party," Dréa commented.

Duncan nodded. "They've been doing this for many years, but somehow they've outdone themselves with this one."

The decorations were more elegant than usual, with floral centerpieces and small jars with candles placed on all the tables. There were more strings of lights hanging between the trees than in past years, and candles floated on the surface of the lake surrounding the dock.

Dréa looked ravishing in a red sundress with her dark locks curled and flowing. Duncan reached over and ran his fingers through a curl that was resting against her cheek and tucked it behind her ear. She looked up at him, and he leaned in and softly pressed his lips to her cheek.

They mingled with guests for a while, and when she went to sit with her family, he walked over to where Shannon was refilling the punch bowl. "Hey, is Micah coming?"

"Yeah, he's driving in from Virginia tonight. He'll be here soon."

"Is he back for good?"

"Not yet. He has to get his house sold and wrap up some other things down there before he finds a place here."

"And then what? Are you guys getting married too?"

Shannon eyed him. "We *just* got back together, D. Give us a little time to get to know each other again."

That might have been a jab at his quick engagement to Dréa, but he let it go.

"Is Jamie coming?" He didn't know why he'd asked, but he hadn't seen her around since that day he introduced the family to Dréa.

"She left town."

His mouth fell open. "You're kidding."

"Afraid not. She's been gone for weeks." Shannon frowned.

"She didn't ... I mean, it wasn't because of me, was it?"

Shannon's eyes met his. "What do *you* think?"

His shoulders drooped, and sadness washed over him. "Is she coming back?"

"I don't know." There was something in Shannon's demeanor that said she was more upset about this than she was letting on. "I have to go help in the kitchen."

"Okay." He watched his sister until she disappeared inside the house, and he tried to pretend it didn't bother him that Jamie leaving town was his fault.

The sound of Papa's fork tapping against glass gained everyone's attention. He and Mama stood alongside Dréa's parents in front of everyone.

"We wanted to take a moment to welcome Dréa's family tonight. They've traveled all the way from Denver to be with us and celebrate Duncan and Dréa's engagement."

Everyone clapped and a few friends and cousins cheered and whistled.

"We've been praying for years for our children's future spouses, and we couldn't be happier that God brought Dréa into our Duncan's life. Dréa, you are a special woman and we are elated to welcome you into our family."

Dréa lay her hand over her heart and gazed over at Duncan lovingly.

Duncan stood and took his fiancée's hand, and they joined their parents in front of the crowd. They exchanged hugs, then Duncan faced everyone, scanning the faces of his family that he loved before turning to Dréa. He was marrying this woman. She would become a part of the McGregor family. The enormity of that suddenly hit him, and he was at a loss for words.

She looked at him expectantly, waiting for him to speak. But when his silence hung heavy in the air, she took over in that eloquent way of hers. Speaking was her job, after all.

He didn't hear everything she said, but a few phrases broke through.

Never expected to meet someone.

God brought us together.

She finished with, "I can't wait to marry this man," and wrapped her arms around his waist, snuggling into him.

He squeezed his arms around her and kissed her cheek, and everyone clapped.

Dréa leaned close to his ear. "Aren't you going to say anything?"

He shook his head. "You said it all perfectly."

She looked disappointed but gave him a weak smile.

"I Don't Want to Set the World on Fire" began to play over speakers set up in the yard by cousin Tim, the musician of the family.

Nana walked toward them. "May I have this dance?" she asked.

Duncan looked at Dréa with eyebrows raised.

"Be my guest." She moved aside as he took his grandmother for a slow turn under the twinkly lights.

Nana held onto his hand and wrapped an arm around his back. "What happened up there?"

"What do you mean?"

"I know you, my boy."

"I don't know. I guess I froze."

"Why?"

"It hit me that we're getting married, and she'll soon be part of our family."

"That's what happens after you get engaged."

"I know. And I'm happy about it. I just had a moment of panic, I guess."

"It's normal to be nervous. If that's what this was."

"It is."

"All right." Nana eyed him.

"Just say whatever it is you want to say, Nana."

"Have you been talking to God about everything?"

He hadn't. He'd made himself busy with a design job, pushing aside all thoughts of what had happened with Jamie. And he hadn't been praying about his and Dréa's issues over where to live either. He kept thinking everything would work itself out, but he knew deep down that's not how it worked.

Nana waited for his reply, but he remained silent.

"Trying to ignore your problems will never end well. Give it all over to Him, Duncan. You'll be amazed at how things work out when you do."

"I know, Nana. I will."

They swayed back and forth to the song, slowly turning. Duncan glanced around and noticed Mama dancing with Papa and Dréa with her dad. Dréa's brother, Kyle, had Melissa and both of their daughters in his arms. Even Aunt Paulie was enjoying a dance with Max.

At the final lines of the song, Duncan saw Jamie, standing in the doorway of the house, scanning the crowd. Her face lit up when she spotted Shannon, and his chest tightened at the sight. She moved toward Shannon, who looked delighted to see her and immediately wrapped her up in a hug before whisking her away into the house.

Duncan had the strongest desire to follow them and talk to Jamie, but Dréa was standing before them now.

"May I cut in?" she asked with a wink.

"Of course," Nana replied and gave Duncan a hug and kiss on the cheek before taking a seat next to her sister.

Dréa wrapped her arms around his neck and leaned into him as they danced to "Put Your Head on My Shoulder."

He kept looking toward the house, wondering if Jamie and Shannon would emerge soon.

"Hey." Dréa touched his face. "Where are you tonight?"

"I'm right here."

"No, you're not. What's going on? Why didn't you say anything earlier?"

"I'm not great at public speaking. That's your thing."

"You could've at least thanked everyone for coming. Two words aren't so hard to say."

His brow furrowed. "Are you mad about this?"

"I thought you'd be more excited, I guess. This is our engagement party, Duncan. We're supposed to be celebrating."

"I'm sorry. I'm just feeling off today."

They danced quietly for a minute before she spoke again.

"We need to pick a date."

He immediately tensed, and she stepped out of his arms.

"You said we would when I got here."

"We will."

"Let's do it now."

"Right now? Let's finish our dance."

"Fine, but we're announcing a date before the fireworks start."

Chapter 15

Shannon dragged Jamie through the house, up the stairs, and into the closest bedroom. She walked across the room, closed the french doors leading to the balcony, and turned to face her.

"You're glowing," Shannon said.

"My mom kept saying that. I don't think I look any different."

"You do." Shannon looked absolutely giddy. "You're still pregnant, right? Tell me you're still pregnant."

A little smile crept over Jamie's face. "I'm still pregnant."

Shannon shrieked so loudly that Jamie was sure all the guests in the yard below heard her, and she practically knocked Jamie over when she ran across the room and wrapped her up in the tightest hug she'd ever received.

"I was worried you left because ... well, I thought you wouldn't come back pregnant."

"I know."

"So, what does this mean? Are you keeping the baby?"

"I'm keeping the baby."

Tears filled Shannon's eyes. "Oh, Jamie. I prayed and prayed something would happen to change your mind. I asked God to break the machines at the clinic or have a freak power outage or have your car break down on the way there. Something, anything."

Jamie laughed. "Well, it worked."

"What happened?"

"I was planning to take the abortion pill, but when I got there, they told me I was too far along for that."

Shannon's eyes widened. "Wow, you actually went."

"Yeah. My only other option was surgical, and I couldn't do it. Especially not after seeing the baby on the ultrasound."

"You saw the baby?"

Jamie nodded as she moved to the french doors, peeking through the glass. "Now I have to figure out how to tell your brother."

When she turned back, Shannon was seated on the edge of the bed, brushing a tear from her cheek. "You should probably know that this picnic is also Duncan and Dréa's engagement party."

"What?" Jamie's stomach dropped, and she felt all the color drain from her face.

"You showed up right after the speeches."

"No." Jamie's hand rested against her belly as a wave of nausea hit, and she raced out of the room toward the bathroom at the end of the hall. Her knees hit the tile in front of the toilet just in time. Morning sickness was a total lie. Hers hit at all hours of the day. And this news certainly hadn't helped.

Engagement party?

She groaned as she stood, flushed the toilet, and went to the faucet, filling her cupped hand for a drink. In the top drawer of the cabinet, she found a tube of toothpaste, squeezed a little on her fingertip, rubbed it across her teeth and around her mouth, then rinsed her mouth once more.

Why did she have to come here today of all days? She planned to show up, find Duncan, ask to talk privately, and spill the news. But she couldn't do that at their engagement party. Their entire day would be ruined.

She stared at her reflection in the mirror. Was she really glowing? Could people tell she was pregnant? She did feel different now that she'd made the decision to keep the baby. Part of her was unwilling to admit it, but she felt excited. It wasn't what she had originally planned for her life, but since she'd decided, she couldn't help but feel a bond forming between her and this baby.

"Well, Peach, I guess we'll have to wait a little longer to tell your daddy." She had nicknamed the baby after reading an article comparing the growth of a baby each week of pregnancy to a similarly sized fruit. At thirteen weeks, the baby was roughly the size of a peach.

Jamie opened the bathroom door, smiling down as she rubbed her palm back and forth over her belly, and ran straight into a broad, solid chest. Strong hands gripped her upper arms to steady her.

"Hey, you."

Jamie's eyes lifted to meet Duncan's, and they both stared for several long beats. She knew she should move away, but she found herself locked in place by his hands and their mutual gaze.

"Hey," she squeaked out. She cleared her throat and tried again. "Sorry. I wasn't watching where I was going."

"You were rubbing your stomach. Are you sick?"

"I was, but I'm better now."

"Something you ate? Or should I be worried you'll give me the stomach flu?" There was a twinkle in his eyes.

"The first one," she replied, still staring and wondering why he hadn't let go yet.

"So, you're back." He finally loosened his hold and took a step away.

"Just got into town and came to see Shannon." It was a half-truth.

His gaze turned to a watercolor painting of the lake hanging on the wall beside them. "Did she tell you ... this is our ... mine and Dréa's engagement party?"

Hit me while I'm down, Duncan. Go ahead.

"Y-yeah." She tried to force herself to congratulate him, but the words wouldn't come. It would've been a bald-faced lie, anyway. She wasn't happy for them. Not at all. And as selfish as it was, she secretly hoped it wouldn't work out. Though she knew that was a long shot. Compared to Jamie, Dréa seemed perfect in every way, and he would be crazy not to marry her.

"Where did you go?" he asked.

"Back to Hershey to visit my parents."

"Pennsylvania?"

She nodded.

"That's nice. I bet they miss you."

Small talk wasn't their thing, and she wondered what was behind it.

"You didn't leave town ... well, it wasn't because of me, was it? Because Shannon said—"

"What did Shannon say?" Her heart rate kicked up a notch. She wasn't going to be happy with Shannon if she had spilled something to her brother she shouldn't have.

"That you left."

"And you just assumed it was because of you?"

He shrugged his shoulders. "Was it?"

"It's complicated."

"I know you were unhappy that day you came over to the house for dinner, and I know I hurt you when I didn't call from Denver."

"Yeah, you did."

"I was a jerk."

"Glad you can admit it, at least."

"I'm sorry. I should've called you. It wasn't anything you did—"

Jamie held up her hand, feeling sick over what he was about to say. "Don't bother with the 'it's not you, it's me' thing. What happened between us obviously meant nothing to you. I'm fine. I'm over it." She wasn't, but she wished this conversation was over.

His eyes met hers again. He was giving her that look, the one he'd given her that night, and it sent a zing of electricity through her body. "I never said it meant nothing."

"Then why didn't you call? I wanted you to call." Her voice was low, almost a whisper now.

His gaze dropped to the floor beside them. "It's hard to explain."

"Well, I'd really like to hear it."

"Duncan! Are you up there?" Dréa called from the bottom of the stairs.

"Yeah! Be right down!" he cried.

Apology was written all over his face when he looked at her.

"Go ahead." She nodded toward the stairs. "She's waiting."

Duncan's arms suddenly wrapped around her and pulled her close. "I hope I haven't ruined our friendship completely. I don't want it to be awkward between us now, and I don't want you to hate me."

Jamie's arms moved against her will and rounded his waist. She rested her head against his chest and settled into him. "I could never hate you, Duncan." Her heart ached with the truth she was holding inside.

He loosened his grip but kept his arms where they were as he looked down at her. There was a war going on in his eyes. He looked as if he wanted to say more.

Jamie wanted to tell him. So badly. Standing there in his embrace, she wanted him to know they were having a baby.

His gaze traveled over her face and landed on her lips, and the air between them charged. She felt it like static electricity, raising the hairs on her arms.

She hadn't been expecting this—their chemistry—to still be so strong. He was engaged. And in that moment, she wished she could read his mind. What was he thinking? Did he want to kiss her? It would be so easy for her to lean in and make that decision for him.

But the moment ended as quickly as it began, replaced by Duncan's guilty expression. His arms dropped like bricks, and he stepped back and shook his head as if waking from a fog. "Sorry. I'll ... see you downstairs."

At that, he turned on his heel and raced down the stairs, leaving her alone, wondering what in the world just happened.

Chapter 16

He'd wanted to kiss her. Holding her in his arms, those deep brown eyes of hers gazing up at him, had reminded him of that night, how good they were together, how good she had felt. Thank God he'd come to his senses before he'd given in.

Inwardly, he groaned. He wanted to punch himself in the face. He was standing next to his fiancée while she talked and laughed with their mothers. This beautiful, Christ-loving woman, who he was going to spend the rest of his life with.

So why was he still thinking about the way Jamie felt in his arms?

Dréa took his hand and tugged him along behind her to a quiet corner of the yard. The sky was growing darker now that the sun had sunk below the horizon, and it was nearly fireworks time. He knew exactly what she wanted to talk about before she said a word.

Her phone lit up as she opened the calendar app, moving to his side so he could see too. "I was thinking, if we're going to have a traditional church wedding, I'm definitely going to need a little more time to prepare."

"Right." The idea of more time until the wedding made him happier than he probably should've been.

"Fall is too soon and that leads into the holidays. So, I was thinking maybe January. That's six months from now. I can plan a wedding in six months."

"January's fine." He tried to summon more enthusiasm than he felt.

"How about the fourteenth? That's right in the middle of the month. The only problem might be snow at that time of year. Do you think we should wait until spring?" She lowered her phone and turned into him, wrapping her arms around his neck. "I really don't want to wait that long."

He slid his arms around her waist. "January's fine."

She smiled up at him. "You already said that."

"Because whatever you decide, I'm cool with."

"Okay. Good." She planted a quick kiss on his lips and rushed back to their mothers.

Shannon and Jamie exited the house then and made their way to the food and drinks. He had to force himself to keep his feet planted. Jamie looked beautiful. Even more so than usual. He shook his head and looked toward the lake, where some of his cousins were standing near the dock talking. He headed their way, determined to ignore the ache in his chest.

Chapter 17

When would the timing be right? If Shannon had any say in it, they would already be in a quiet room in the house, where Jamie could tell Duncan the news. But this was huge. She was about to drop a bomb and blow all his plans to smithereens, not to mention possibly ruining his relationship in the process. As much as she didn't want Duncan to get married, she didn't relish the thought of hurting him in any way. But she hadn't done this alone. He was a part of this, and he deserved to know. But when? She couldn't just pull him out of the middle of his engagement party and lay this information on him.

She nibbled on a cracker, hoping nausea would remain at bay, and watched Duncan, who was standing across the lawn talking with some of his cousins. She scanned the crowd to Dréa. Gorgeous Dréa, who fit so well with Duncan's family. She was talking with Mrs. McGregor and another woman, probably her mom based on their similar looks.

"I don't belong here," Jamie told Shannon. "I think I'm gonna go."

"Don't go yet. Stay for the fireworks," Shannon begged.

A hand touched her back as Nana McGregor stepped up beside her. "Do stay for the show, dear."

"Hi, Nana." Jamie smiled at the sweet woman, who had always treated her as her own granddaughter.

"Why leave now? You only just arrived."

"I know." Jamie's gaze found Duncan again. "I'm just very tired these days."

"Well, of course, you are." She lay a palm on Jamie's belly.

Her eyes shot to Nana's and then Shannon's, who looked as shocked as she did.

"What do you mean by that, Nana?" Shannon asked.

"I've been around a long time, you two." Nana lifted her wrinkled hand and cupped Jamie's cheek. "You're glowing, sweet girl."

"Why does everyone keep saying that?" Jamie let out a little laugh, and Shannon giggled.

"It's a dead giveaway." Nana reached down and squeezed Jamie's hand. "He doesn't know yet, does he?"

Jamie looked at Nana. "Who?"

Nana tilted her head in the direction of the lake. "Duncan."

"How did you ...?"

"He told me what happened between you two," she admitted.

Nana's answer was not what Jamie was expecting. He had talked about her to his grandmother? She was dying to know what he said.

"Is that why you're here tonight?" Nana asked. "To give him the happy news?"

Jamie made a face. "I'm not sure how happy he'll think it is."

"Maybe not at first, but he'll come around."

"I don't know." Jamie certainly didn't have Nana's confidence.

Nana was about to say something else when Dréa suddenly called out from across the yard.

"Duncan and I wanted to thank you all again for celebrating with us tonight. And before the fireworks start, we wanted to share some exciting news."

Jamie's stomach flipped.

Oh no! She's not pregnant, too, is she? It would be just Jamie's luck for something like that to happen.

"We've chosen a wedding date," Dréa announced.

The yard filled with applause, but Jamie couldn't bring herself to lift her arms, let alone clap her hands together. Dréa looked so darn happy, but Duncan's smile appeared half-hearted.

"We're getting married on January fourteenth in Denver. Save the date!"

Jamie's heart caught in her throat. *January fourteenth?*

Of course, they chose the baby's due date as their wedding day. Of course they did.

The fireworks over Reeds Lake were spectacular, as always. Jamie sat on a blanket in the grass with Shannon and Micah, watching the explosions of red, white, and blue light up the sky. She tried to pretend she didn't notice Micah running his fingers up and down Shannon's arm and nuzzling her neck the entire time. She was elated that her friend was back together with her first love. Nobody deserved it more than Shannon, who had sacrificed so much and given up that relationship for such difficult reasons.

Jamie stared across the yard at the man whose arms she wanted to be in. Dréa was seated next to him, leaning into his side, staring up at the show. One of Duncan's arms was draped around her back, but he wasn't watching the fireworks.

They made eye contact, and Jamie gave him a weak smile. The right corner of his mouth tilted up in a way that made her heart rate accelerate.

Why was he watching her?

Hope crept its way into her heart, but she tamped it down quickly. She couldn't dare to dream that he might have real feelings for her too. Because if she started to think that way, if she imagined them as a family with their baby, she would be crushed when it didn't happen. She needed to let it go and hope Duncan would at least be a part of the baby's life.

After the fireworks, the crowd thinned out as many of the extended family headed home. Jamie stayed and helped Shannon and her family carry leftover food into the house and clean up trash from around the yard. Duncan and a few of the cousins started up a fire and moved chairs in a circle around it.

"Come on, Jame." Shannon walked toward the fire. "Let's make s'mores."

Jamie wasn't sure her stomach could take that since she was already nerved up on top of the normal "morning" sickness. But sitting around the fire on a pleasant summer evening sounded nice, so she followed.

Duncan placed the last of the chairs in the circle. "Here, Jamie. You can have this one."

"Thanks." She took the seat, disappointed that he didn't stick around.

One of the cousins sat down in the chair she wished Duncan had taken. "Hey, do you remember me?"

Jamie looked at him closely, his face lit by the fire and the warm glow of lights from the house. "You were there when I came to the McGregor's for dinner a few weeks ago, right?"

"Right."

"Was it Mark?" She scrunched up her nose, knowing that probably wasn't right.

He laughed. "Max, actually."

She gave him a sheepish grin. "I'm so sorry. I'm Jamie."

Max smiled and held out his hand. "I remember."

"No, you don't." She gave his hand a shake.

"Of course I do. You were the prettiest girl there."

Jamie snorted. "Dréa was there, so I know you're lying, but thank you."

Max held onto her hand longer than a friendly handshake. "I wasn't lying."

Her cheeks warmed under his stare.

"Hey, guys."

They both looked up at Duncan, suddenly standing behind them. His gaze settled on their connected hands, and Jamie saw the muscle in his jaw twitch, which made her want to do a happy dance.

She slid her hand from Max's and clasped both hands together in her lap as Duncan took the empty seat to her other side.

"Hi," he said sweetly.

"Hi." She gave him her cutest smile.

"Did you have fun tonight?"

"I did."

"Not too mild for ya?" he asked.

Her eyes narrowed.

"Do you want to roast a marshmallow?" He held up a bag containing all the supplies to make s'mores—fluffy marshmallows, graham crackers, and milk chocolate Hershey bars.

"No, thanks." She definitely couldn't handle that much sugar right now, but she was still stuck on his previous comment. *Not too mild? What does he think? That all I do is party?*

"I'll take those." Max snatched the bag from his cousin and disappeared into the shadows to find a roasting stick.

Jamie decided to let Duncan's remark go. She glanced around the circle and scanned the yard. "Where's Dréa?"

"She and her family went back to their hotel."

"Oh, I thought maybe they were staying here or at your parents'."

"They prefer a hotel," he explained.

"So ... January, huh?" She was still in disbelief that they had chosen *that* date.

He shrugged his shoulders. "Yep."

Jamie looked at the others around the fire then glanced at Duncan. His fiancée was gone for the evening. This was her chance. It had to be now.

"Hey, Duncan, can we maybe go somewhere and talk?"

His eyes met hers, and he looked as if he was searching for what to say. "We can't let what happened before happen again."

That's why he hesitated? He thought she wanted to ... what? Sneak off and do it again? She wasn't sure whether to be insulted or not, but it didn't matter. Now was the time.

"That's not ... I didn't mean that. I respect your relationship, and I would never do that." Maybe the old her would have, but not anymore. She wanted to tell him everything that had happened to her when she was in Pennsylvania—the way she had changed, the decision she had made. But first, she needed him to know about the baby.

"I'm sorry." He stared down at the ground. "I shouldn't have presumed."

"There's something important I need to talk to you about ... in private."

His brow furrowed. "All right."

"Where can we go?"

"I know a place." He stood, and she did the same.

Her eyes met Shannon's over the fire, and Shannon pressed her hands together as if to show she'd be praying. Jamie had never felt as many butterflies as were flipping and fluttering around in her stomach at the moment.

She and Duncan walked across the lawn into the darkness and out onto the dock. The boards creaked beneath their feet as they moved to the end.

"These look so pretty," she commented on the floating candles in the water around the dock. Her hands were suddenly sweating as Duncan sat down and patted the boards next to him.

Jamie took a seat beside him, leaving enough room between them to give him space when he heard the news.

"So, what's up?" he asked.

Her heart raced at an alarmingly rapid rate. She took a shaky breath in and let it out slowly as her eyelids closed. Tears burned with the sudden fear of what his reaction might be.

Please, God, please give me the strength to do this. Give me the words to say. This prayer thing was coming more and more naturally to her every day.

"Jamie?"

She opened her eyes and saw his concern.

"Are you okay?"

She shook her head slowly, which caused him to lay a hand on her shoulder.

"What is it?"

How was she supposed to say this? Just blurt it out? She turned her gaze to the dark, rippling water before them and focused on one of the floating candles. "I've thought about this conversation for weeks. Playing the whole thing over in my mind. All the possible outcomes. But now that I have you here ... this is so hard." She was trembling, and her chin quivered as she fought tears.

Duncan took her hand and squeezed. "Whatever it is, you can tell me. We're friends, right?"

She closed her eyes again, then opened them and looked him straight in the eye.

He reached over with his other hand and sandwiched hers between his. "Maybe you don't consider me a friend anymore, but I hope we can find some way to move forward. Because you're my sister's best friend, and I know you'll always be in our life."

An unexpected laugh escaped Jamie before she could stop it. "You have no idea how true that is."

His brow scrunched up.

She took the deepest breath she could and let it out slowly, then shifted to face him, determined to spit it out once and for all.

"I'm pregnant."

Chapter 18

Pregnant? Had he heard her right?

"I'm sorry. Did ... did you just say *pregnant*?"

She nodded sadly.

His stomach dropped, and a wave of dizziness overtook him as he turned his attention to the lake. The reflection of house lights and the glow from the floating candles on the water twisted and skewed. If it had been daytime, he was certain the trees and clouds and blue sky would be spinning all around him. This wasn't happening. It couldn't be.

He looked over at Jamie. "You're saying you're going to have a baby?"

"Yes."

"*My* baby?"

"Yes."

His heart pounded in his chest. "And you're sure it's mine?"

Her breath huffed out, and she looked more than a little insulted. "I had to ask."

"Did you, though?" She abruptly stood and walked up the dock.

Duncan jumped up and followed. "Jamie, wait." He gently took hold of her arm to stop her and turned her to face him.

"You're the only guy I've been with for over a year. You know this."

"No one since me?"

"Only you," she replied, brushing a tear from her cheek.

He let out a breath and raked his fingers through his hair. "Okay."

"Look, I know you need time to let this sink in. I just needed you to know that it's yours, and I've decided to keep it."

He was taken aback. "Were you thinking about not keeping it?"

"Yes." Her gaze fell.

"Without telling me?" She didn't reply, and a flash of anger shot through him. "Is that why you left town?"

"I went home to my parents to clear my head and decide what to do."

"Do you not want the baby?"

"I wasn't sure at first, but I want it now. You can be involved or not. Whatever you want to do. I know this messes things up for you. And I'm sorry about that."

Messes things up? Dréa! How was he going to tell his fiancée he had gotten another girl pregnant?

Jamie stood still and quiet while he paced back and forth on the dock, his mind racing wildly.

"Duncan?" Jamie's voice was soft and filled with concern.

He stopped in front of her. "I don't know what to say right now."

"It's okay. You don't have to say anything. Just sleep on it."

There was no way he would be able to sleep after hearing this news. "I can't believe this is happening," he whispered.

"I know it's not what you were expecting to hear."

Her voice held such sadness, and it broke his heart. And before he knew what he was doing, he'd pulled her into his arms.

She stood there stiffly at first, arms hanging at her sides, until she eventually softened and wrapped her arms around his back, letting him hold her.

"I'm sorry, Duncan." Her voice caught on his name.

"Don't apologize. I was there too."

"I remember." Her breath tickled his neck and sent the best kind of chills up his spine.

He remembered too. Every detail. Every moment. He would never be able to get her out of his head. And now they would have a little reminder of that night for the rest of their lives.

The fire was almost completely out. Most of the family were long gone. Jamie had gone home. But Duncan sat staring into the dying embers, Jamie's words playing on a loop in his mind, reeling with the news that he was going to be a dad. A dad? He could barely wrap his mind around it. He thought about his father and his grandfathers. All family men, who married the women they loved and made good Christian homes. They had settled down with the right girl, provided for their families, and never made the kind of mistakes Duncan had made.

He leaned forward, resting his elbows on his knees and his head in his palms. He wasn't ready for this. And what would it look like for him? Married to Dréa and living where? In Denver? While Jamie and his baby lived in Michigan? How would that even work? He didn't want to be that far away during the first years of the baby's life. Dréa would surely understand that, right?

His mind returned to their past conversations. Dréa was so set on staying in Denver, working her DJ job. She would never agree to move. But maybe he wouldn't have to worry about that. She might not want to marry him once she learned about the pregnancy. Maybe this would be too much for her to forgive. He wouldn't know until he talked to her, but he couldn't do that tonight. He couldn't wake her, even though he was dying to get this off his chest.

He pictured Jamie's face on the dock earlier when she'd told him. He wished he'd been a little more supportive and asked some questions. How long had she known? That day she came to the house and met Dréa? Had she told Shannon? Was that why she came there tonight? To tell them both?

A hand on his shoulder startled him.

"Can I sit?" Shannon asked.

He nodded.

"Are you okay?"

"Not really." His throat tightened as tears threatened to fall. "Do you know?"

"Yes, I know. And it's going to be all right, D."

As soon as his sister wrapped her arm around his back and pulled him into her side, the tears spilled down his cheeks. He couldn't hold it in any longer. A mixture of fear, confusion, and worry churned inside him. He'd never felt such an intense ache within his heart. Sobs ripped through him as he let it all out.

Shannon sat with him and let him cry until he couldn't cry anymore.

He moved his arm up, resting it around her shoulders, and leaned his head against the side of hers. "Why did this have to happen?" he murmured. "I just found Dréa. We have this perfect plan."

"You'll make a new plan."

"What if she doesn't want me now?"

"Then it wasn't meant to be."

"I did this," he said with sadness in his voice. "I ruined everything."

"You don't know that. Don't think the worst. I truly believe there is a reason for all of this, and we're going to see God work in this situation in big ways. Trust me."

"I did something I shouldn't have, and now I'm dealing with the consequences of that choice. I'm being punished, and it serves me right."

"This child is not a punishment." She got choked up, and he knew it was because of her PCOS.

"I'm sorry, Shan. I didn't mean ..."

"I told her I'd adopt the baby," she blurted.

"You did?"

"If she didn't want it, and you didn't want it, I wanted to raise it as my own."

"Shannon ... I don't know what to say."

"Do you want it?" she asked.

"It's my ..." He could barely say the words. "It's my baby."

"That's not an answer."

He stared into the ashes. "Of course I want it."

She looked over at him with a raised eyebrow. "Is that how you actually feel, or are you saying it because you think it's what I want to hear or what you're supposed to say?"

"I mean, I'm kind of in shock right now. This is the last thing I was expecting."

"I know."

But from the moment he'd heard the words, he had felt a sudden and undeniable connection to this baby, a need to protect it at all costs.

"I want it," he said confidently.

"Good." She squeezed her arm tight around him then let go, resting her hands in her lap.

His eyes went to the remnants of the fire again. "I don't know how I'm going to tell Dréa. This is a nightmare."

"Just be honest with her about what happened. It was before you guys even met."

"True, but I don't think that will make her feel much better about the situation. I should've told her when we first got together. I told her about my past, just not about this."

They were quiet for a few beats before Shannon spoke.

"Can I ask you something?"

He nodded.

"If there was no Dréa, do you think something would happen with you and Jamie?"

"I don't think so."

"Why not?"

"Because of all the reasons I told you before. We don't have much in common. She doesn't share our faith. And she's not the kind of girl you settle down with. She's the kind of girl—"

"You sleep with?" Shannon's disapproval was obvious.

He shrugged his shoulders. "I mean, she's the party girl, Shannon. You know this about her."

"I know she has been in the past, but what if being a mom changes her?"

"I just don't see a future with her. I'm marrying Dréa."

"Because you met her and you just knew?"

"That's right. Is that so hard to believe?" Why did he suddenly feel like he needed to defend his relationship?

"I don't know, Duncan. It seemed really sudden to me."

"You don't like her?"

"I didn't say that. She's a wonderful person, and if she's the one you truly love and want to spend your life with then I'm happy for you."

"Well, she is. Why else would I have proposed?"

She eyed him. "I don't know. Why else would you?"

"What exactly are you trying to say?"

"I'm not saying anything. I just want you to be sure."

"I *am* sure." He stood and looked down at her. "I'm going to say goodnight to everyone and head home."

"Don't be mad at me."

"I'm not ... it's just been a long day."

Shannon nodded. "I understand."

"I'll talk to you later."

"Okay."

"Night." He walked across the lawn. Conversations with Shannon usually made him feel better, but he was more confused than before. Maybe his relationship with Dréa *had* been fast, but his reasons for wanting to marry her were sincere. What was Shannon getting at?

He thought about the first time he met Dréa. The instant attraction—not only to her beauty, but to her personality. And it wasn't long before he saw how much she loved Jesus too. She was what he'd been waiting for his whole life.

His mind returned to Jamie sitting beside him on the couch at her apartment, leaning closer, their lips about to touch. The complete adoration in her eyes had drawn him in. He'd been powerless against it and had absorbed every look she'd given him all night long.

He tried to remember the look in Dréa's eyes the first time he'd kissed her, but he couldn't. Their kiss had given him butterflies, but it hadn't consumed him the way kissing Jamie had.

And now he felt despicable, comparing the two women like this. What was wrong with him? He really needed a good night's sleep, and hopefully, when he woke, he'd see things more clearly.

Chapter 19

Jamie lay on the couch in her living room, staring up at the spinning ceiling fan, as her hand rubbed over her nearly imperceptible baby bump. The apartment had been closed up for the three weeks she'd been at her parents', and the small air conditioner in her bedroom window hadn't managed to lower the temperature in the stuffy space very much since she'd arrived home.

She didn't mind sleeping on the couch. It had been her bed many nights when she needed to escape the memory of Duncan in her room. There was no way she could escape that memory, though. Not now. Not ever. Their child would be a constant reminder of what they'd shared.

A tear slid from the corner of her eye and over her temple, wetting her hair.

Duncan had been understandably shocked. But even though she'd dropped a huge bombshell on him and his future, he'd been sweet and comforting. His hug had surprised her at first, and she'd fought hard to keep from sobbing into his chest, but she let him hold her, and she held onto him because it was exactly what she needed. And she had left with a good feeling about the situation.

Three soft knocks on her door sent a nervous chill through her. She glanced over at the clock, which read twenty after one in the morning, and tiptoed toward the window, slowly moving the edge of the curtain back to see who it was.

Her brow furrowed, and she unlocked the door. "Duncan? What are you doing here?"

He looked completely defeated. "I couldn't sleep."

She gave him a little closed-mouth smile. "Me neither."

"Can I come in?"

She stepped to the side, and he walked past, leaving her in the wake of his musky cologne and campfire scent. He went instantly to her couch.

The scene of the crime. Well, that's where it had all started.

She tried to ignore how good he looked sitting on her couch again and sat down, leaving a foot between them.

The room was silent. She knew he wanted to say something, but he sat with his elbows resting on his knees, staring down at his clasped hands.

"Duncan." She spoke in a near whisper.

He looked over at her.

"What are you thinking?"

"A lot of things. Like, I thought you said you were on the pill."

She expected this to come up. "I am. Well, I was. I just ... I forgot to take a pill and then I took it as soon as I realized, but it must've been too late."

"Oh."

"It's my fault." Her throat tightened as she continued. "I'm so sorry, but you have to know I didn't do this on purpose. I didn't remember the missed pill until I skipped a period. I wouldn't blame you if you hate me for this."

"I don't hate you, Jamie." His voice was soft on her name. "I just wish I hadn't gotten so carried away. I should've been more responsible."

She nodded sadly. He regretted it, and that cut deep.

"Do you know when the baby's due?" he asked.

She pressed her lips together, dreading telling him the date.

He gave her a questioning look. "Is something wrong?"

"The baby's due January fourteenth."

"January fourteenth," he repeated.

She stared at him, wondering if he'd realized the importance of that date.

"Okay, that gives us six months to figure things out."

"Aren't you forgetting something?" she asked.

He looked at her, clueless.

"Dréa."

"I know I need to tell Dréa. I will."

"That's good, but that's not what I meant."

Again, he looked clueless.

"January fourteenth." Did she really have to spell this out for him?

His jaw dropped. "The wedding."

"Yes, the wedding."

"We'll change the date," he blurted.

"I think you should discuss that with your *fiancée*." That word tasted bitter on her tongue. She was insanely jealous that Dréa had Duncan for the rest of her life.

"I'm so sorry," he said.

"There was no way you could've known when you picked the date."

"If only you would've told me sooner."

"When? The day I came to your parents' house and you were there with her?"

He lowered his head.

"I couldn't stick around after that. I had to get out of there, out of here. But I came to talk to you the second I got back to town."

"What happened when you were at your parents'? Did you see a doctor?"

"I went to a clinic. They told me I was eleven weeks along."

"Like a walk-in clinic?"

A few beats passed. "Something like that."

He searched her eyes. "You mean an abortion clinic."

"I thought it would be easier for all of us if I just got rid of it."

He swallowed hard. "What changed your mind?"

"The ultrasound. I saw this little round head and arms and legs. There's a baby in here. Our baby." She touched her belly. "And I couldn't do it after that. I just couldn't."

He reached over and lay his hand atop hers.

She was surprised to see tears in his eyes.

"I know this is a mess," she said, "but we can make it work, right? We can figure it out."

He nodded. "I want to be part of the baby's life."

"I hoped you would, and I know it's going to be kind of complicated—"

"More complicated than you know." He looked down at their hands. "I think I'm moving to Denver."

"Denver?" It came out as a whisper as she pulled her hand from beneath his.

"With my freelance job, I can work from anywhere. Dréa has a steady job there that she loves."

Jamie didn't know what to say. She hadn't considered that they might live in another state.

"We'll figure it out, Jame."

She stood and paced across her apartment and back.

"I thought I'd come back here and tell you and, somehow, we'd raise this baby together. I never thought you'd be all the way across the country. How would that even work?"

Duncan's eyes trailed her. "I don't know."

"It can't. It's so far. You'd have to travel here or something. I can't afford to fly out there. Especially when the baby's little."

Duncan stood and stepped toward her as she passed him again. Taking hold of her forearms, he turned her to face him. "Calm down."

"You calm down!"

His eyes were wide with surprise at her outburst, and his lips were tilted to one side like he was holding in a laugh.

A laugh of her own burst out, effectively cutting through the tension, and he laughed with her, which felt natural and comfortable.

When they quieted, they were left staring at each other, his hands still holding her arms. His deep brown eyes had always mesmerized her. In a certain light, they were almost hazel, with the tiniest flecks of green and gold. She wanted to get lost in them, but she knew she couldn't.

His head moved side to side. "The way you look at me …"

"How do I look at you?" She had never tried to hide her affection for him in all the time they'd known each other, and if that was what he was seeing, she wasn't ashamed of it.

"Like you … care."

"I do."

He let go of one of her arms and brushed a loose hair back from her face. "I care about you too." His gaze fell between them. "And I care about our baby."

"Really?" She couldn't help getting choked up. This pregnancy was making her an emotional mess.

He nodded. "Let's just take things as they come. One thing at a time, okay?"

"Okay."

"So, your parents already know, but mine don't. After I tell Dréa, I'd like to tell them. Together."

"You want me there?"

"Yeah."

"Oh." She hadn't expected that.

"Why? You don't want to be there?"

"I don't want them to hate me for seducing their son."

He snorted.

"What? That's what happened."

"We were both there, Jamie. We both flirted that night."

"We've always flirted, but that was the first time I ever dared you to take it further."

"And I didn't have to kiss you, did I?"

She looked down at the floor. "No."

"But I did, because I wanted to. And I'm a grown man. I know how to stop myself, but I didn't want to. I'm pretty sure it wouldn't have gone farther than a kiss if I hadn't pushed for more."

"No way. I practically dragged you into my bedroom."

"I went willingly, and you know it."

Jamie raised an eyebrow at him. "Are we seriously arguing about whose fault this was?"

He let out that adorable laugh of his once more. "We were equally responsible."

"Irresponsible, you mean," she said with a smirk.

"Yeah." He smirked too. "My family won't hate you for this, Jamie. They all love you. You know that."

"I'm afraid of how they'll react."

"They'll be supportive. And they'll love their grandchild."

"Wow." She was suddenly struck by a thought.

"What?"

"I've always loved your family and wished I was a part of it." She lowered her head, a little unsure if she should say this out loud. "I guess now a part of me will be."

When Duncan didn't say anything, Jamie stepped over to the coffee table and took a drink from a glass of water she'd left there earlier.

"You know, this is probably the most we've ever talked at one time," Duncan said.

"Probably." She set her glass down. "Too bad this little peach is the reason." Her index fingers pointed to her belly.

"Peach, huh?" he chuckled.

"I read online that the baby is the size of a peach right now."

"You're comparing our baby to fruit?"

"The internet is."

They both chuckled. At least they had a sense of humor about the situation.

"Do you know if it's a boy or a girl?" he asked.

"Not yet. I have a doctor's appointment set for next week. I don't think they do the ultrasound for another month or so. I've been trying to read a lot online, so I know what to expect."

"I want to know what to expect too. Can I go with you to the doctor?"

"Maybe you should talk to Dréa first."

"I'll still want to go, even after I talk to her."

"Of course you can go. It's your baby too." Her heart warmed when she thought about sharing this experience with Duncan. She wanted him to be involved, but she had tried not to get her hopes up. And she couldn't be happier to hear him say these things.

Jamie yawned as lack of sleep caught up with her.

"I should let you rest. And I need to get some sleep too. I have a feeling tomorrow's going to be a very long day." He walked toward the door.

"Duncan." It felt like there was so much more to say.

He turned back to her expectantly.

"Thank you. For everything. You ... you're just so great."

He closed the space between them and pulled her into a hug.

She wasted no time wrapping her arms around him, soaking in every moment she was in his arms.

"You're pretty great too," he said.

"You're just saying that because I'm your baby mama."

His body shook with laughter. "You're funny."

She felt his arms loosen, and wished he'd kept holding on, that they could stay like that forever. He leaned in and pressed a kiss to her forehead before releasing her.

"Get some rest," he told her.

"I will."

"I'll see you later."

"Good night."

He smiled back over his shoulder as he let himself out, and she locked the door and leaned back against it. That had gone way better than she'd expected.

She took the glass to the sink and decided to sleep in her bed for once, not minding the memories of Duncan that floated around in her brain tonight.

Her stomach flipped when she thought about facing his family. At least Shannon and Nana knew and were on her side. She didn't doubt that his parents would be supportive, but the idea of standing before them with this kind of news felt more than a little intimidating.

Chapter 20

As usual, the sun came up, the birds chirped outside Duncan's window, the wind gently rustled the leaves in the trees, and the scent of coffee wafted through the house. Papa was at the kitchen table with his nose buried in a newspaper, Mama was reading her daily devotions, and Nana sat on the back porch with her morning tea and a book. But today was not like any other day. Not for Duncan.

After the shock of Jamie's news had worn off, their conversation at her apartment had given him the answers he needed and had also reminded him why he'd always liked her. She had a lightness about her, an ability to laugh, even in the middle of the most difficult situations.

He wished he was more like her. He'd tossed and turned all night, thinking about the next hard conversation he needed to have, trying to come up with the right words to say to Dréa. He wasn't sure how she would take it because he didn't know her well enough to anticipate her reaction.

He knew it needed to happen in a private place, without people around, so they could talk openly with no interruptions. He wasn't sure when or where, but the sooner the better so they could move forward. No matter what her decision.

As he was about to head to her hotel, the front door opened, and Dréa walked in with her parents, carrying bagels and coffee.

"Good morning." She greeted him with a smile, and he wondered if it was the last one she would ever give him.

"I was coming to the hotel to get you."

"Why?" She whooshed past him into the kitchen and set breakfast on the counter. "I told you we'd be over in the morning."

He followed her. "I wanted some alone time."

She spun around and sauntered toward him, slipping her hands around his neck. "Why didn't you just say so?" Her lips pressed against his in a sweet kiss, which he tried his best to return, but he couldn't manage much enthusiasm. She pulled back. "What's wrong?"

"Nothing." Now was not the time.

Dréa wandered leisurely to the porch, and Duncan could hear her chatting with Nana. He helped himself to a bagel and coffee and joined them, stopping in the doorway to catch their conversation about favorite Jane Austen books since Nana was reading *Sense and Sensibility* for probably the hundredth time.

"*Pride and Prejudice* is my favorite." Dréa looked over at Duncan. "Are you my Mr. Darcy?" She winked.

The women in his family had subjected him to more Jane Austen movies than he'd ever cared to see, so he was familiar with the men of those stories. "I think I'm more Willoughby than Darcy," he replied under his breath.

She glanced up with quirked brow. "What was that?"

He shook his head and took a seat, finishing off his bagel and coffee while the ladies chatted. His eyes kept landing on the clock, watching the hands creep down from nine. When they hit nine-thirty, he could stand it no longer. He stood and held his hand out to Dréa.

"Can we go somewhere and talk?"

She glanced up at him. "Sure. See you later, Nana."

"Of course, dear," Nana replied.

Duncan caught Nana's eye, and she gave him an encouraging smile as Dréa took his hand and followed him into the house.

"We're going for a drive," he called out to their folks as he moved toward the front door.

"Okay, drive safe," Mama replied.

He glanced over at his fiancée and saw her concern.

"Should I be worried?" They might not have known each other well, but she was still pretty good at reading him.

He didn't know how to respond to that. Of course, she should be worried. He was about to potentially destroy their life together. He continued to lead her out of the house and into his car, but before he could start the engine, she lay a hand on his arm.

"Just tell me now. If this is bad news ... something I'm not going to like, then I don't want to drive somewhere and have to sit in the car with you all the way back."

"Dréa." Duncan breathed slowly, trying to calm his nerves.

She wrung her hands in her lap. "Just say it. Whatever it is. I can take it."

"Okay. Here it is." Time to rip off the bandage. "I told you about my past and how I had changed, but I neglected to tell you I slept with someone the night before I left for Denver."

Her jaw dropped.

"It was a one-time thing. A slip-up."

She swallowed hard. "Why didn't you tell me before?" There was a sudden iciness to her tone.

"I was ashamed it had happened after all that time."

"So, why are you telling me now?"

He gulped back tears.

"Duncan." She stared at him.

"Because she's pregnant."

It broke his heart when her chin quivered, and he wished he could go back and undo everything.

"I'm so sorry, Dréa. I never meant for this to happen."

She was speechless, staring ahead at the house for several long, torturous minutes.

"What are you thinking?" he asked quietly.

"Who is she?" Dréa demanded.

He blew out a deep breath. "It's Jamie."

Her mouth fell open, her eyes as big as saucers. "Jamie? Your sister's best friend, Jamie?"

He nodded.

She pressed her lips into a hard line. "That doesn't surprise me," she spit out.

His eyebrow raised. "What does that mean?"

"She seems like the type."

What she'd said was not okay. At all. And he almost said something, but he figured he'd done enough to ruin their relationship today. Why add more fuel to the flame?

"So, she's keeping the baby?" she asked.

"Yes."

"And where does that leave us?"

"Is there still an us?" He clung to this little shred of hope. "Because that's what I want."

She continued to stare ahead with a scowl.

"I know this changes a lot of things for us, but—"

Her eyes shot to his. "It changes everything."

He was silent, waiting for her to say more.

"I need to think." She opened the door and climbed out, walking at a rapid pace toward the house.

Duncan jumped out of the car. "Dréa!"

Over her shoulder, she gave him a look that could kill, so he followed at a distance.

She pushed the door open and went to the kitchen. "I need to go back to the hotel for a while."

"Did you forget something, dear?" her mother asked.

"We just have to go. Right now," she snapped.

Their parents all stared at her in surprise.

"Sorry. I will explain on the way. Can we go?" Her tone was cold and clipped. She crossed her arms over her chest, angling toward the door.

"Of course," her father said.

They said rushed goodbyes and followed her out.

The click of the door as they left the house felt final, and Duncan sank into the nearest kitchen chair and buried his face in his hands, wanting to disappear.

Mama's tender touch brought him back to reality. "What's going on?"

"I think I just ruined everything."

Later that day, the doorbell rang, and Duncan's stomach flipped, knowing it was Jamie. He headed to the front door and opened it to find her bent over, heaving between two bushes.

"Oh no. Are you okay?" he asked.

She looked up, horrified, and covered her mouth. "I'm so sorry. I was really nervous. I thought morning sickness would be over soon, but it still strikes when I least expect it."

He gently took her arm and guided her into the house with his hand on her lower back. "Want to freshen up?" He reached into his pocket and pulled out a stick of gum. "Maybe this will help."

She laughed and took the gum. "Thanks. I'm gonna use the bathroom. I'll be out in a second." He watched her disappear down the hallway, feeling awful for her.

When she returned, she was chomping on the gum he'd given her, looking more radiant than ever. Nobody would've been able to tell she'd been throwing up in the bushes not five minutes earlier.

"Ready?"

"Is anybody ever really ready for something like this?"

He shrugged his shoulders. "Probably not." His hand found a place on her lower back again as he ushered her through the house to the back yard. His family was waiting patiently, seated on the patio, sipping iced tea and lemonade.

They looked up as Duncan took Jamie's hand and guided her before them.

Mama's face showed confusion, while Shannon wore a supportive smile.

It probably seemed wrong for him to be holding anyone's hand but his fiancée's, but given the situation, he felt like holding onto her through this, and she seemed to want the same.

Duncan cleared his throat. "I know you're probably wondering what this is all about after the way Dréa left his morning." He looked over at Jamie, who gave him a little smile of encouragement, then back at his family. Nerves skittered through him. "Jamie's pregnant, and come January, you'll be getting your first grandchild." He nodded at Nana. "Great grandchild for you, Nana."

They were all quiet at first. Shannon and Nana exchanged glances. Papa's brow was furrowed, while Mama's eyes filled with tears.

Nana broke the silence. "Congratulations." She stood and walked over to them, took one of Duncan's hands and one of Jamie's and squeezed.

Shannon came over and hugged each of them.

Mama wiped away a tear. "When did this happen?"

Duncan went to sit next to his mother. "It happened before I went to Denver."

"What about Dréa?" she asked.

"I don't know what's going to happen there. She said she needed to think."

"Do you still want to marry her?"

"Yes."

"Well, she has a good head on her shoulders. I'm sure she'll forgive you."

"Maybe." He glanced over at Jamie, whose head had fallen. Hearing them talk about his relationship with Dréa probably hurt her.

Mama spoke softly to her son. "*How* did this happen?"

"A moment of weakness, Mama. I'm sorry for disappointing you."

She reached up and lovingly touched his face. "God is merciful and forgives us when we fail."

"I know."

Mama turned to Jamie. "How far along are you?"

"Thirteen weeks." Her response was quiet.

"Have you seen a doctor?" she asked.

"I saw one in Pennsylvania when I was visiting my parents, and I have another appointment coming up with my doctor here. Duncan's going with me."

"Good. That's good." Mama stood and walked over to Jamie, cupping her cheek with her hand. "This baby is a blessing, and we're here for you. Whatever you need."

It warmed Duncan's heart to hear his mother's words.

"Thank you for saying that." Jamie sniffled and brushed away a tear.

Papa cleared his throat to speak. He was a man of few words, so when he spoke, they listened. "This isn't an easy situation. It's going to take a lot of maturity and communication on everyone's parts to make it work. Especially if Duncan and Dréa's wedding happens as planned. But I believe God will get us through it."

Jamie looked down at her hands, which were resting against her belly, and Duncan was reminded again that she didn't share their faith. That was going to make raising a baby together even trickier.

"How are you feeling?" Shannon asked. "Do you need anything to drink? Are you hungry? Can I do anything for you?"

Jamie giggled at her friend. "Okay, we get it. You're going for the title of Best Aunt, but I'm fine, Shan. Really."

"I will be the best aunt in the world."

"Only because Sophia is never around."

"That's not why. I am the best at spoiling, and I plan to spoil this baby so good."

They laughed together, and Duncan liked the sound. It felt so natural, having Jamie there, but Dréa was still at the forefront of his mind. He wondered if she would be in his life after today or if she would throw the ring in his face the next time they saw each other. He hoped there was still room in her heart for him and that maybe there would be room for his baby as well. Like Papa had said, it would take a lot for them all to come together and make this work, and he wanted so badly for things to work with Dréa.

But more than anything else, he wanted this baby to have the best life possible. He already knew Jamie would be a great mom. Shannon *would* be the best aunt in the world. And he planned to be the best dad ever. But would Dréa want to be a stepmom?

Chapter 21

Awkward. The whole situation had felt more than awkward. But the McGregor's hadn't freaked out or yelled, and Jamie hadn't felt judged like she thought she might. Their support meant everything to her. But it had hurt to hear them talking about Duncan and Dréa's wedding.

She wondered what was going to happen. Would they stay together? Would the wedding go on as planned? She wondered if they'd spoken since yesterday when the pregnancy was revealed. The sooner she knew the state of their relationship the better, so she would stop obsessing.

Jamie stared at her computer screen on her half of the brand new shared studio space Shannon's boyfriend, Micah, had secured for them. This was the space they'd dreamed of having in East Grand Rapids, and it felt surreal that it was theirs.

While she'd been away at her parents', Shannon had furnished the place and set up a workspace for her, all without knowing whether she'd be coming back. There was a lot of catching up for her to do after being gone the past few weeks. She had pictures to edit from the wedding she'd photographed the weekend she found out she was pregnant. Normally, she would've posted a sneak peek of pictures on her website within a few days of an event, but the news of the baby had sidetracked her. Her clients were the best, though—completely understanding and offering their congratulations—but she still felt bad for the delay.

Shannon was out for the morning with a client meeting and engagement session, so Jamie had the entire space to herself. She went to work, sorting through the gallery of beautiful images, and edited highlights of the day.

The silence was beginning to get to her, though, and with her mind still reeling from all that had happened, she found it difficult to concentrate. She stared at more images of the lovely couple on the screen, then abruptly pushed back on her office chair, rolling across the room toward the long console table along the wall.

Jamie turned on the small stereo Shannon had set up there and cycled through the channels to find something to break the silence. As she rotated the dial, she heard the notes of the song "Stronger" by Mandisa, which she'd first heard at her parents' last week while Mom was on the treadmill. She rolled back to her desk and let the words and music pour over her. The antsy feeling she'd had since returning to town faded, and she felt calm, the way she had that day in Hershey when she finally accepted Jesus into her life. No matter how hard things seemed, the song reminded her that it was only going to make her stronger. God had started a work in her, and though this was all new, she believed He was with her through it all. She felt like a different person, and she was excited to see what God had planned for her life.

Jamie went back to work, leaving the stereo set to the Christian music channel, and worked straight through lunch. Her stomach growled as the front door chimed.

"Hey." Shannon walked in and stopped beside the stereo. "You could've changed the station if you wanted."

"I chose this channel." Jamie grinned.

"You know this is Christian music, right? Not your usual grunge or metal band."

"I don't listen to metal. And I like this stuff. Every song is so uplifting and hopeful."

"Yeah, it is. I thought you didn't liked my music."

"Well, a lot changed in my life while I was gone."

Shannon rolled her office chair over to Jamie and took a seat. "Do tell."

"When I got home, I found out my parents had suddenly become big-time churchgoers."

"They weren't before?"

"They've never gone to church in their lives, but somehow they started going, and I could tell they were different. Not that they were awful people before or anything, but there was this new kind of joy about them. I went to church with them while I was there, just to see what it was about."

"They didn't have to drag you?" Shannon winked.

"I went willingly if you can believe that. And what I found there really changed me." She started at the beginning then, spilling the whole story, from clinic appointment to church with her parents. "I felt so welcomed from the moment I walked into my parents' church, but I wondered if they would see me differently if they knew my situation. Only, I found out some of them already knew, because my mom and her prayer group had been praying for me since I got to town. They accepted and encouraged me, and I wanted to know more. I listened so intently to the pastor, and after church, I asked my parents to tell me what it was that had changed them. They shared all that God has done for us by sending His Son, and that they had accepted Jesus into their hearts, that He was the reason for their joy. I told them I wanted that joy too, so they prayed with me."

Tears slid down Shannon's cheeks.

"I didn't mean to make you cry."

"Believe me, they're happy tears. I only wish I'd been in a better place in my relationship with God all these years so I might've helped you learn all this sooner."

"I think you did. Maybe you didn't tell me with words, but I could tell you were different than my other friends."

Shannon gave a weak smile. "I was angry at God for years because of my diagnosis, and while I believed it was the right choice to let Micah go so he could have a chance at a family with someone else, I blamed God for the whole thing. After Micah came back, a lot of those feelings were brought to the surface again, and thankfully, I made my peace with God."

"I'm glad."

"Me too. It's hard when you're in the moment, and you don't know what's going to happen. Things can seem so hopeless. But He knows everything, and He sees the whole story when we only see the chapter we're in. If we trust that He knows what's best for us and keep flipping the pages, there are better days to come."

Jamie smiled. "I like that."

"I'm so happy for you, Jamie."

"So, I guess we're sisters in Christ now. My mom referred to Gloria that way, like being a sister because they both belong to the family of God."

"Yes, we are." Shannon rolled her chair closer and hugged Jamie.

"At least I'll be part of your family in that way," Jamie said with a shrug.

"Hey, you don't know what's going to happen."

Jamie rolled her eyes. "He's going to marry her. It's obvious. She's perfect and has never made a mistake like this in her entire life. How could I even compare?"

"But you're the one carrying his baby, Jamie. And I know he cares about you. I know it."

"Thanks for saying that, but I'm not so sure."

"You need to tell him about this decision you've made."

Jamie smirked. "I'm sure he won't care. He never mentioned God or church or faith to me before, so why would it matter now?" That fact suddenly struck her. Why *hadn't* he ever told her about Jesus?

Shannon shook her head. "Everyone will be thrilled to hear your news. This is a big deal, Jamie. We need to celebrate it. It's your spiritual birthday."

"I never thought of it like that."

Shannon jumped up. "I want to throw you a party."

"That's not necessary."

"Why? We could make it a baby shower too."

Jamie laughed. "Shouldn't that be a little closer to the baby's actual arrival? What if something happens before then."

"Like what?"

Jamie shrugged. "I don't know. What if I lose the baby?"

Shannon's jaw dropped. "Don't even say that."

"I'm just saying, we should wait on baby showers until later in the year."

Shannon's shoulders sank. "Okay. But can I at least call up a couple of friends and throw a little celebration dinner?"

Jamie gave her a look.

"Just dinner."

"Who with?"

"Maggie and Sarah."

Jamie grinned. "I'd love that, actually." She hadn't seen them since she and Shannon had photographed Maggie and Simon's wedding in early spring.

"Okay. I'll make a plan. Leave it all to me."

Chapter 22

"Please don't leave town without talking to me." Duncan ended his voicemail to Dréa and threw himself back on the bed.

They hadn't spoken since yesterday when she left the house with her parents, and their flight home was scheduled for tomorrow evening. He wondered if maybe they'd gone back to Denver early and she hadn't informed him.

Duncan wanted her to have the time she needed to think things over, but he was worried she would leave and they wouldn't get to have this very important conversation.

His phone sounded with an incoming text message.

Dréa: This wasn't how I thought our life together would start.

His heart broke when he saw it.

Duncan: Can I call you right now?

Some time passed before a response came through, and he was sweating bullets waiting for that reply.

Dréa: I'm not ready. My parents and I booked an earlier flight home in the morning. I'll call you soon.

Duncan: Okay. I'm so sorry.

Dréa: I know you are.

Duncan: I love you.

No reply came, and he was certain his future with Dréa was over.

When Duncan shuffled out of his room the next morning, he could hear Shannon's voice coming from the kitchen. She was there awfully early. He went into the bathroom to brush his teeth, but her enthusiastic tone had him standing near the door to eavesdrop.

"I wanted to do a baby shower, but she said it's too soon."

"Well, yes, Shannon, I agree. A baby shower is a little premature," Mama said.

"But it's okay if I have a little intimate dinner in the back yard, right? Just a few of us. I'd rather it be private than at a restaurant, and it's much nicer here than my tiny apartment."

"You're welcome to have friends here whenever you want. You know that. But will it be awkward for her?"

"I want her to know we accept her and the baby with open arms. She's going to be around here a lot, and I want her to feel comfortable. And I want to celebrate this decision. It's so huge."

Decision? What decision? Keeping the baby? He spat into the sink and walked into the room just as his sister said, "I've been praying for this for her."

"I know. We all have," Mama replied.

"It's wonderful news," Nana gushed.

"What's wonderful news?" Duncan asked as he stopped next to the kitchen island.

"Jamie got saved while she was visiting her parents," Shannon told him.

His heart fluttered in his chest. "She did?"

Shannon nodded excitedly.

"Wow! That's ... wow!" He couldn't seem to form a coherent sentence. Jamie was a Christian? This news floored him.

"Isn't it exciting?" Shannon was beaming. "I'm having a dinner here for her tonight to celebrate her spiritual birthday."

Duncan nodded and swallowed hard. "Uh ... that's great."

"Do you want to be here?" Shannon asked.

"What? No." He was too confused to honestly consider it. "But that's great. Really great. Just great." Why did he sound like such a bumbling idiot?

The ladies all looked at him strangely.

"You already said that. What is the matter with you?" Shannon asked.

"Nothing. It's …"

"Great?" Shannon finished.

He groaned. "Whatever. Leave me alone. I just woke up."

"That's no excuse for you being such a weirdo."

"Loon."

"Psycho."

"Doofus."

"Okay," Mama cut in. "You'd think you two would've outgrown this by now."

"Never!" they both cried in unison.

Mama and Nana shook their heads as the two of them cracked up laughing.

Duncan returned to his room with a nervousness in the pit of his stomach. As he got ready and went about his day, he found it impossible to concentrate. He was supposed to be focused on a design scheme for a new client, but all he could think about was Jamie's newfound salvation.

He wasn't surprised that God could change a heart. God had changed his, after all. But he hadn't expected it to happen to Jamie. She knew their family's beliefs, and it had never made a difference for her before. So why now?

He wasn't upset that she was a Christian. Not at all. This was truly amazing news. It was just that she was Jamie—fun-loving, uncommitted, unbelieving Jamie. Her lack of faith in God had been his primary reason for never dating her in the past. And besides that one night of weakness, it had kept him away from her for a long time.

So, now what?

What if Dréa didn't forgive him? Could he have some kind of future with Jamie?

Questions like this swirled around in his head all afternoon until he felt as if he was losing his mind. He tried to force himself to work, but after two hours of staring at the cursor on his screen, he slapped the laptop closed and went for a run around the lake instead.

The fresh air did him good. He ran and ran. He should've been praying, seeking God, and getting right with Him, but he'd found himself unable to talk to God since he got to Denver. He couldn't find the words to pray. And it was worse now that Jamie was pregnant.

The laughter from the back yard floated in through the open kitchen windows and down the basement staircase to Duncan. He'd made himself scarce all evening, trying to watch a TV show, but he had no interest in what was happening on the screen.

He clicked the television off and made his way upstairs, walking through the house to the sunroom, where he stayed out of view. He felt a little like a stalker, but he was curious.

Shannon had set up a little table for four with candles and flowers. Strings of bare bulbs were hung in a zigzag pattern between the house and the trees and gave the yard a warm glow. Their photographer friends, Maggie and Sarah, were there. Maggie had a camera in her hand and was taking a picture of Sarah, who was bouncing a baby girl on her knee. Jamie was smiling at the baby and holding her tiny hand. The sight pulled at something deep inside him.

He hadn't planned to join them, but he found himself pushing the back door open with a squeak, his feet moving him across the yard.

"Hey, D," Shannon said when she spotted him.

"Ladies." He greeted them with a wave and bent down to get closer to the baby. "Hello, pretty girl."

"This is Claire," Sarah said as the baby cooed at Duncan.

His heart melted in his chest, imagining his own baby looking at him like that. He glanced over at Jamie, who was giving him that familiar look of adoration.

"Take a seat." Shannon pointed at one of the nearby patio chairs.

He waved her off. "I don't want to impose." He straightened and turned to Jamie. "I'm really happy for you, Jamie, for the decision you made. It's really exciting."

She smiled up at him. "Thanks. I feel ... different. Peaceful."

He nodded, knowing exactly what she meant.

Shannon stood suddenly. "Maggie, Sarah, remember that thing in the house I wanted to show you. Let's go look at it now."

They both stood along with her.

"Oh, right," Maggie replied with a smirk.

"Take us to it," Sarah declared.

Duncan stared after them as they walked hurriedly toward the house. "That wasn't obvious or anything."

"Not at all." Jamie laughed.

"May I?" He pointed to the chair beside her.

"Sure."

He moved the chair closer and took a seat.

"Do you want some water?" She reached for the pitcher.

"Nah, I'm good."

"Okay." She lowered her hands to her lap.

"I was a little surprised to hear the news," Duncan told her.

"More surprised than the fact that I was pregnant?" She quirked her eyebrow.

"Almost."

"Why so surprised?"

"I don't know. I shouldn't have been, because I know personally how God can change someone. He changed me."

"Yeah?"

"I used to be a bit of a partier myself."

"You? I don't believe it."

"Believe it. I drank a lot and slept with a lot of girls."

She focused intently on his lips as he spoke, which was distracting.

"I was kind of out of control."

"What changed?"

"Nana told me to grow up."

"Nana did?"

"My dad caught me in bed with a girl here in the house."

Jamie's eyes widened. "Embarrassing much?"

"To say the least." He shook his head, remembering the humiliation. "When Nana found out, she told me to get my act together and be a better man. And it was after that when I decided to listen to God and see what He could do if I gave my life over to Him."

"That's good."

"That was five years ago. No more drinking. No more girls." His eyes met hers. "Until that night with you."

Her head dropped forward. "I'm sorry."

He reached over and lifted her chin to get her to look at him. "I'm the one who's sorry. I'm sorry I couldn't control myself with you."

"I feel like I corrupted you or something." A tear slipped down her cheek, and he brushed it away with his thumb.

The way she was staring at him made his stomach flip. What was this connection between them? Why was it so strong? He lowered his hand and leaned back, giving them a little space.

"I'm happy we'll be able to share our faith with the baby," he told her.

"Me too. It's weird. I've never really considered the church or religion of any kind. I didn't grow up that way, and it seemed like a waste of time. But when I went home, there was something so different about my parents since they started going to church. I could just tell. Mom introduced me to a friend of hers at a family clinic, and she took the time to listen to my fears about this baby and talk to me about my options."

"I wish you had told me sooner so I could've helped you figure things out."

"I found out right after you came home from Denver. I was scared you'd hate me for messing up the birth control and for putting you in this situation when you just got engaged. And it wasn't like you were talking to me then."

He cringed, feeling awful for his behavior.

"But it was a good thing I went home. If I hadn't, I might not have found Jesus or decided to keep the baby."

"That's true."

She gave him a sweet smile. "I'm kind of excited about the baby now that you and your family know. I was terrified before that I would have to do it all alone, but now I know I won't."

"You won't." He reached over and took her hand. "I'll be with you the whole way through this pregnancy, and I think we'll be amazing parents."

She shook her head. "This is so weird. I never would've thought we'd end up having a baby together."

He laughed a little. "Me neither."

"It's gonna be okay, right?"

He reached up and touched her face without thinking. "More than okay."

Her fingers wrapped around his wrist, holding his hand in place.

His skin tingled where she touched him, and his heartbeat accelerated.

"Duncan," Shannon's voice suddenly called out from the doorway. "You have a visitor."

Dréa stood just outside the door, staring at them with mouth hung open, clearly disgusted.

Duncan's hand dropped lightning fast, and his heart jumped into his throat as he stood. "Hey, I thought you flew back with your parents this morning."

"I can see that."

He glanced over at Jamie then back at Dréa.

"I changed my mind about going home, so we could talk," she snapped. "I guess I should've gone."

"No, let's talk." He walked toward her.

She spun on her heel as he approached. "I don't think so."

"Nothing's going on with us," Jamie offered.

Dréa spun around and glared at her. "It sure looked like I was interrupting something."

Duncan went to Dréa and gently took her arm. "We were talking about the baby is all. And as Jamie said, nothing's going on between us."

She stared up at him. "I beg to differ."

The silence was excruciating. Dréa had been standing quietly in the driveway with her arms crossed over her chest for the past ten minutes. Duncan waited for her to speak. He'd already done plenty of talking over the past couple days and all she had done so far was listen. She was the one who had come to the house to talk, so he waited for her to do just that.

When ten more minutes had crawled by, he could take it no more. "I'm sorry about all this. I know I've said it before, but—"

She held up a hand to stop him. "All I've done is think since you told me. Part of me wants to end this now and pretend I never met you."

"Dréa." His heart ached over the pain he was causing her.

"I always saw myself marrying a man who had never been with anyone but me, someone who had waited for me like I waited for him. But when I met you, and I heard about your past and how God had changed you, I was willing to look past that, because I believed God had brought you into my life."

She closed her eyes, clearly fighting back emotion.

"But you lied to me when you left out what happened with Jamie. You told me all that stuff from your past, yet you had just slept with her weeks before we started dating."

"That was wrong. I know that."

"You bet it was wrong. And I should throw this ring in your face right now and get on the next plane home."

"But ..." He looked at her with hope.

She sighed. "But the other part still wants to marry you and start the life we've been planning."

He took her hands in his. "We *can*. We *can* start that life. I know this complicates things, but we're all adults, and we can figure out a way to move forward in this."

She pressed her lips together and pulled her hands from his. "I haven't decided yet. I feel like maybe everything happened too quickly between us. Maybe we jumped into this without knowing each other well enough."

"Don't say that. This wasn't a mistake. I know how I feel about you."

"Maybe so, but I think you might be in denial about how you feel about Jamie."

"What does that mean?"

"You must've felt something for her to have done what you did."

"She's my friend, and we made a stupid mistake. It was a moment of weakness, that's all."

"I know we haven't known each other for a long time, but I think I know you well enough to say you wouldn't have slept with her if there weren't some kind of feelings there. If God truly changed your heart in the way you see women and sex, and you viewed it as only right within a marriage commitment, like you told me you did, then that means you would've seen Jamie differently and maybe you acted on those feelings because you saw her as someone you could be with for life."

Duncan shook his head. "That's just it. I didn't see her that way. I've only ever thought of her as my sister's flirty friend. And yes, I've always been attracted to her, but that's all it was. Physical attraction. I knew she wasn't a virgin, that she liked to party and sometimes slept with guys. Definitely not someone I saw a life with. I still don't know why I did it, only that the temptation was there, and I gave in to it."

His mind flashed back to that night again, and he did his best to push those memories away.

"I won't be your second choice, Duncan."

"You're not! I swear!" He took hold of her arm to stop her from walking away. "Please don't go. We can work it out."

"I don't know if we can."

He gently turned her. "Listen. I've waited five years for God to bring me the woman He wants me to marry, and it's you. I wouldn't have asked you to spend your life with me if I was in love with someone else. If you need to go back to Denver and think, that's what you should do. Take all the time you need." He took hold of her left hand and lifted it. "But please do it with this ring right here on your finger."

Dréa was quiet for a minute before she slid her arms around his waist and rested her head on his shoulder.

He wrapped her up in his arms and held her tightly. "I love you."

"I love you," she whispered back.

Her admission released all the tension he'd been holding, and for the first time in days, he felt like things might be okay after all.

Chapter 23

The waiting room at the obstetrician's office was nearly full when Jamie arrived. After checking in, she managed to find a couple of open seats off to the side and took one, placing her purse on the other to save it for Duncan. She had told him the date and time, but there was a little insecure voice in her head telling her he wouldn't show.

She knew she wasn't alone. God was with her and would get her through this. But not growing up knowing such a thing, she had to keep reminding herself of that fact. She did have a newfound peace, but it was still scary.

It had been a week since Dréa went back to Denver. Shannon had told her as much. She felt bad for the situation this put Duncan's fiancée in. It couldn't be easy knowing that the man she loved had impregnated another woman, even if it was before they got together. All Shannon knew was Dréa had gone home, and as far as she knew, they were still engaged.

Jamie fidgeted nervously. At her last appointment, she'd had her mom with her as a second set of ears in case she missed anything the doctor told her. This time, she might have to write things down so she wouldn't forget.

A woman seated across from her glanced up from a Parents magazine. "First pregnancy?"

"Is it that obvious?"

The woman chuckled. "I can remember my first. I was terrified. And you have the same look I'm sure I had back then."

"Are you seeing utter confusion and pure terror?" Jamie asked. "Because that's probably what I'm putting out there."

Her laughter somehow took Jamie's nerves down a notch.

"How many kids do you have?" Jamie asked.

"This is my third," the woman told her. "Two boys, and I finally got the girl I've been wanting."

"How nice. I can't wait to find out what I'm having."

"How far along are you?"

"About fifteen weeks."

"They'll schedule you an ultrasound soon, and then you'll know."

Jamie didn't know what Duncan thought about finding out the gender ahead of time, but she was dying to know if she should buy blue or pink for this child.

"Jamie Linde," the nurse called out.

Jamie's heart stuttered in her chest just before disappointment settled over her. Duncan hadn't come. She clutched her purse tightly as she stood. "It was nice talking with you."

"You too. Congratulations." The woman gave her a friendly wave.

"Thanks." She returned the wave and walked toward the smiling nurse.

"Hi, Jamie. Right this way." The nurse led her down a hallway. "We're going to be in this room today."

Jamie entered, and the nurse proceeded to take her weight and blood pressure.

"We received the records from your doctor in Pennsylvania."

"Oh, good. I was hoping you would get them in time."

"Did you just move here?"

"No, I had only just found out I was pregnant when I was home visiting my parents, and I wasn't sure how long I was staying, so I went to our family doctor while I was there."

A sudden knock on the door interrupted.

"Yes," the nurse answered.

Another nurse opened the door. "I have someone here for Jamie Linde's appointment."

Jamie was sure her smile lit up the room at the sight of Duncan walking through that door. "You came!"

"I told you I would." He moved to the chair beside hers.

"The father, I presume," the nurse said.

"Yes," they replied in unison and laughed.

The nurse finished her tasks. "Okay, Doctor Dearing will be in to see you in a few minutes."

"Thank you."

She left the room, and then they were alone.

"I thought you weren't gonna show," Jamie admitted.

"Hey, I meant it when I said I'd be with you through all of this."

"I'm glad you're here."

He gave her a cute smile that made her stomach flip.

"How was your week?" she asked, trying to make the situation lighter.

He shrugged his shoulders. "It's hard to focus right now, and I'm behind on a project."

"I'm sorry. This is all my fault."

"Not all your fault." He tilted his head until he got her attention. "I think I'm going to have to come up with some kind of penalty every time I have to remind you of that."

She raised an eyebrow.

"Like, every time you say it's your fault, you owe me a coffee."

Jamie chuckled. "You're funny."

"Hmm, I like this idea. I have a feeling it will get me a lot of free coffee. I am implementing this plan starting now."

"What? No! You can't just do that."

"I just did." He chuckled.

"Unfair. How can I get free coffee?"

"You shouldn't drink coffee while you're pregnant."

"I can have decaf."

He snorted. "Decaf doesn't count."

"Better than none."

"Is it really, though?"

She smiled. "Okay, you have a point. What will I do without coffee?"

"It's probably okay if you have a cup now and then."

She glanced down at her belly. "Oh, Orange! What are you doing to me?"

"It's an orange now?" Duncan asked.

"Yep! Fifteen weeks is the size of a navel orange."

He grinned as he reached over and lay his hand on Jamie's midriff. "I like that."

Butterflies flitted every which way in her stomach. It was the first time he had touched her there since that night.

Their eyes locked, and she swallowed hard.

The door opened then, and Duncan took back his hand.

"Hi there," the doctor said. "How are we feeling today?"

"Fine," Jamie replied.

"Let's have you hop up onto the table and lie down, and we'll give baby's heart a listen."

Jamie did as the doctor requested, and he squirted a warm gel onto her abdomen and proceeded to press a fetal doppler against the area until a steady whooshing sound filled the room.

"There we have it," the doctor announced. "147. Nice and strong."

Duncan stood and moved to stand beside Jamie, his eyes filled with wonder. "That's the baby's heartbeat?"

"Yes, it is," the doctor replied.

Jamie reached for Duncan's hand just as he reached for hers, and they held on tightly.

"Oh my gosh," Duncan said. "That's so fast. Is it supposed to be that fast?"

"Completely normal," the doctor explained. "A good range, and exactly where we want it to be at this point in the pregnancy."

Jamie didn't hide the tears that had welled up and were now spilling down her cheeks.

The doctor continued with routine questions and measured Jamie's belly. "Everything's right on track, Jamie. We'll get your ultrasound set up to see how the baby is developing, and we'll see you back here in a month."

"Okay, thank you."

The doctor shook Duncan's hand on his way out. "Congratulations."

"Thank you. Oh, hey, one more thing," Duncan said before the doctor left the room.

"Yes?" He looked back from the doorway.

"Is it okay for her to drink coffee while pregnant?"

"A cup of coffee is okay on occasion," he told Jamie, "but make sure you're drinking plenty of water too."

"Of course," she said.

"Thanks," Duncan said.

When the doctor left the room, Jamie started laughing. "Now, to find a way for me to get free coffee from you."

"That won't be happening," he replied.

"We'll see about that."

Duncan walked Jamie to her car after the appointment, and they stopped by her door. She wasn't sure whether to hug him or just get in, but then she remembered something.

"Hey." She reached into her purse and pulled out the ultrasound picture she had received from the clinic the day she nearly ended her pregnancy. "Here. It's Orange."

His face lit up as he took it.

"Although, the baby was more like the size of a lime then. It was taken a few weeks ago when I was in Pennsylvania."

His lips spread into a huge smile as he stared at the picture. "Thank you." He looked up at her. "This is crazy, right?"

"Having a baby together? I think we've established how crazy this is."

He shook his head. "That's not what I mean. You have a baby growing in there." He touched her stomach again, sending the same butterflies darting about deep inside. "We're going to meet our child in like six months." He leaned back against her car. "I always thought I'd have kids one day, but I never thought it would be this soon. I thought I'd get married and then ..." He stopped mid-sentence, obviously realizing what he'd said.

She avoided eye contact. "Then you and Dréa would have a bunch of kids and live happily ever after. I know. I'm very aware that I've ruined your life."

"Hey, you haven't ruined anything. And you owe me a coffee."

"No way."

"I told you what would happen if you tried to take the blame."

Jamie rolled her eyes and couldn't hide her smile.

He elbowed her gently in the arm. "It's just going to take some getting used to, but we'll figure it out. Don't worry. I'm all in, Jame. I'm going to be the greatest dad on the planet to our kid."

"I believe that."

His eyebrow raised. "Was that a compliment?"

"Maybe."

"Can I borrow this?" He held up the picture.

"It's yours."

"I'll scan it and make a copy for you when I get home."

"That's fine."

"And I'd like my coffee tomorrow for breakfast," he informed her.

"Oh my gosh." She laughed.

"We can go to Starbucks, by your studio."

"It's a date." She said the words before she thought about them, but he didn't seem bothered by it.

"See ya tomorrow." His smile melted her heart.

For her emotional well-being, she needed to get past her longing for him. It did her no good to harbor feelings he didn't reciprocate. He was engaged to another woman, and as far as she knew, still planned to marry her.

But she couldn't help the way her body reacted when he was close or how her heart pitter-pattered when he touched her. She couldn't help but appreciate the man he was and the amazing father he was going to be. And when he smiled at her like that, all she wanted was to be his in every way for the rest of their days.

She climbed into her car, slammed the door, and leaned her head on the steering wheel, knowing that was never going to happen.

Chapter 24

The chime on the front door sounded, and Jamie looked up from her computer. Her heart skipped a beat at the sight of Duncan. His auburn waves were still damp from a shower, the T-shirt he wore stretched perfectly across his broad chest and muscular arms, and those jeans hung just right on his hips.

Shannon chuckled as she noticed Jamie checking out her brother. There was no pulling one over on her. They knew each other too well.

"Morning, Shan." Duncan gave his sister a bear hug.

"Morning. To what do we owe this visit?"

"Jamie's buying me coffee." He smiled over at Jamie.

"Is that right?" Shannon raised an eyebrow at her.

Jamie shrugged. "I lost a bet, I guess."

Shannon returned to her desk. "Well, don't let me keep you from it."

"Wait, did you see this?" Duncan pulled the ultrasound picture of the baby out of his pocket. "It's our little orange."

Jamie's heart warmed at the pride he displayed.

"Oh my goodness." Shannon stared at the picture. "Look at the little head. Are those arms and legs?"

"Yep." Duncan looked at Jamie. "At least I think so. It's hard to see much."

Jamie nodded. "It's arms and legs."

"We get to see them again in a few weeks for her ultrasound."

"And we'll find out what we're having," Jamie added.

His eyes shot to hers. "You want to know?"

"Of course. Don't you?"

He shrugged his shoulders. "I don't know."

"I hate surprises, and it will make it easier to plan and buy things the baby needs."

"And buy gifts for the baby," Shannon interjected. "So many gifts."

"Don't go overboard," Duncan told his sister.

"This is my first niece or nephew. Of course, this child will be spoiled."

"Oh, boy," he replied.

Jamie grabbed her purse. "Should we go get that coffee now? I have a lot of work to do today."

"Okay," he agreed. "See ya, Shan."

They walked out onto the street and fell into an easy pace as they moved toward Starbucks.

"How are you liking the new studio?" he asked.

"I love it. Shannon had everything all set up by the time I got back."

"It's a great space and in such a great part of town."

"I know. That was the dream. At least it was Shannon's. I'm just sort of along for the ride."

"I think you're more than that. You may share the space for your separate businesses, but you two are partners. I've seen you work together. You compliment each other very well. And you're both so crazy talented. I'm blown away when I see the pictures you two take."

"Thanks." She was touched by his kind words. "I'm lucky to have found a friend like her."

"And she's blessed to have you too."

Jamie wasn't used to all these nice things being said to her and about her. "You don't have to butter me up to get your free coffee, by the way."

"I'm not. I mean it."

"Well, you're pretty great too."

"I know." He winked then laughed when Jamie rolled her eyes at him.

Jamie's steps slowed as they passed by a new baby boutique. She'd strolled past several times since returning to town and fell in love with the most beautiful baby bassinet displayed in the front window.

She couldn't help but dream of setting it up in an adorable nursery with her sweet baby resting peacefully within. Too bad it was way out of her price range.

"I guess we'll have to buy baby stuff soon, huh?" Duncan said.

"Yeah." She picked up the pace. "But we have plenty of time to think about that."

When they reached Starbucks, he held the door for her, and his hand landed softly against her lower back as he led her inside. As soon as he moved it away, there was an instant longing for him to put it back. It felt so nice each time he touched her. She knew it was meant in a friendly way, but she still couldn't help but crave every connection.

The barista interrupted her train of thought when he asked what she wanted.

"Oh, uh, I'll just have a bottled water."

"Okay." He handed one over the counter to her.

When she had paid for their drinks, she assumed they would walk back to the studio, but Duncan nodded toward an empty table by the window. "Do you have time?"

"Sure." There was no way she would turn down time with Duncan. Ever.

"So, I wanted to talk about what will happen when you go into labor."

Her stomach twisted at the thought and an uneasiness settled there. "We've got time before we have to worry about that. And honestly, I've thought nothing about it and don't want to until I absolutely have to." That was a total lie. Labor terrified her. She *had* thought about it. A lot. But she was trying to pretend it wasn't going to happen.

"Are you scared?"

"Heck yeah, I'm scared. I have to push a *watermelon* out of me."

A loud laugh escaped Duncan, and a few snickers from customers made her realize her volume level had gone up a little too high.

"You think it's funny, but it's true. It's going to hurt."

"They have drugs for the pain. It will be fine."

"Fine? If you think it will be so fine, then *you* have the baby."

They stared at each other for several beats before bursting into laughter.

He reached over and squeezed her hand. "I know it's scary, but I'll be there. You won't go through that alone."

"What if I go into labor and you can't make it here from Denver?"

"We'll work it out. Maybe I can work from here when it gets closer to your due date."

"Okay. I like that plan."

"Don't worry. Stress isn't good for the baby."

"I feel better knowing you'll be with me."

He lifted her hand to his lips, pressing a kiss to the back. "Good."

Her eyes met his, and she saw a hint of embarrassment there.

She took a swig of her water as he sipped his coffee. "Can I ask you something?"

He sat up straight and tall. "Anything."

"Do you wish it hadn't happened? You and me."

His lips pressed together and twisted to the side as he thought about her question.

"It's okay if you do. I know this was an unexpected outcome of that night."

"Maybe I shouldn't answer that question."

She looked down at the table. "Maybe."

"If I answer one way, I'll hurt you. If I answer the other, I'll seem unfaithful to my fiancée."

"You're right. I should've never asked." She stared down at her hands, wrapped around her water bottle, then back at Duncan. "I don't, by the way."

He eyed her questioningly over the top of his cup.

"I don't wish it hadn't happened."

His throat moved as he swallowed hard.

Their eyes locked, and her pulse began to race. *Was he thinking about that night like she was? Did he still want her as much as she wanted him?*

He pressed his lips together and looked down at the table. "I think from now on it's best if we don't talk about that night. I really can't go there, Jamie, okay?"

"Okay. I get it. I'm sorry."

They chatted about surface things after that—her photography, his graphic design jobs, the weather. When he walked her back to the studio, there was no goodbye hug, and she wondered if it was because she had pushed too hard with her question about their night together. It had made him uncomfortable, of that she was sure. But was it the kind of uncomfortable filled with regret or the kind that had him remembering just how good they were together?

"Things aren't good between them." Shannon spun her office chair around before going back to work editing wedding photographs.

"Why do you say that?"

"She doesn't return his calls. She thinks something more is between the two of you than a one night stand."

Jamie glanced at her computer screen. "That's not true. He's the baby daddy, nothing more. He's made that very clear."

"He has? What did he say?"

"He doesn't want to talk about us, about our night together. And I get it. It isn't something he's proud of, I'm sure. But that tells me he's not as concerned with how I felt than he is with how it will affect his relationship with Dréa going forward."

"Like I said, I don't see that happening."

"It's going to happen," Jamie replied.

"He's going to Denver next weekend to see her, so we'll see."

Jamie's heart sank at that news. The idea of him and Dréa working it out and settling down in Denver worried her. Living across the country was not an ideal situation. He said he would be there for her, but if that was the case, she knew he wouldn't be able to be present for her and the baby. It just wasn't logical.

"I have a feeling she'll be giving him back his ring." Shannon turned back to her computer.

Jamie stared out the window at the passing cars and people walking along the sidewalk. She didn't want to take hope from what Shannon had said, but if anyone knew Duncan and the workings of his mind, it was his sister. She shook her head and went back to work, trying not to think about how happy she'd be if Duncan was no longer engaged.

Chapter 25

There were extra cars in the driveway when Duncan returned from his trip to Denver. He recognized Jamie's right away, and a zing of excitement rushed through him, which he immediately shoved down deep inside.

After the past few days with Dréa, things were good. They had made progress, and she had forgiven him and wanted to move forward. They had even started on their wedding plans, moving their wedding date to early December instead. He had left Denver feeling like they were on the right track, yet there was still this underlying uncertainty about Jamie and the baby.

He needed to ask if she would be willing to move to Denver since he knew that's where he and Dréa would end up. He just wasn't sure how to broach the subject. Her life was here. Her business was here. And he wasn't sure if Jamie living close by him and his wife would make life easier or more difficult. He only knew that once the baby was born, he didn't know how he would be able to stand living so far away from them.

Them? He shook his head. He'd been thinking of both Jamie *and* the baby, and he knew that wasn't right. He was committed to his fiancée.

He took a deep breath as he opened the door and paused on his way to his room when he heard voices and laughter. He glanced out the picture window in the kitchen, and what he saw sent a sudden rush of blood through his veins.

Jamie and Shannon sat on the patio with his parents and Nana ... and his cousin, Maxwell. Max had his arm across the back of the love seat, resting against Jamie's shoulders, his gaze fixed on her as she laughed.

Duncan's stomach knotted, and he dropped his suitcase where he stood and made his way to the back yard.

"You're home," Shannon said. "How was your trip?"

"Fine." He couldn't take his eyes away from his cousin and Jamie.

"How's it going?" Max asked.

He released his gritted teeth. "Can't complain. You?"

"I was just telling everyone that I got a promotion at work. Senior V.P. of marketing."

Duncan wanted to lift his finger in the air and twirl it around with a great big whoop-de-do, but instead, he went the polite route. "Congratulations."

"Thanks. Shannon said you were in Denver. How's your lovely fiancée?"

"She's good." He noticed Jamie glance at the ground.

He took a seat and listened to the group's discussion of the morning's church service. Jamie had yet to make eye contact with him, and he couldn't ignore Max's arm around her. His mind recalled the Fourth of July, the way Max had been staring at her when he'd come upon the two of them by the fire. He didn't like this. Not one bit.

When his parents and Nana headed inside, Jamie went to use the bathroom, and Max followed, carrying glasses to the kitchen.

Duncan looked at Shannon.

"I know what you're thinking," Shannon said.

"What?"

"I think he really likes her."

"No," Duncan said firmly.

Shannon's eyebrows pinched together. "You can't control who she dates."

"Watch me."

Shannon shook her head. "She could do a lot worse than Max. He's a great guy with a good job and a good head on his shoulders. What if they're meant to be?"

Duncan rolled his eyes. "You need to stop thinking like such a romantic."

"You never know what God might be doing. He might've brought her into our lives so she and Max would find each other."

He snorted. "That's ridiculous."

"Why? Why does this bother you so much?"

"It just does. She's carrying my baby. She shouldn't be dating my cousin."

"You don't want her to find someone who can help her raise the baby?"

"*I'm* going to help her raise the baby."

"From Denver? I don't think so."

He felt irrationally panicked and desperate.

"That's *my* baby." He pointed his finger at his chest. "I don't want another guy raising it."

"Duncan, you can't do that to her. You can't plan your life with Dréa and tell Jamie she can't have a life too."

His shoulders sank. She was right. She was always right. But he couldn't shake the uneasiness he felt when he saw another man's arm around Jamie.

Rationally, he knew it wasn't fair of him to expect her to stay single. He should want her to find happiness as he had.

"Think of it from Jamie's perspective," Shannon continued. "She's going to have to let you and Dréa have the baby sometimes for visitations and stuff. The baby will have Dréa as a stepmom. You can't expect Jamie to be alone forever."

He didn't say anything more, and Shannon put her arm around him.

"Unless there's more to this that you're not saying."

"What does that mean?"

"That you have real feelings for her you aren't admitting to and that's why you don't want her with anyone else."

"Now you're being even more ridiculous."

"Am I?"

"I'm engaged to a great girl. I love her. Jamie and I ..."

Shannon eyed him. "I know you, Duncan, and I could see it in your eyes. You care about her. Maybe more than you realize."

"I do care about her. But it's not like that."

"You sure about that?" She stood and walked toward the house, stopping halfway. "Do you want to go to a movie with me and Micah tonight?"

He shook his head. "No, thanks. Long weekend."

"Are you sure? It'll get your mind off things."

"I'm sure."

"Okay." She left him alone, his brain spinning.

Of course, he cared about Jamie. And of course, he had felt something for her before their night together. He couldn't deny that. But he couldn't dwell on that or think about that night because it stirred things inside him he needed to tamp down, longings that needed to be reserved only for Dréa from now on.

But they were still there. And maybe that's why he didn't like Max's arm around Jamie. Maybe that's why he was feeling so territorial over her. Residual feelings. There couldn't be a future for them. He had his future all set, all planned out now. And it was going to be good.

So why did his heart ache at the thought of Jamie with someone else?

Chapter 26

Was Duncan jealous? He had been focused on Max's arm around her and looked like he might attack at any moment. If they hadn't gone into the house when they had, she thought he might actually do it, which was confusing. She wondered how his trip to Denver had gone. Were he and Dréa still getting married? Maybe they weren't together anymore. Maybe he seemed so upset because he wanted to be with her and have that family she was hoping and praying for.

Sometimes her mind wandered to a picture-perfect family—them and their sweet little avocado—but it was a fantasy. And even though it felt good to think about, it wasn't realistic to imagine waking up in his arms every morning, their kid jumping into bed with them. The picture her mind conjured up gave cozy, warm feelings of her childhood. She'd had a good upbringing, despite the way she'd lived her young adult life. Her parents had given her safety and security, and she hoped she would give that to her baby. She was learning and growing and changing, especially now that she had found Jesus and was going to be a mom, and she knew she needed to be realistic. But she still longed for the happy images in her mind's eye.

She shook her head as she washed her hands and stared at herself in the McGregor's bathroom. "He doesn't want you. Accept it and move on."

Could she move on? She didn't know how that would be possible while she was pregnant.

She thought about how attentive Max had been to her all day. He'd been visiting from the east side of the state, and they'd all gone to church together that morning. She found it easy to talk to him, and he made her laugh. Nobody had mentioned the baby yet, but she was pretty sure Max would be saying *not interested* faster than she could say *stepdad*.

In the kitchen, she found Shannon, Micah, and Max talking.

"Hey, do you want to go see the Captain America movie with us?" Shannon asked.

"Who's us?" she asked.

"Me, Micah, and Max," she replied.

"And me," Duncan interjected as he entered the room.

Shannon raised an eyebrow. "I thought you didn't want to go."

He shrugged. "I changed my mind."

Jamie noticed a nonverbal exchange between siblings, and she wondered what that was all about. "Uh, sure."

The five of them climbed into Max's SUV and headed to Celebration Cinema. When they arrived, Max opened the car door for her just as Duncan ran around to do the same. Duncan grabbed the outer door to the building, then Max held the inner door. Max ushered her into the line with a hand on her lower back and let it linger there. Duncan bought her popcorn and a drink. And when it was time to sit down, she ended up between the two men.

She looked over at Shannon, who was seated on the other side of Duncan. She must've noticed their behavior too because she rolled her eyes and started laughing, which made Jamie laugh.

"What's so funny?" Duncan asked.

"Nothing," Jamie replied as she settled back into her seat.

When the movie started, Jamie couldn't focus on the story, even though Chris Evans was not hard on the eyes. All she could think was that Duncan had no right to act the way he was acting. He was engaged, for heaven's sake.

She reached into the popcorn bucket that was resting on her knee just as Duncan did, and their fingers brushed. He kept his hand there, gently rubbing his pinky against hers, and she yanked her hand away, nearly knocking the bucket over. Her eyes were glued to the screen, fury pulsing through her.

Out of the corner of her eye, she saw him toss a handful of popcorn into his mouth, losing a few kernels down his front.

She shoved the bucket into his lap. "I have to go to the bathroom," she declared as she stood and excused her way along the row and headed for the restroom.

Her mind was reeling, and she stayed in the stall longer than necessary to calm herself. What was Duncan doing? He was a twenty-six-year-old man, engaged to be married, but he was acting like a jealous teenaged boy. And why? Because of the baby? That had to be it. Because he was in love with Dréa. Wasn't he?

Duncan eyed her when she returned, but she didn't care. She took the empty seat on the other side of Max, which Duncan seemed none too pleased with.

"Everything okay?" Max whispered.

She nodded. Max really was a nice guy, but it could only be friendship between them. It would be an awkward situation to put him in the middle of.

When the movie ended, they headed home, and Jamie was quiet. She made sure to sit far away from Duncan and avoided talking to him. Back at the house, she said goodnight and hugged Shannon before heading to her car. She noticed Duncan moving toward the door, glancing over his shoulder at her and Max, who had hung back from the others.

Max approach her once everyone had gone inside. "Hey, it was fun hanging out with you today. Do you think I could get your number? Maybe we could do it again sometime."

Jamie was about to tell him she couldn't when she spotted the curtain in the front room window move to the side to reveal Duncan. "You know what, yes. Let me see your phone." She entered her number for him and handed it back.

"Thanks." He typed on his screen and hers lit up. "There, now you have mine too."

"Great." She opened her car door. "Goodnight, Max."

"Night."

Jamie got into her car and started the engine. She glanced at the window and saw the curtain drop into position as Duncan moved away.

Chapter 27

Over the next week, Jamie's phone lit up daily with messages from Max. He was a funny guy, sending her jokes and internet memes, which she wasn't usually fond of, but found amusing. He asked how her day was going and told her how his day was in return. She liked the steady stream of attention, but she didn't like the uneasiness she felt over not telling him everything there was to know.

As Jamie was finishing up an album design from a June wedding she had photographed, her cell phone rang. She almost didn't answer when she saw her friend Quinn's name on the screen. When Quinn called, it usually meant she wanted to go out for a night of bar-hopping, but Jamie answered anyway.

"Hey, Quinn!"

"Jamie! How are you, girl?"

"Good. What's up?"

"A bunch of us are going out tonight. You in?"

"Can't."

Quinn groaned. "Come on! It's been months since we've seen you. Come out with us."

"No can do."

"You never say no to a party, are you sick?"

"Not sick. Pregnant."

Silence.

"Quinn? Are you still there?"

"Wow! I can't believe you got yourself knocked up."

"I know, but it'll be good."

"You could still come out. You don't have to drink."

"I don't think that's my scene anymore," Jamie told her.

"Why's that?"

"Something pretty important happened in my life recently."

"Oh, girl. Are you in AA?"

"No, nothing like that. I went to church with my parents and—"

Quinn snorted. "Oh no, we lost you to the Bible-bashers?"

Jamie shook her head. She could picture Quinn pretending to gag and rolling her heavily mascara'd eyes that matched her jet black hair. "Not Bible-bashers, Quinn. My parents."

"Yeah, you know how I feel about organized religion."

"I know, and I thought the same thing, but I changed my mind."

"Well, good for you."

"Maybe we can go to dinner sometime and catch up, though," Jamie offered.

"Yeah, maybe some other time. I'll call ya."

"Okay, that sounds—"

Quinn hung up.

"Okay. Bye." Jamie stared at the screen, her mouth agape. She shouldn't have been surprised by Quinn's blow off, but it bothered her. She rolled her eyes as she dropped her phone onto her desk. At least she knew who her true friends were.

Her phone rang again, and she snatched it up and answered without looking at the number. "Jamie Linde Photography." Still feeling insulted by Quinn, her tone wasn't exactly the friendliest.

"Hello, Jamie Linde Photography, this is Max McGregor."

"Max, how are you?"

"I'm great. It's good to hear your voice."

"Yours too."

"Hey, I'm coming to Grand Rapids again this weekend, and I wondered if you'd like to have dinner with me on Friday."

Her heart skipped a beat. "Really?"

"Is it so hard to believe I'd want to have dinner with the most beautiful girl in the state of Michigan?"

"You're so smooth," she replied.

"I try. What do you say? Dinner?"

She paused, still uneasy. "Okay. That sounds nice."

"Great. Text me your address, and I'll pick you up at seven."

"I will. See you then."

"Can't wait," he said sweetly.

She sat back in her chair and stared at her phone. He had asked her out. Now what? She had to be honest with him from the start or this would never work. And she had a feeling this would be their only date after the truth came out.

Shannon was on the phone across the room. She wore that smile she only got when it was the man she loved on the other end of the line.

Jamie waited for Shannon to get off the phone and rolled across the room in her office chair. "I need advice."

Shannon spun to face her. "Shoot!"

"Do you think it's okay for me to go out on a date with someone without first telling them that I'm pregnant?"

"Date?" Shannon's eyebrow raised. "Who are you going out with?"

"Max."

"Max asked you out?" She practically shrieked.

Jamie held her hand up to try to calm her friend. "Whoa there."

Shannon laughed. "This is so exciting."

"Ya think?"

"It's great, Jamie. But I had no idea you were into older men." Shannon giggled.

"He's not that much older than me."

"Four years. He's robbing the cradle."

"If he knew there'll soon be a baby in the cradle, he might not want to go out with me at all."

Shannon cracked up.

"Seriously. Should I have told him? I feel dishonest going out with him and not telling him first."

"Max is a good guy. When you explain the circumstances, he'll be honest with you about how he feels about it."

"So, you think I should still go?"

"Absolutely."

"Are you sure? Because I feel like calling him back right now and telling him my situation."

"It's up to you, Jame, but honestly, it's just dinner, right? If things go well, then tell him. If you don't feel anything for him, then don't."

"What about Duncan?"

Her eyebrow raised again. "What *about* Duncan?"

"You saw how he was acting at the movies."

"It's not his life, it's yours. He should want you to be happy too."

"Yeah, I guess."

Shannon rolled forward and took Jamie's hands in hers. "Everything's going to work out how it's supposed to. No matter what happens, God has a plan. He's got a reason for this happening and this baby coming into all of our lives. Just trust Him and pray for His guidance. He'll get you through it all. Even going out on a date with my cutie pie cousin."

Jamie smirked. "He is pretty cute."

"He's a real catch."

"Why hasn't been caught before now?"

"He had a steady girlfriend a year or so ago, but they broke up. Not sure why. I don't think he's found the right girl yet." She squeezed Jamie's hands before letting go. "Maybe it's you."

Jamie laughed. "Okay, let's see how the first date goes before you go marrying me off to your cousin."

They laughed and rolled back to their desks.

Jamie thought about what Shannon had said. She did believe God had a reason for all of this. But waiting to see what that plan was ... well, patience was not her strong suit.

Chapter 28

Nerves had Duncan's stomach churning as he rapped on the door to Jamie's apartment. He'd been trying to think of a way to ask her about Denver. It had been constantly on his mind all week. Well, that and seeing her with Max, which still ate him up inside. He didn't have a great argument for why she should move to Denver, nothing convincing that would get her to agree. He only knew he wanted to be close to his baby.

Dréa's reasons for wanting to stay in Denver were completely valid, but it felt like she wasn't taking into consideration how he felt about being away from his child. Why should she, really? She hadn't signed up for this. She was now in the middle of a situation she didn't want to be in because of his choice.

It was selfish of him to ask this of Jamie, but he had to give it a try.

When the door opened, the sight of her knocked the wind out of him. Her hair was curled and half twisted up. Her face was made up and lips were glossed. His gaze journeyed down her body and back, taking in her flowery dress and sandaled feet. She looked stunning.

"Hi" was all he could manage.

She fidgeted and glanced behind her nervously. "What are you doing here?"

"Not exactly the greeting I was expecting. I thought maybe we could go get some ice cream and talk. There's something I want to discuss with you."

"Oh, well, I ..." She glanced back again. "I sort of have ... plans, Duncan. Can we do this another time?"

"Plans?" His eyebrows squeezed together, and an uneasiness settled over him. Why was she all dressed up? "Are you—?"

"I have a date," she admitted before he could get the question out.

His lips fell open. "A date?"

The sound of a car pulling up had him turning to see his cousin, Maxwell, step out.

His attention returned to Jamie. "You're going out with Max?"

"Why shouldn't I?" she asked.

"Should you be dating ... in your condition?"

"Why not?"

"Did you tell him about the baby?"

She shushed him. "I'm going to. Tonight. But it's none of your business who I date."

"The heck it isn't." His voice was probably louder than she wanted it to be as Max reached them.

"Hey, Duncan," Max said. "Didn't expect to see you here." His eyes turned to Jamie. "Everything okay?"

She nodded. "Duncan was just leaving," she said as she stepped out of her apartment and locked the door behind her.

Duncan was ready to spit nails, and he was sure it showed.

Max looked from Jamie to Duncan and back. "You ready?"

"Yes." She silently pleaded with Duncan to let her pass.

He stepped out of the way, and she moved to Max's side.

Max held his arm out like a gentleman, and she wound her arm through his. "See ya, Duncan."

It took everything within him not to run after her and stop this whole thing now. His gaze never left Jamie as he moved along the sidewalk to his car. When Max opened the door for her, she smiled up at him, and Duncan wanted to punch his fist through the window. Once inside his car, he glanced over in time to see her laugh, and an ache twisted deep inside.

He knew he had no right to keep her from dating. But he didn't have to like it.

Chapter 29

This was the most fun Jamie had ever had on a first date. The conversation was easy, Max was funny and sweet, not to mention handsome, and she found herself forgetting she was having a baby with another guy. At least for a little while.

When they returned to her place, he walked her to the door, and the nerves in her stomach kicked up a notch.

"I had a really good time with you, Jamie."

Max leaned closer on his way to her lips, but the baby popped into her mind, and she turned away at the last second.

"What is it? Was I being too forward?" he asked.

"No, it's just ..." Oh, how she wished she didn't have to tell him this. Because the moment the words were out, she knew this would be over. "I need to tell you something before this can ever become anything more."

"Okay." His eyebrow raised as he waited for her to speak.

"There's no easy way to say this, so I'm just going to." She took a deep breath and exhaled through her nose. "I'm pregnant."

He was silent for several beats. "That's ... not what I was expecting you to say."

"I'm not with the father or anything. I never have been. It wasn't a relationship. Just one night together."

"Wow."

"I know, and I understand if this is it as far as we're concerned. I had a great time with you, but I get it. Don't feel bad at all."

"Now wait a minute, I never said I didn't want to see you again, did I?"

Her mouth fell open. "Wait, what?"

"I like you, Jamie. I've never had such a great first date before."

She smiled. "Neither have I."

"I don't know about you, but I'd like to spend some time together and see if there's more between us. And we can deal with the rest. I'm not going to judge you for a bad life choice. We've all made them."

"Thank you for saying that, but you might change your mind when I tell you the rest."

"Maybe, but I doubt it."

She blurted it out before she lost her nerve. "Duncan is the baby's father."

Max was quiet for long seconds that stretched into a minute.

"So, that's why he was here and acting so weird when I came to pick you up."

"I don't know why he was here. He just showed up and said he needed to talk."

"He did *not* like me taking you out."

"That wasn't it. He's engaged."

"He didn't like it. I could see that plain as day."

"Probably because I'm having his baby."

"I don't know. It seemed like more than that, but I could be wrong."

Jamie lay her hand on her belly. "I get it. Like I said, don't feel bad about this. I probably should've told you before we went out. I felt really guilty about that."

"I'm going to talk to him," Max replied.

"Duncan? Why?"

"To make sure he's okay with us seeing each other."

"You still want to see me?"

"Yes."

"Well, it's not Duncan's choice, it's mine."

"I like you a lot, Jamie, but Duncan's family, and I can't pursue you if it's going to cause a rift between us."

Jamie nodded. "You're a good guy, Max McGregor."

He shrugged his shoulders. "Maybe too good."

She stood on her tiptoes and pressed a soft kiss to his cheek.

He gave her a quick hug before heading down the sidewalk with a cute wave.

Jamie went into her apartment and plopped down onto the couch. She rested her head back and stared at the ceiling fan. Max was the nicest guy and showed her such respect, which she hadn't experienced much with other guys in her life. He made her feel like she was worthy of that kind of attention.

Her mind returned to the look in Duncan's eyes when he realized she was about to go out with his cousin. Why did the thought that he might be jealous cause more butterflies in her stomach than almost kissing Max had?

A knock at her door made her jump. She opened it, thinking maybe Max had forgotten something, and found Duncan standing there again. He ran his fingers through his hair, causing it to stand on end, leaving him looking disheveled in the sexiest way.

"Why are you back here?"

He glanced over her shoulder into the apartment.

"He's not here," she said.

Duncan said nothing as his gaze met hers.

"What is wrong with you?"

He glanced down for a heartbeat and then suddenly stepped into her space, his arms winding around her back, pulling her firmly against him.

She gasped but didn't fight him. She wanted nothing more than to be right there as close to him as possible. "Duncan, what are you doing?" she whispered.

"Hugging you," he whispered back. His breath was warm against her neck, which sent shivers up her spine. He pulled back and looked down at her belly. "I felt your baby bump."

She didn't respond to that because their eyes connected, and he leaned in until his forehead rested against hers, their breaths mingling.

His lips hovered millimeters from hers. They were so close. All she'd have to do was lean in.

"I don't want you going out with Maxwell," he whispered.

She lifted her head to look at him. "What?"

"I'd rather you not date him."

"That's what this was all about? Staking your claim or something?" She eyed him. "Are you jealous?"

"No, I—"

"Screw you, Duncan." She left his arms, and immediately felt the loss of his warmth. "Just because I'm having your baby doesn't mean you have the right to tell me who I can and can't date. You can't expect me to sit on the sidelines alone while you marry Dréa and start your happy life together. And you sure as heck can't hold me like that and almost kiss me when you're engaged to another woman. What is the matter with you?"

Duncan reached out to touch her arm, but she jerked away from him. He raked his fingers through his hair again. "I'm sorry."

"You should be. Now go home and leave me alone." She marched toward the bathroom. *Darn bladder.* "You can let yourself out," she snapped over her shoulder.

The tears flowed freely once she was in the bathroom. She thought she heard the front door close, and she was glad for that. Having him hold her the way he had, nearly kiss her, it was confusing, and it hurt.

When she finished, she expected him to be gone, but he was leaning against the wall across from the bathroom door. She had to shake off the memory of him pressing her up against that very wall and kissing the breath out of her the night they spent together.

"I can't leave if you're upset with me."

"I am."

"I care about you, Jamie. So much. You know that. I didn't mean to hurt you."

"Well, you did. Because I want you to kiss me, Duncan. I want to be with you. I always have."

His eyes widened at her confession.

"There, I said it. I have always liked you, and I don't regret that night we shared. It was the best night of my life. But I can't have you. Pomegranate and I have to go it alone and find someone else to make us happy. It can't be you. So, please just go. You can be part of his or her life, but you can't be a part of mine."

"Jamie." Her name sounded strangled on his tongue as he neared her again.

Her tears were flowing steadily now. "Please," she whispered. "Go."

Chapter 30

He took her face in his hands, tilting it up until she was forced to look at him. "Pomegranate?" He smirked. "What happened to Orange?"

"The baby grew again."

"I liked Orange better. I was thinking OJ might be a good baby name," he joked.

"Don't try to make me laugh right now. I'm not done being mad at you."

He didn't know what had possessed him to come back there. But sitting home, wondering what was happening on her date with Max, wondering if he was kissing her goodnight, drove him insane. And when she stood before him again, with those beautiful eyes and kissable lips and that feisty attitude he loved so much, he couldn't help himself. He'd needed her as close as he could get her. It had felt so good, so right, never wanting to let her go, not wanting her with anyone but him.

She was his weakness. Clearly, he couldn't control himself around her. He had wanted to taste her lips again after all these months without it. And he nearly had. The guilt over that betrayal to Dréa was already eating him alive.

He was frustrated. With himself for almost kissing her. With his out of control emotions over her dating Max. Was he jealous? Heck yes, he was. But Jamie was right. She deserved happiness and someone to love her.

He hadn't expected her to admit her feelings for him, though, and that made things more complicated.

"I'm sorry, Jamie. You're right about everything."

"Of course, I am. And you're a jerk."

He nodded. "That's accurate."

Jamie sniffled as she stepped away from him and took a seat on the couch. "I told you to let yourself out, didn't I?" She tilted her head toward the door.

"I'm going." He headed in that direction.

"Wait, what did you want to talk about when you stopped by before?" she asked.

He turned around. "It's not relevant anymore."

"What isn't?" Her brow furrowed.

There was no way Jamie would move to Denver. Not after admitting how she felt about him. To ask her to live near him and his new wife would be like pouring lemon juice on a paper cut.

"You have to tell me now or I'll wonder what it was, and that will drive me crazy. Please don't torture a pregnant woman with overactive hormones."

"It had to do with Denver," he replied.

"You're still moving there then?"

He nodded. "It makes the most sense."

"Not for the baby." Her tone was snarky.

He hesitated but wanted to be honest with her. "I was going to ask if you'd consider moving there."

Shock spread over her face. "Excuse me?"

"I found a great apartment with a short-term lease when I was down there last weekend. I'm going to rent it for myself, for now, so I have a place to stay until the wedding, and I thought it would be a great place for you and the baby to live. It's a nice neighborhood, good schools, not far from where Dréa and I are looking for a place." He paused to look at her. "But I know it's probably not going to happen."

He could almost see steam coming out of her ears as she held her reaction in. It scared him that she was probably going to burst at any moment. And then she did.

"Probably? I'm not moving. I'm not upending my entire life for you. My business is here. I've got a support system in place for this baby with your family. Why would I move to a strange city, where I only know you and your new bride, where I have to start all over establishing photography clients? Have you not thought this through?" She didn't give him a chance to reply as she continued, growing louder the longer she talked. "Apparently not. You only thought about how it would be for you, having the baby closer. And I get that you don't want to be so far away, but that's *your* choice, Duncan. So, go! Move to Denver! But I'm staying here with your sister and your family—"

"And Max?" he added.

Jamie tilted her head. "I barely know him, Duncan. You know that. But who knows ..." She quirked her eyebrow, knowing full well what saying that did to him.

"I get it. No Denver," he grumbled.

"No Denver."

When Duncan arrived home, he was surprised to find Max sitting at the kitchen table with Papa. He loved his cousin and was usually happy when he visited, but Max was the last person he wanted to see tonight of all nights.

"What are you doing here? Your date end early?" His tone was unkind and he knew it.

Papa stood and patted Duncan on the shoulder. "Are we still on for golf tomorrow morning?"

"Sure, Pop."

"Night, boys," he said as he headed upstairs to his bedroom.

"Are you staying over?" Duncan asked as he glanced at the clock.

"No, I'm on my way home, but I wanted to talk to you about something."

"If it has to do with Jamie, don't bother."

"It does."

"Then don't bother," Duncan snapped.

"Look, she told me about the baby."

"Yeah?"

"And I get why you aren't thrilled about me taking her out."

"Do you?"

"You're protective of her because she's having your kid. If I were in your situation, I'd probably feel the same way. But you know me, man. We're blood. You know I would never treat her with anything but the utmost respect."

Duncan did know that. Maxwell was a McGregor. They'd been raised to care for and protect the women in their lives. It was in their DNA or something.

But it was Jamie. And Max. And when he thought of them as Jamie & Max, he felt sick to his stomach. It just didn't feel right. Even without the baby in the mix.

"I want to get to know her and see if there's something more between us."

Duncan said nothing.

"But I wanted to make sure you were okay with it while she's pregnant. I know it's a little awkward."

"No," Duncan replied.

"Would you rather we wait until after the baby's born? I understand if that's what you want, and I'll respect that."

"No."

"No what? You need to be more specific."

"I don't want you dating her."

"While she's pregnant?"

"Ever." He knew how crazy that sounded, but he didn't care.

"What? Why?"

"It's too weird. You'll be the baby's cousin and, what ... stepdad too? I don't like it."

"Whoa! Slow down there. I'm talking about dating her, not marrying her."

"The answer is no."

Max pressed his lips together, his nostrils flaring. "Hey, I came to you because you're family, but you're not being rational here. Jamie is a great girl, who I like very much. She's funny and beautiful ... and single. Last time I checked, you were marrying someone else, so why are you so dead set against us being together?"

Duncan had no good answer to that question. He couldn't very well tell Max that the thought of them dating made him murderous. That he was so confused, he felt like he was losing his mind.

"You know what, you and Jamie do whatever you want." He pushed the chair back with a loud squeak and went to his room.

He couldn't talk about this anymore. Maybe things would've been different if he had stopped seeing Jamie as a girl to flirt with and seen her as a girl who needed Jesus.

That thought popped into his mind seemingly out of nowhere, but he knew where it had come from. From the One who loved him and Jamie and their baby more than anyone else possibly could, the One who was working all things together for His good—even though it felt far from good at the moment. From the One he'd been giving the silent treatment for weeks.

Guilt and confusion overwhelmed him, leaving him tossing and turning all through the night. There should've been room in his mind for thoughts of Dréa and the wedding, but all he could think about was Jamie and the baby and where he'd gone so wrong.

In the early morning hours, Duncan wandered into the kitchen and found Papa seated at the table with the Bible open in front of him.

"You're up early."

"Couldn't sleep," Papa said.

Duncan poured himself a glass of water and sat down beside his father. "What are you reading?"

"The Psalms."

"Which one?"

"Fifty-one. It's David's repentance to the Lord after sinning with Bathsheba."

Duncan tensed. He knew the story of David and Bathsheba well. King David saw a beautiful woman bathing, found out who she was, and though she was married, he had her brought to him anyway and slept with her, which led to her getting pregnant. He committed adultery, which was in that time punishable by death. He even went so far as to have her husband put on the front lines in battle so he would die and David could have her for his own.

"David's sins were great, but God sent his friend, Nathan the prophet, to open his eyes to the error of his ways. And David threw himself at the mercy of his Lord, admitting he had sinned against Him. No matter what we've done, God offers us his pardon. If we admit what we've done and seek His face, He offers us forgiveness."

"I know, Papa."

"Do you? Because you've been walking around here lately wound up so tight. I feel like there's a reason for that."

"Yeah, the reason is I slept with someone and got her pregnant, I'm engaged to someone else, I'm moving to Denver after the wedding, I'll probably never see my baby, and now the mother of my child wants to date my cousin."

Papa's gaze was sympathetic. "I'm sorry you're going through all this, Duncan. But I have a strong feeling you're not talking to God about any of it."

Duncan shrugged his shoulders.

"Well, when you get to that place, remember this Psalm. God's forgiveness and grace are limitless. He wants you to come to Him rather than try to handle things by your power."

Duncan didn't reply.

"Just think on it."

"I will."

Papa stood and left the Bible open to Psalm 51. "I'm going for a walk. Care to join?"

"No, thanks." He watched his father walk out of the kitchen and turned his attention to the open Bible before him. He skimmed a few of the verses and stopped on one.

Create in me a pure heart, O God, and renew a steadfast spirit within me.

The guilt and shame struck him again, and he closed the Bible and went back to bed.

Chapter 31

This was the day. The day Jamie would learn whether she was carrying a boy or a girl. All morning, she'd been jittery and anxious to see the baby on screen again.

Normally, any day she got to see Duncan was a good day, but she still wasn't happy with him about Max or Denver. So when she opened the door to head to her appointment and saw him walking up the sidewalk, she was taken aback. "I thought we were meeting at the hospital."

"I thought we'd go together. Is that okay?"

"I guess." Her answer was clipped as she locked the door, then turned to face him, only to discover him standing in her personal space. He smelled so good, and she angled past him before she did something foolish, like lean in and inhale his scent.

"We can take my car." He rushed ahead and opened the door for her, which would've been sweet if she wasn't still annoyed. Duncan wasn't hers and never would be, so she knew she shouldn't get used to this special treatment.

On the drive to the hospital, Duncan chattered nervously, talking about his latest design job, mostly, and she let him talk, because her bladder was full for the ultrasound, and his random story was working as a distraction.

"You're quiet," he stated. "Are you still mad at me for asking you to move to Denver?"

"Yes, but that's not why I'm quiet. I have to go to the bathroom really bad."

He chuckled. "We'll be there soon. You can go before the appointment."

"No, I need a full bladder for the ultrasound."

"Oh. I didn't know."

"I feel like I might pee my pants."

He laughed at that.

"I'm not joking. Not even a little."

"Don't pee on my seat."

"Don't make me laugh," she snapped, "or I will."

A few quiet beats passed between them.

"You know I want to know my baby, right? And I want the baby to know me. That's why I asked you to move. I don't want to miss out on things."

His words warmed her heart, but there was no easy solution. "We'll have to send each other videos and figure out a visitation schedule that works."

"This is just … really hard." His fingers tightened on the steering wheel.

"I know it is. We should pray about it. I'm sure God has a better plan than we could come up with anyway."

He didn't respond to that.

When they parked at the hospital, he jumped out and rounded the vehicle to help her out. "Do you need a wheelchair?"

Jamie raised an eyebrow at him. "Seriously? I have to pee. I didn't lose my ability to walk."

"Don't pregnant women get wheeled into the hospital?"

"I'm not in labor, Duncan." Jamie winced. "Oh, stop making me laugh."

"Just trying to be helpful."

She shook her head as they walked toward the entrance. "Thank you, but I think I can get there. Although, every time I take a step, my bladder screams at me to find a toilet."

Duncan chuckled. "I could carry you if you want."

"You're funny."

"I'm serious."

"How would carrying me help?"

"I don't know. Less jostling."

"Oh my gosh." She cracked up laughing as the automatic doors opened before them, and they went to get checked in at the front desk.

"We're here for an ultrasound," Jamie said, laying her hand over her little baby bump.

"Well, let's get you all checked in." The receptionist directed them to a small office to the right, where a woman took Jamie's information and got her registered.

A mix of nerves and anticipation had her knees bouncing. Duncan reached over and took her hand in his and squeezed, and she let him because she needed the support right now. He never let go all the time they were at that desk or when they were waiting to be escorted into the ultrasound room.

"I don't know why I'm so nervous. I guess I just want the baby to be okay."

"It will."

The sonographer came out soon after, and once they were in the exam room, Jamie felt calm. She lay on the table as instructed and lifted her shirt to reveal her belly, and Duncan came to stand at her side. She glanced up and found his eyes on her baby bump. Her cheeks warmed, remembering the last time he'd seen her bare stomach. His gaze met hers, and he grabbed hold of her hand again as the woman squirted a warm gel onto her bare midriff and moved the ultrasound wand over the area.

Jamie's eyes were locked on the screen with fascination.

"There's the baby's head," the woman said.

"There's the left foot. And the right."

"Five fingers there. And here are five more."

"That's the baby's heart. See it beating?"

She shifted the wand to just the right angle for a perfect silhouette of their child, and hot tears spilled down Jamie's cheeks.

Duncan squeezed her hand and leaned down until his forehead was against her temple. "That's our baby," he spoke softly.

Jamie's eyes twinkled. "Our baby."

They both turned back to the screen, enraptured by the arms and legs and the little silhouette of their child.

As the sonographer moved the wand lower and at a different angle, she paused. "Would you like to know the sex of the baby?"

Duncan replied, "No," just as Jamie enthusiastically said, "Yes!"

Their eyes met.

"You really don't want to know?" she asked.

"You do?"

"I mean, we talked about it. I said I wanted to know so I could plan better."

"I'd rather not know. I want to be surprised."

Jamie looked at the sonographer. "Is it possible for me to be told without him knowing?"

"Sure. I can write it on a piece of paper and put it in an envelope for you."

"Yes, that would be perfect."

"No way," Duncan protested.

"Why not?"

"Because then you'll know, and I won't."

"It's not my fault you don't want to know."

He pouted. "Fine. But do *not* tell me. And don't tell my sister."

Jamie laughed. "You know I can't keep this from Shannon."

He grumbled.

She couldn't help but giggle at his expression.

"What?"

"You're cute when you pout."

His brow furrowed, and his lower lip remained stuck out. "I'm not pouting."

She laughed again, which made her let out a sudden groan.

"What? What is it?" He gently took hold of her forearm. "Is it the baby?"

She shook her head. "My bladder."

The sonographer chuckled, and Duncan smiled. "Oh."

When they were finished and Jamie had finally relieved herself, they headed out with a picture of their little pomegranate in hand. Jamie stared at it as they walked along the sidewalk. "Is it weird to say I think the baby looks like you?" She held the picture up next to Duncan's profile.

He laughed and took hold of her hand.

She instantly stopped and pulled her hand from his. "You can't do that, Duncan."

He looked down at the ground. "I know. It's just ..."

"It's just what?"

"I can't help myself. We're having this baby, and that makes me feel close to you."

She understood. Completely. "I feel close to you too, but when you do things like that ... it's confusing for me. After everything I told you, you get that, right?"

"I get it, and I'm sorry. I don't mean to hurt you."

"I know you don't."

"This is just a really weird situation we're in, that's all."

"That it is."

"And I want to be supportive, but I'm not sure how to show that."

"Just keep showing up for us. And I guess, just be my friend. Even if that's hard for me for a while. I'll get over it."

"I can do that."

"We have to. For the sake of the baby."

He nodded. "For the baby."

Duncan dropped her off at her place, and she insisted on walking herself in. She wasn't sure she could handle a hug at the door. It would've either been awkward or wonderful. Probably wonderful, which was not healthy for her right now.

As she collapsed onto her couch, she felt like a puddle of goo, remembering the grin he'd given her before she walked away from his car. When would it get easier to be close to him without catching all the feelings? How would she live her whole life having Duncan close, yet not able to be with him like she wanted? She closed her eyes and started to pray aloud.

"Dear God, I've never really prayed like this before, so I will probably sound ridiculous. But I just want to thank you for this baby. It's a blessing. I know that. But You know how hard this is for me and how hard it's going to be. I love him, God. I love Duncan. I have for so long, and I need Your help to get over this because he's marrying someone else. He's going to spend his life with her. And I have to be in his life because of the baby, and that's going to be so tough. Because there is no future for us ... romantically. There's only parenting and visitations and taking turns caring for our child. I want us to be partners in this. To be a family, the three of us. But that will never be."

She broke down crying then. It was the first time she let the floodgates open and allowed the disappointment in. She'd dealt with her feelings about the pregnancy, but really crying over Duncan and the fact that they would never be a couple was something she hadn't let herself do.

She lay back on the couch, placing her hand over her belly. "It's going to be okay, Pomegranate. We're going to get through this. You're the only thing that matters, the most important thing in my life. And I'm going to be the best mom to you."

In that instant, she felt a tiny flutter deep inside, and she bolted upright.

"Was that ...?"

She felt it again, positive it was the baby.

"I know you heard me, didn't you?" She thought she was all cried out, but tears of joy now streamed down her face.

Not wanting Duncan to miss a thing, she grabbed her phone and sent him a text.

> **Jamie: I felt the baby move.**
> **Duncan: What? Are you serious?**
> **Jamie: It was like a tiny little flutter.**
> **Duncan: That's amazing. I wish I could feel it.**
> **Jamie: I wish you could too. It was the weirdest sensation.**
> **Duncan: Tell baby Daddy loves him.**
> **Jamie: Or her.**

Duncan replied with a winking emoji and a heart. If only he loved her too.

Chapter 32

After the ultrasound, something shifted between them. Duncan didn't know if it was their conversation that day about being just friends for the sake of the baby, but he could feel the change in her. Like they had a new understanding.

They'd been talking on the phone a lot over the past couple weeks, trying to come up with the best possible plan for after the baby arrived. Jamie had asked if he could stay in town for a couple of weeks to help her and bond with his baby. Thankfully, Dréa was on board. She'd even suggested he stay in Michigan for the first couple months and she would travel back and forth on weekends, which only confirmed what a wonderful, selfless woman he was marrying.

There was still much to talk about and plenty to do before January, but on this particular afternoon, Duncan and Jamie were about to check a big to-do off their list—the overwhelming task of registering for gifts at Babies R Us.

The automatic doors slid open, and they walked through, both stopping just inside, scanning the room with great intimidation. The store was filled with aisle after aisle of everything one could possibly need for a baby—bottles, pacifiers, burp cloths, blankets, baby monitors, and on and on.

"Where do we start?" Duncan asked.

"Over here." Jamie walked toward a customer service desk, and Duncan followed.

The nice woman behind the desk set up their registry and gave them a hand-held device to scan the items they would need, and they headed off into the unknown.

Jamie led, walking up and down each aisle, looking as confused as Duncan felt.

"How do we know what we'll need?" She stopped at a display of bottles.

Duncan came up beside her and noticed her chewing on her bottom lip. "What's wrong?"

"I wanted to breastfeed." She glanced up at him then back at the bottles.

"I know you do."

"But is that even realistic in our situation?"

"Of course it is."

"How? When the baby will be with you in Denver sometimes."

He wanted nothing more than to take away her sadness.

"Don't worry. For however long you want to feed the baby, I'll come to you or you can come to Denver too. I know you'll have to be close to the baby to make that work, and I know you want the baby to have the best start in life."

"I do."

"So, we'll figure it out. We can postpone any kind of visitation schedule until the baby is a little older and off the boob."

Jamie laughed. "Off the boob?"

He shrugged.

That seemed to lighten the mood, and Jamie picked up a bottle. "I guess the baby will need a bottle for times when I can't be there. I'll have to pump and you can feed ... him or her."

He scowled. "I hate that you know what we're having."

"Hey, you could know too."

"No!"

She laughed again. "Fine. This one?" She held up the bottle.

"Sure."

They continued through the store, scanning baby supplies, a car seat, a stroller, a high chair, and only neutral colored clothing so Jamie wouldn't give away the sex of the baby.

Just as they were about to finish, Duncan froze and darted across the aisle.

"This!" he declared as he grabbed hold of a onesie and held it up. "We have to get this."

Jamie let out a laugh at the *Star Wars* onesie with Yoda on the front that read "Too Cute I Am."

"No, this one!" He grabbed the one beside it. "Jedi In Training."

"I love them!"

"You like *Star Wars*?" he asked.

"Who doesn't?" She pointed the scanner at the onesie in his hand, but he blocked the barcode.

"You don't want them on the registry?"

"No, I'm buying them now. My first purchase for our kid."

A smile lit up her face, and he tried to ignore the sudden flutter in his stomach.

They walked to the customer service desk to return the scanner, then paid for the onesies and headed to his car.

"What's your favorite *Star Wars* movie?" he asked.

"*Empire*. No contest," she replied.

"I would have to agree with that. Second favorite?"

"*Return of the Jedi*."

"Not *A New Hope*?"

She shook her head. "What can I say? I love the Ewoks."

"Who can resist the Ewoks? I would say mine are *Empire*, *A New Hope*, then *Return of the Jedi*. What about the prequels?"

She snorted. "Never happened."

He eyed her as he opened her door. "Not a fan, I take it?"

"I mean, midichlorians? Jar Jar Binks? Come on."

Duncan laughed heartily, and they spent the drive to her studio debating the merits of the prequels and the downfall of Anakin Skywalker.

They arrived at the studio in a blink, and he felt disappointed, wanting to continue their conversation, so he followed her into the building. "Despite all the ridiculousness, there are plenty of redeeming qualities to the prequels. Don't you at least like knowing the history of the characters? How they got from that point to where they are in the original trilogy."

Jamie shrugged. "I guess. But I could've done a better job, and I'm not even a writer."

"Are you talking about *Star Wars*?" Shannon asked when they walked in.

"Jamie doesn't like the prequels," he explained.

"I don't mind them," Shannon said, "but the originals are the best."

"We're not debating that," Jamie said.

"Don't you have a senior picture session at four, Jame?" Shannon asked as she shut down her computer and gathered her things.

"I do. I didn't think registering was going to take all afternoon." Jamie took her camera from the cubby behind her desk.

"I'm outta here!" Shannon announced. "See you tomorrow."

"See ya," Duncan said.

"Bye." Jamie waved her arm without looking back, too focused on getting ready for her photo session.

Duncan followed Jamie into the studio space at the rear of the building. Afternoon sunlight flooded the room through a row of windows that were covered with white shades to filter out the harsh light.

Jamie spun around suddenly and ran into him.

"Sorry." He let out a nervous laugh.

"I forgot my other lens." She grabbed his forearms and turned them both so she could pass.

His skin tingled where she had touched him, and he shook it off. *Friends.*

When she returned, he watched in silence as she made sure the room was ready for her next client. She was in the zone until she stopped and stared over at him.

"Are you staying?"

He shrugged. "I could stay."

She walked to the corner, grabbed a reflector, and shoved it in his direction. "Then I'm putting you to work."

The chime on the door signaled her client's arrival, and she rushed out of the room. When she returned, a teenaged boy was on her heels. He fidgeted and stood stiffly to the side until Jamie directed him to sit on the stool she had set up. She had a firm yet gentle way about her, and it wasn't long before the kid was comfortable with her.

Duncan did all Jamie asked of him, holding the reflector just right to light the boy's face. He was in awe of her talent and ability to bring out a person's real personality in photos. That boy had walked in completely nervous, but once Jamie talked to him, asking him questions about himself, showing an interest, it was as if he was a different person. By the end of that session, he was smiling and laughing like he'd known her forever, which made him appear confident and natural in front of the camera.

After the boy left, Duncan followed Jamie to her desk and stood behind her as she loaded the images into her computer.

"Can I see a few?" he asked.

"Sure." Her hand moved the mouse and clicked to open a preview of the pictures she had just taken.

"Somebody knows how to work a reflector," he joked.

She laughed, and he liked the sound. He'd never realized how cute her laugh was before. He shook off his thoughts and watched her click through a few more photographs.

"You are so talented, Jamie."

"Thanks," she replied.

"I mean it. That kid was so awkward at the beginning, but look at him in this picture." He leaned forward, resting his hand on her shoulder, and pointed at the screen. "That's a real smile. Nothing fake or awkward about it."

Her eyes lifted to meet his. "Thank you."

He didn't look away, and he was very aware that his thumb and index finger were touching the soft skin of her neck. "How did you know you wanted to do this for a living?"

"You'll probably think it's weird." She tilted her head away shyly, and he released her shoulder.

He turned and took a seat on the corner of her desk. "Tell me."

"I never wanted to photograph people," she admitted.

"Really?"

"I wanted to be a macro photographer."

"Like the closeup pictures of bugs and stuff?"

She nodded. "My parents gave me my first SLR camera when I was twelve, and I kept trying to take pictures of things really close up, but I didn't have the right lens. It was so frustrating. So I saved up and bought a macro lens, and it was like a whole new world opened up for me. I went through so much film back then. My parents freaked out on me every time I needed another roll developed. Then in college, I got my first digital SLR, and I was in heaven because I could take as many pictures as I wanted and delete the ones that didn't turn out. And I wasn't broke all the time from taking film to the photo lab."

Duncan chuckled. "Did you take those pictures that are hanging in your apartment? The closeups of the flowers?"

"Yep."

"Wow. I've always thought those were cool."

That earned him a smile.

"So, how did you switch over to weddings?"

"I realized I needed to focus on more than just macro to be able to make a living. I majored in photography and started second-shooting for some wedding photographers in the area and doing engagement sessions for friends, and I fell in love with capturing those moments for people."

He loved hearing that, knowing more about how she got to where she was today.

"And then I got in with the area photographers, and I met Shannon."

"And me," Duncan added.

"And the rest is history." She touched her belly then looked at him again. "Thanks for helping in there."

"You're welcome." He glanced toward the door. "I should probably get some work of my own done today."

Jamie chuckled. "Probably."

He fought the urge to stay, forcing his legs to move to the exit.

"I'm glad we got the registry done," she called after him.

He looked back at her. "Me too. I hope we didn't miss anything."

"We got a Yoda onesie. What more does the baby need?"

Duncan laughed. "True." He gave her a wave and headed out.

As he drove home, he couldn't stop picturing moments from the day, and his chest tightened. He took slow, deep breaths, trying to release whatever tension he was holding, and thought about Jamie's Yoda comment. That made him smile, but the tension was still there.

Being friends with Jamie was easy. It always had been. The attraction and flirtation had been there all along. But this ... this ache that had settled itself deep inside his heart the moment he was away from her ... this was different.

Chapter 33

Jamie was getting far too comfortable at McGregor family gatherings. She was glad to fit in and be accepted and supported by the family, but it made her heart ache the more she was around them because she wanted so badly to be one of them. Officially. And she knew that was never going to happen.

This Labor Day picnic, in honor of Nana's ninety-seventh birthday, was bound to be interesting. Max would be there, which she was happy about. They weren't officially dating, but they talked and texted often and had seen each other a few times over the past month. Max hadn't said much about his conversation with Duncan, only that it hadn't gone well, and that it was best if they kept things casual. Jamie wasn't sure how to feel about that.

Dréa would be in attendance too. The last time she'd been in town was the night of Jamie's spiritual birthday party at the McGregor's, and that hadn't ended well.

Things between Jamie and Duncan had been good since the ultrasound. It felt like they were going to make it through all this with their friendship intact, and she was happy about that. If she couldn't be with Duncan, at least he would be in her life.

Shannon and Micah had insisted on picking Jamie up on their way to Aunt Pauline's, and she had agreed because, honestly, she was feeling tired most days. She thought when she reached the second trimester, she would have more energy than this. That's what she'd been told to expect anyway. But it was probably different for every woman.

Her belly had finally popped when she passed the twenty-week mark. Well, she was probably the only one who noticed, but she was proud of her bump.

"How's Coco doing?" Shannon asked.

Jamie shook her head. "You're making me regret telling you the baby's the size of a coconut right now."

Shannon giggled. "Are you feeling more movement yet?"

"A lot, and the kicks are getting stronger."

"Do you think I could feel it?"

"Not yet." Jamie lay a hand on her baby bump as she felt a kick. "But I don't think it will be much longer."

When they arrived at the house, Micah got out and opened Jamie's door, offering her a hand to help her out of the car.

"Thanks, Micah. Such a gentleman. Shannon's a lucky girl."

Micah grinned. "I'm the lucky one."

Shannon walked around the car and gave him a kiss, then looped her arm through Jamie's as they walked up the sidewalk.

"Maybe I shouldn't be here," Jamie said.

"Why?"

"It's been just me and Duncan for the past couple months, and I dread seeing him and Dréa together again."

"I know. I'm sorry, Jame."

"It is what it is, right? I got myself into this situation," she said as they walked in and found Duncan in the living room with his dad.

He gave her a look. "Do you owe me a coffee again?"

She blushed a little, liking their inside joke. "Maybe."

He rubbed his hands together. "Excellent."

Jamie playfully punched him and a smile spread across his face. She walked past on her way to the kitchen with Shannon and glanced back to see him shake his head, the smile still hanging on his lips.

But the moment was spoiled as soon as she stepped into the kitchen and noticed Dréa. She was wearing an apron, helping Nana, Aunt Pauline, and Mrs. McGregor. Shannon instantly joined them, which left Jamie feeling a little out of place just standing there.

"Can I help with anything?" she asked.

Nana looked over at her. "Jamie dear, how are you feeling?"

"Pretty good, Nana. Thank you for asking." Jamie caught Dréa's unhappy stare and gave her a weak smile before she was startled by a kiss on her cheek.

"Hey, beautiful." Max's facial hair scratched against her skin.

"Hey." Jamie reached up and touched his beard, and she noticed how pleased Dréa looked at their interaction. "Wow! This grew fast." When they'd last seen each other two weeks ago, he'd had a little bit of scruff, but this would become a full-on beard if he let it go.

"I know. Once in a while I decide to stop shaving. You like?"

She had a weak spot for guys with beards. "I like." She reached up to run her fingers through it just as Duncan walked into the room. The look on his face told her he didn't like what he saw. Not one bit. And deep down, that pleased her.

Duncan walked over and wrapped his arms around Dréa's waist, leaning in to kiss her cheek, and Jamie thought she was going to lose her breakfast, even though she was long past having morning sickness.

"I'm going to get some air," she announced as she moved past Max and headed for the back yard.

This was exactly what she feared, witnessing their lovey-dovey displays of affection. She may be the one having his baby, but seeing them together drove home the fact that she didn't have his heart.

Max followed her outside, and they sat down in a couple of lawn chairs. He talked about work and everyday things that had happened since they'd seen each other last, but she struggled to pay attention, especially when the baby moved. This baby was a constant reminder of Duncan, and it always would be.

"Jamie? Did you hear me?"

She shook herself out of the fog. "I'm really sorry. My mind is somewhere else right now."

"I asked how work is going."

"It's fine. I'm staying busy." The inquiries were steady, but she had been shooting less than usual. She had turned down a couple of engagement shoots recently, mostly telling herself it was because of how tired she was, but it was hard to photograph happy couples lately. It wasn't a smart decision to turn away clients. She needed to keep a steady income, especially with the baby coming, but her hormones were messing with her head, and the last thing her clients needed was a weepy, emotional photographer who couldn't see through her tears to shoot their session.

"Do you want something to drink?" Max asked.

"Water," she replied.

"Okay, be right back."

The yard had filled up quickly with family members. Jamie loved that Shannon and Duncan were close with their extended family, especially Nana's side. Jamie had aunts and uncles, but not many cousins. The McGregors were blessed to have a large, loving family. And now her baby would be a part of that too.

Jamie was sure they would welcome *her* in as well, because of the baby, but she knew she would always feel like an outsider.

The smell of barbecue pork floated across the lawn, and Jamie's stomach growled. This pregnancy made her more hungry than usual. For being petite, she had always been known for her voracious appetite and quick metabolism, allowing her to eat pretty much whatever she wanted and never gain weight.

Now, though, she was gaining all sorts of baby weight, and she didn't mind one bit. She had taken to looping an elastic hair tie through the button hole of her favorite jeans so she could keep wearing them. But she knew she would have to figure something else out soon because, over the next few months, those jeans were no longer going to fit. Maybe she would size up in jeans because she didn't want to wear maternity clothes. Shannon had taken her shopping, and she hated every frumpy maternity outfit she saw. Nope. She'd wear leggings and long shirts for the winter if she had to. But no jeans with cotton panels and elastic waists. Not for her. No way.

It was crazy to think of winter clothing when the sun was beating down on this warm September day. There wasn't much of a breeze either, which was causing Jamie to perspire. Her attention turned to some of the cousins and their kids, jumping off the dock into the cool blue water.

"Hey, Jame, do you want to go swimming?" Shannon came across the yard with a towel wrapped around her.

"You read my mind."

"I put our stuff in the balcony room at the top of the stairs."

"Okay, thanks." She stood and headed into the house, passing Max on her way.

"Where ya goin'?" He handed her the glass of water he'd fetched for her.

"Swimming. Wanna come?"

"Maybe later."

"Okay. Thanks for the water."

Jamie went upstairs and threw on her pink polka dot bikini, then examined her pregnant form in the mirror. Her chest was ampler and her baby bump stuck out, which made her feel more beautiful than she ever had. It amazed her the way her body was changing to accommodate this baby, and tears sprung to her eyes, thinking she might not have experienced any of this if she'd made a different decision.

She rubbed her hand over her tummy as she felt little Coconut move and kick inside.

After wiping away a few stray tears, she tossed a towel over her shoulder and made her way downstairs, where Max was standing by the back door, chatting with some of the guys. She didn't miss the way his eyes skimmed over her baby bump, and she wondered if seeing her this way would change his mind about dating a pregnant woman, but she wasn't going to worry about that now. A day of swimming and fun was exactly what she needed.

Chapter 34

Duncan was sure his eyes would betray him. The second Jamie stepped out of the house in that bathing suit with all her smooth skin on display, he couldn't keep his eyes off of her. And this was a problem for a few reasons—the most important being his fiancée, who stood no less than three feet away from him since Jamie's arrival. Dréa was obviously having trust issues, and she was right to be concerned. Duncan hated himself for staring.

But despite that, and knowing Jamie was his weakness, he still headed down to the lake to swim with the rest of them. He fixated on her as he strode across the grass, watching her and Shannon jump from the end of the dock with triumphant cries as they flew through the air and dropped into the shining water below.

He glanced over his shoulder to where Dréa was talking to Mama, then picked up the pace, jogging across the yard and along the dock. As he reached the end, he let out a cry of his own and jumped over the girls' heads. He hit the water in a hard cannonball, sending a large wave their way.

When he emerged, Shannon was already splashing him, and he splashed in return.

"Thanks a lot." Jamie pushed her plastered hair back from her face.

"What do you think, Jame?" Shannon moved closer to Duncan. "Does he need to pay?"

"I think he does," Jamie replied.

He kicked and moved his arms through the water, hoping to escape, but they were faster. Both girls jumped up on either side of him, grabbed his head and shoulders, and pushed him under. He came up and spit water at his sister, who was then grabbed by Micah and dunked.

Duncan laughed. "Serves you right." He backed up, running into Jamie, who was floating beside him. His hand skimmed her thigh, and he felt her fingers brush against the middle of his back. Heat instantly spread through his body, and though he knew he should've gotten the heck out of that lake, he remained still, floating next to her, allowing the dark water to hide the fact that they were touching each other. He let the backs of his fingers drift down the outside of her leg and over her knee, and fought the urge to spin around and pull her against him.

She removed her hand from his back and pulled her leg away from him.

He rotated slowly to face her. "How are you feeling?"

"Fine." Her cheeks were pink, and not from the sun. "Baby's kicking. A lot."

"Right now?" he asked.

She nodded. "A little."

His hand glided through the water, his palm coming to rest against her belly. Her sharp intake of breath sent the blood pumping through his veins.

"I don't think you can feel it yet." Her voice was shaky.

He felt a little shaky himself. But he waited, holding his hand still, staring at her, the sound of his heart beating in his ears. She was looking at him in that adoring way he loved, but there was a hint of uncertainty there as well.

"You look good." He shouldn't have said that, but it was the truth.

"Thanks." Her eyes flicked to his bare chest and back. "You too."

His thumb slid back and forth against her skin. He had to stop touching her. This was insane and wrong, but it felt so good.

A sudden splash of water hit them. "Dréa's on her way over," Shannon said under her breath.

Duncan dropped his hand and floated backward away from them.

He didn't make eye contact with Jamie. He had crossed a line, but he wasn't sure how to break their connection.

He swam to the dock and pulled himself up as Dréa joined him. "Are you coming in?" he asked.

"No, thanks."

He wrapped his arms around her, and she shrieked. "Duncan! You're getting me all wet!"

He angled her toward the water, threatening to drop her in. "Are you sure? It's a nice day for a swim."

"Let go of me!" She wasn't happy at all, so he did as she asked.

She gave him a look of disapproval before marching across the yard, mumbling about having to change her clothes.

Duncan let out a deep breath, grabbed his towel, and walked up the dock. He glanced toward the water once more before going after Dréa, and he wished he hadn't. Jamie coming out of the water, dripping wet, was a sight he wouldn't be able to get out of his mind for the rest of the day. Especially with that cute little belly—that belly that was carrying their baby. And that only put the memory of how they'd made that baby back into his mind again.

He was in trouble, and in his desperation, he did the only thing he knew could truly make a difference. Instead of following Dréa across the lawn, he took a detour to the waterfront at the far edge of Aunt Pauline's property. He dropped onto the bench there, squeezed his eyes closed, and finally talked to God.

I need your help, God. You know my thoughts are in the gutter right now. I don't want to be unfaithful to Dréa, but I can't stop thinking about Jamie. Why can't I shake her? I've tried and tried. Please forgive me for these sinful thoughts. Please help me get through this. Help me to think of her as only my friend, as the mother of my child. I want to be a faithful husband to Dréa, but right now, I just don't know how I can be when I can't get Jamie out of my head.

The more he prayed, the more he realized he should've gone to the Lord with all of this the moment it had happened. He wasn't sure why he thought he could get past it on his own, but his guilt and shame over the whole incident had kept him from reaching out. But now, the words flowed freely from his mind as he cried out to God.

Forgive me, Lord. Forgive me for sleeping with Jamie. For giving in to lust for one night of pleasure. I wanted her, and I took her when I knew better. I know I've sinned against you, as David did. And I know I've wasted a lot of time trying to figure all this out on my own, but I'm here now, God. Show me what to do. Because I can't get through this without You.

He opened his eyes and gazed out across the glistening water.

Create in me a pure heart, O God, and renew a steadfast spirit in me.

Chapter 35

With the sun sinking low in the sky, Jamie and Max sat on one of the benches by the bonfire. It had been a good day, but her mind couldn't stop going back to the way Duncan had touched her in the water. At that moment, she wished they were the only two people in that lake. But she couldn't read too much into it, because it would only lead to disappointment.

She looked around the yard at the family milling about, talking, and laughing. Shannon and Micah passed by the fire, walking hand-in-hand across the yard, then out onto the dock together. Jamie watched them sit down together, Shannon between Micah's legs, letting their feet dip into the lake. Jamie's heart ached at the sight. She wanted that kind of love, but she wasn't sure she'd ever have it. She could only pray that God would bless her like that one day.

"Want to play cornhole?" Max asked.

She wrinkled her sunburned nose. "You go ahead. I'm kind of tired from all the swimming."

Max went to play the game with some of the cousins and left her alone. She kept watching her friends on the dock until they stood and walked to the end. If only she'd brought her camera along. It was a moment she wished she could capture for them. The pink glow of the sunset off the water, their perfect silhouettes with hands held between them.

Someone sat down beside her just as she saw Micah turn toward Shannon, take her hands in his, and get down on one knee.

Her hands shot to her mouth. "Oh my gosh!"

"What's wrong?"

She turned to see Duncan beside her, not Max as she had thought it was.

"Look!" She pointed toward the dock.

They watched as Micah held out a ring box, and Shannon's head bobbed up and down. Then Micah was on his feet, wrapping his new fiancée up in his arms, lifting and spinning her around.

Duncan and Jamie clapped, as did several of the others who had taken notice. Whistles and cheers filled the yard.

Warm tears spilled down Jamie's cheeks, and she covered her face and cried. She was so happy for her friends but sad for her own predicament, and these days, she seemed to cry at the drop of a hat.

"Hey." Duncan lay his hand on her back. "Are you okay?"

She stayed hidden and shook her head.

He moved her hands, revealing her tearstained cheeks.

Their eyes locked for what seemed like forever, and his gaze slipped to her lips then back to her eyes. The electricity sparked between them. Even more so when he reached up and brushed his thumb against her damp cheek.

"Duncan," she whispered and swallowed hard.

"Duncan, sweet boy." Nana's voice came from behind them.

He immediately dropped his hand and stood to face his grandmother. "Yeah, Nana?"

"Can you come help us move some chairs around the fire so more people can enjoy it?"

"Of course, Nana. I'm on it." He took off across the lawn to help move the Adirondack chairs and lawn chairs into the circle.

Nana walked up and lay a hand on Jamie's shoulder, giving her a wink and a squeeze. Jamie smiled. Even though Nana seemed to have bonded with Dréa, Jamie had a feeling she was secretly rooting for her and Duncan.

A few minutes later, Shannon and Micah came walking up from the dock, holding hands, and Jamie jumped up from her seat and rushed over to hug her friend.

"I am so happy for you guys!"

"Thanks, Jame."

Jamie hugged Micah, then reached for Shannon's hand. "Lemme see!"

The beautifully simple round diamond solitaire fit perfectly on Shannon's slender finger. "It's gorgeous!"

Shannon was beaming. Ten years had gone by since they split up after high school. Ten years to find their way back to each other. Shannon and Micah's love was special, and their second chance made Jamie believe anything was possible where love was concerned.

The sound of acoustic guitar music filled the yard as cousin Tim led a round of "Happy Birthday" for Nana. Shannon carried a cake out of the house and set it on the table in front of her grandmother, who blew out the candles to loud applause from her family. The song turned to "You Are My Sunshine," and Nana sang along as she enjoyed a slice of her cake.

There was a chill in the night air, so much that Jamie wished she'd brought a sweater or jacket. She rubbed up and down her arms to keep warm.

"Here." Duncan peeled his sweatshirt off and handed it to her.

Jamie smiled up at him from her seat by the fire, but as she reached to take it, she noticed Dréa standing behind him, staring at her with that unhappy expression she'd worn earlier. She pushed it back at him. "Thanks, but I'll be fine."

"Are you sure?"

"Yeah." She tried not to shiver. "I guess I should've brought a jacket. I wasn't thinking about it getting colder when the sun went down. It was so warm earlier."

"Fall will be here before we know it," he replied.

There was suddenly a commotion to the side of the house.

"Sophia!" Shannon jumped up from her chair and ran to embrace her sister.

Duncan followed, and Dréa tagged along behind.

Jamie had only met Shannon and Duncan's sister once. Sophia had left Michigan after her high school graduation and had been living in New York City, working in fashion, for nearly a decade. From what Jamie knew, Sophia hadn't been around much in all of those years, missing many family functions and holidays, even Christmas. But here she was, clearly loved by her family, as they surrounded her and smothered her with hugs and kisses until she was laughing and waving people away.

Jamie heard Duncan introduce Dréa and glanced over just as the two soon-to-be-sister-in-laws embraced. Her heart ached at the sight.

Sophia made a beeline for Nana next.

"Oh, my Sophia." Nana cupped her cheek as she leaned in and kissed her on the cheek.

"Happy birthday, Nana. I missed you."

"I've missed you too."

Jamie's heart warmed at their interaction. She loved being with the McGregor family, and she couldn't imagine why Sophia would stay away as long as she had.

After a conversation with Nana, Sophia joined them by the fire, taking a seat between Jamie and Shannon. The music suddenly shifted to a rendition of "New York, New York."

"Very funny, Tim," Sophia cried, which brought on a round of laughter.

"Soph, you remember my friend, Jamie, right?"

Sophia nodded. "You're the one our baby brother knocked up, right?"

Jamie choked on a laugh. "Uh ... yeah, that's me."

The sisters' laughter blended as if it came from one person.

She glanced around to see if Duncan and Dréa had heard her, but they were nowhere in sight.

"When are you due again?" Sophia asked as she flipped her long brown locks over her shoulder.

"January," Jamie replied.

"A New Year's baby?"

"Mid-January, actually. Will you be coming home after the baby is born?"

Sophia shrugged.

"We didn't think you were coming home for this," Shannon said.

"Yeah, well, I missed another picnic on the Fourth, and I felt bad about it. Figured it was about time I showed my face around here again. Plus, I didn't want to miss Nana's birthday."

Shannon wrapped her up in a hug. "I'm so glad you're here."

Sophia forced a smile. Maybe Shannon didn't notice, but Jamie did. Sophia seemed a lot like Jamie's old friends—into herself and her own life. Jamie had been like that once too. But not now that she was carrying another life inside her. Not now that she knew the goodness of God in her life. She knew Sophia's type, though, and she wondered what was so great about her life in New York that kept her from her wonderful, loving family.

"I've never been to New York," Jamie said, hoping to get some information out of Sophia. "But I'd love to shoot a wedding or some engagement pictures in Central Park." She glanced past Sophia to Shannon and gave her a hopeful look.

Shannon grinned.

"You must've been to more than a few New York weddings in your time in the city," Jamie said.

"A few," Sophia replied. "I worked with a wedding dress designer before I moved on to work at DVF."

"I don't know what that is, but I'm sure it's cool."

"Diane Von Furstenburg. She's a famous designer," Sophia stated.

"I've heard the name before," Jamie replied. "Is that where you work now?"

"Uh ... no, not right now. I'm working on my own stuff and in between designers."

"You are?" Shannon looked surprised. "I thought you got that job at Givenchy."

"I did, but it was a short term gig."

"Oh," Shannon replied with a shrug. "But you're doing okay, right?"

"Of course. I love New York."

"Any guys in the picture?" Shannon leaned into her sister's shoulder.

"Guys suck."

Shannon held her hand up in front of Sophia's face. "Not all guys."

"Shannon! What? You're engaged? Why didn't you tell me?"

Shannon's giggle was adorable. "It just happened tonight."

Sophia threw her arms around her sister.

It was the first honest emotion Jamie had seen Sophia exhibit since she'd sat down.

"You should totally go to New York to find a wedding dress, Shannon," Jamie suggested. "Sophia could help you since she works in the industry."

"I do know a few dress designers, but—"

"I love that idea," Shannon blurted. "And you can come too, Jame."

"That would be awesome." She had always wanted to go to New York.

Shannon looked back and forth between the two of them. "Hey, since you're both here together, I have a question for you." She paused for suspense. "Will you be my maids of honor?"

"Of course," Sophia replied like it wasn't even a question.

"Yes!" Jamie couldn't wait to share the day with them.

"So, how about New York, Soph?" Shannon said with excitement.

Sophia shrugged. "New York, here we come."

Jamie found Sophia's lack of enthusiasm strange, but Shannon didn't seem to notice at all, probably due to her excitement over her engagement.

Chapter 36

"I don't understand this attitude you're giving me?" Duncan stared at his fiancée in disbelief after she snapped at him for everything from his driving to dropping his jacket on the floor inside her hotel room.

"There's no attitude." She hung her jacket up in the closet and went about picking his up and hanging it as well.

"You've been finding one thing after another to argue about since we left Aunt Paulie's. What's wrong?"

Dréa stared at him.

"Just tell me. We've got to be able to work through our problems."

"Fine. You want to know what's got me so upset?"

"I wouldn't have asked if I didn't."

She raised an eyebrow at him. "Jamie."

"What about her?"

"I saw the way you looked at her today."

"What do you mean?"

Dréa sighed. "I've been trying to ignore it, hoping it wasn't true, but it is."

"What is?"

"You're in love with her."

Duncan snorted. "What? That's crazy."

She crossed her arms over her chest. "I wish it was, but I saw it with my own eyes. All day long, you kept watching her. And if Nana hadn't interrupted you two by the fire …"

"There was nothing to interrupt. We were just talking."

"Duncan, I need you to be honest with me, okay. Life is too short to waste time with the wrong person."

An unease settled over him. "What are you saying?"

"Are you in love with Jamie?"

"No." He shook his head adamantly. "No. I'm ... I don't ..."

The look in her eyes and the almost imperceptible shake of her head told him she knew he wasn't being honest.

He stared out the hotel window into the parking lot below, unable to look her in the eye any longer. It was no use. He felt more for Jamie than he had admitted, especially to himself. Even Dréa saw it.

"I'm sorry, Dréa. I'm really confused right now." He ran his fingers through his hair.

"I know you are. I saw you go off by yourself for a while. Were you praying?"

"Yeah. I've been avoiding talking to God for a while now and everything sort of came to a head today." He paused to consider his words. "What happened between me and Jamie, it was a moment of weakness. I knew she wasn't the kind of woman you settle down with and marry. She wasn't a Christian, for one thing, and then I met you, and ... you were everything I wanted—the perfect Christian girl, passionate, driven, beautiful, good family. You checked off all the boxes."

Dréa's face lacked any emotion. "Nobody's perfect, Duncan. Not even me. And I don't want to be the girl you marry because I meet all the criteria of what you think a good Christian wife should be. I want someone completely and unconditionally in love with *me*, someone who wants to build a life with me. I was willing to overlook your night with Jamie and the aftermath it's brought into our relationship because I love you, and I thought you loved me too." Her chin quivered.

"Dréa." He stepped toward her, but she held a hand out to stop him.

"I won't settle for less than I deserve, and I deserve more than this, Duncan. So much more than the small part of your heart you're willing to give me. Because the rest of it doesn't belong to me, does it?"

Duncan shook his head sadly, realizing she was right.

Dréa straightened her back, took in a deep breath and let it out. She pulled Duncan's jacket back out of the closet, and handed it to him. "You need to go."

He reluctantly took the jacket. "I'm sorry."

"I know you are."

"I don't know what else to say."

"You don't have to say anything."

He stepped into her space, and she folded her arms across her chest again. "You are an amazing woman, Dréa. The best. And I pray you'll find the right man because God knows it's not me. I wish I'd figured all of this out sooner and not dragged you into it. I never meant to hurt you."

"I believe you. We all make choices in our lives, and we have to live with the consequences. Mine was saying yes to you." She twisted the engagement ring from her finger and held it out to him.

Duncan hung his head as he took it.

"I don't regret knowing you, Duncan. You're one of the good ones."

"I don't know about that." He felt like the lowest of the low.

"You are. And don't let anyone tell you differently."

"How can you say that after all of this?"

"Because I've known jerks in the past, and you're not one of them. You're kind and thoughtful and you want everyone around you to be happy. You were willing to move a thousand miles away from your baby for me."

Duncan pulled her in for a hug, which she stiffly returned. He kissed her cheek as he let go. "Thank you for loving me."

She wiped a tear away as she nodded. "I hope you and Jamie and the baby will be very happy together."

"Well, that's not going to happen since she's dating Max now."

Dréa gave him a pointed look. "That's nothing, Duncan. It's obvious she loves you too."

"I don't know."

"I do. And so does everyone else when you two are together. I just didn't want to see it."

He gave her a weak smile as he stepped outside the hotel room door.

"Goodbye, Duncan."

"Bye."

The door clicked behind him and a wave of sadness washed over him. Did that just happen? Did he and Dréa break up?

He shook his head as he walked the hallway, his mind turning to Jamie. His steps increased in speed on his way to the elevator, which closed and went down just before he reached it. With no patience to wait for it to return to his floor, he opted for the stairs and pulled out his phone as he raced the three flights to the lobby, texting Shannon as we went.

Duncan: Are you still at Aunt Paulie's?
Shannon: Yes. Why?
Duncan: Is Jamie there?
Shannon: Yep.
Duncan: Please keep her there. I'm on my way.

Chapter 37

Jamie wasn't sure so much laughter was good for the baby, as much as it was making her stomach hurt. She, Micah, Shannon, and Sophia were being entertained by Max's silly shenanigans around the bonfire.

"I'm serious. You have to stop, or I'm going to go into labor right now."

Max's eyes widened. "It's a little early for that. You aren't even showing yet."

Jamie frowned. "Yes, I am." She tugged her shirt, flattening it against her stomach to show the baby bump that had formed.

He held his hands up in defense then squinted at her belly. "I'm sorry. I see it now ... I think."

She punched him playfully in the arm.

He clamped his hand around her wrist and gently pulled her toward him, sliding his other arm around her back until she was tucked into his side.

Her stomach somersaulted at the flirtatious look he was giving her.

"You're cute when you're feisty," he whispered into her ear.

"I guess you bring out that side of me," she replied.

His lips brushed against her ear before pressing against her cheek. "Can we go somewhere more private to talk?"

Her stomach flipped again. "Okay."

He took her hand and led her into a darkened corner of the yard.

"I like you, Jamie." He wasted no time saying what was on his mind.

"I like you too, Max."

He squeezed her hand as he turned toward her. "What's happening here?"

"We like each other, and we enjoy spending time together."

"But is there more than that?"

"I don't know." Jamie shrugged. "I mean, can there be more? With the baby and everything?"

"I know it's a little complicated, but you're worth it, Jamie."

Nobody had ever said such a thing to her before, and it filled her with hope that maybe she could find happiness, that maybe she and the baby wouldn't be the third and fourth wheel to Duncan and Dréa's happy little marriage.

She was about to reply to him when he suddenly cupped her cheek with his free hand, leaned in, and pressed his lips to hers. The kiss was soft and tentative at first, but when she responded, he dropped her hand and slid his arms around her back, pulling her into him.

It was nice, and she experienced all the feelings and sensations that accompany a passionate kiss, but there was a little nagging thought in the back of her mind that he wasn't Duncan.

She pulled back at that thought and touched her lips with her fingertips.

"Was that okay?" Max asked.

"I wasn't expecting it, that's all."

He smirked. "I couldn't help myself."

Jamie smiled up at him then glanced toward the yard and was taken aback by the sight of Duncan standing not far away, his mouth agape. He shook his head and huffed, then spun and marched across the yard.

"Duncan!" She was torn as she looked back and forth between the two men.

"Go ahead," Max said.

She noticed Max's sad expression. "I just need to talk to him."

"I know. But we need to finish our talk too."

"We will. I'll be right back." She rushed across the lawn, following the path Duncan took, rounding the house as his car backed out of the driveway. "Duncan, wait!"

He made eye contact with her as he pressed the gas and squealed his tires.

Jamie stared after him, her mind spinning. She knew he wasn't happy about her relationship with Max, but his reaction was a little overdramatic.

"What was that all about?" Sophia was suddenly at her back.

"I have no idea."

"He didn't seem very happy." She moved to Jamie's side. "What did you do?"

"I think he saw Max kiss me."

Sophia laughed. "My brother is so hung up on you."

Jamie looked at Duncan's sister with surprise. "He's engaged to be married."

Sophia raised an eyebrow and pursed her lips.

"He's just upset about me starting a new relationship when I'm having his baby in a few months."

"Look, I know my brother, and he's got it bad for you."

Jamie blew out a deep breath. "Well, that's tough. He slept with me, went away to Denver, completely blew me off, and came home with a fiancée. I think I have the right to find someone who will make me happy too."

"Whoa there, girl. I'm on your side. I'm just telling it like I see it."

"He's so confusing."

"He's figuring all of this out right now. Trust me. He's got feelings for you."

Jamie huffed in frustration then looked at Sophia. "Can I ask you something?"

She shrugged. "Sure."

"Why don't you want Shannon to get her dress in New York?"

Sophia kicked at a stone in the driveway. "What do you mean? I said yes to that."

"I could tell you didn't want to. What aren't you saying about New York?"

"It's complicated."

Jamie pointed at her belly. "I think I know a little something about complicated."

"I don't work for Givenchy or DVF or any big-name designer," Sophia admitted. "I never have."

This was huge news. News Sophia should've shared with her family long ago. "So what have you been doing there for all these years?"

Sophia opened her mouth to answer.

"Hey, you two." Shannon joined them. "Was that Duncan squealing his tires?"

"He's jealous that Max kissed Jamie," Sophia blurted, seemingly happy for the interruption.

"Max kissed you?" Shannon's eyes sparkled.

Jamie nodded, distracted by Sophia's admission.

"Duncan saw," Sophia told Shannon. "Don't you think he's got it bad for Jamie?"

"He does."

"You guys, Duncan is engaged to be married. I told you, this is all about the pregnancy."

Sophia laid her hands on Jamie's shoulders and looked her in the eye. "You keep telling yourself that, sweetie."

Shannon laughed and headed back toward the house. "I'm going to find Micah so we can get out of here. I have a ton of editing to do tomorrow."

"And by editing, you mean making out, right?" Sophia said.

Shannon glanced over her shoulder and stuck out her tongue before letting out a tell-tale giggle.

"I need to talk to Max before we go." Jamie began to follow her but was stopped by Sophia's hand on her arm.

When Shannon was out of earshot, Sophia spoke with a lowered voice. "Please don't tell my family what I told you."

Jamie's brow furrowed. "I won't. But you should."

Max McGregor was everything Jamie was attracted to in a man—handsome, kind, great sense of humor—and when she walked into the house and spotted him on the couch, chatting with one of the cousins, shivers traveled up her spine at the thought of their kiss.

She liked him, that much was for sure. She liked the attention he gave her, the laughs they shared, the looks and touches, the flirtation. It was the beginning. It was new and exciting. And the fact that he was willing to overlook the pregnancy and get to know her in spite of her mistakes was a huge draw.

But whenever she thought about Duncan marrying Dréa, it ached deep down inside. His reaction to her relationship with Max both excited and infuriated her. She liked that it bothered him, but it wasn't his business who she dated. Once the baby was born, he would have someone in his life to help with baby duties. She wouldn't. Unless she took this chance to see where things went with Max.

Jamie took a seat next to him on the couch and leaned close. He reached over and wound his fingers through hers as he continued with his conversation. She sat quietly, enjoying being close to someone who cared about her and only her.

When his cousin departed, Max turned to her. "Did you talk to him?"

She shook her head. "He left too quickly."

"He doesn't want me dating you."

"Too bad." She was tired of Duncan telling her what to do—asking her to move to Denver, not wanting her to date Max, giving her mixed signals.

Max's eyebrows raised. "Does that mean you want to date me?"

"I want to take things slow, but I definitely want to get to know you better."

"Me too." He squeezed her hand and leaned close to her ear. "Does this mean I can kiss you again?"

Jamie gave him a coy look. "It does."

He squeezed his hand into a fist and pulled it into his side with a loud "Yes!"

She laughed, appreciating his silliness, as he leaned in and pressed a soft kiss to her lips.

Chapter 38

All for nothing. That's what this was. His relationship with Dréa was over. He didn't have Jamie. She was going to end up with his cousin, instead of where she belonged—with him and their baby. Why hadn't he figured all of this out sooner? Why hadn't he been honest with himself about how he felt about her? Why hadn't he just prayed for God's forgiveness and guidance sooner?

Seeing Max and Jamie kissing had sent adrenaline racing through his veins. His flight reflex had him rushing out of there as fast as his legs and his car would take him. If he'd stayed and talked to her at that moment, he would've said things he didn't mean. And with his engagement ending, what he really needed was a good night's sleep to clear his head. But that hadn't happened. He'd tossed and turned all night with the image of her lips on Max's.

But today was Jamie's checkup with the doctor, and he had a plan. He was going to tell her how he felt. He had to let her know he was single again and that he wanted her in his life. She and the baby. The three of them as a family. And then it would be up to her.

If she chose Max, it would kill him, but he would have to accept her decision, just as she had accepted his engagement to Dréa.

Duncan stared at his reflection in the mirror as he wiped away leftover shaving cream. He ran his fingers through his hair. What a mess he'd made of things.

Before leaving for the hospital, he kissed his mother and grandmother goodbye and headed off with their well-wishes and greetings to pass along to Jamie. He hadn't told anyone about the broken engagement yet. He needed Jamie to know first.

When he walked into the waiting room at the doctor's office, his heart sank at the sight of Max seated next to Jamie.

"Morning," Max greeted him.

Duncan took an open chair across from them. Crossing his arms and leaning back, he stared at Jamie with a straight face until she met his gaze.

They said nothing, so Max broke the awkward silence. "Hope it's okay I tagged along. Jamie said it was all right."

"Well then it must be okay," Duncan replied sarcastically, still staring at Jamie.

"Knock it off, Duncan," she said. "I didn't know if you were going to show up today after the way you took off last night."

"I'm the dad," he stated. "Me. Not him. This is about you, me, and the baby."

Jamie's eyes darted around to the other moms seated in the room. "You're making a scene, Duncan."

He got to his feet. "You want a scene? I'll give you a scene!"

"Duncan, sit down!" She gave him the look of death, which made him one-hundred percent positive she would be great at disciplining their kids. *Kids?* Why was he suddenly thinking about having more kids with her at a time like this?

"Maybe I should wait out here for you," Max said softly.

"Yeah, maybe you should," Duncan snapped.

Jamie looked at Max with affection, which pierced Duncan straight through the heart. "That might be best."

"No problem," Max replied.

"Jamie Linde," the nurse called out.

Jamie stood and walked away, ignoring Duncan.

"Hey, sorry, man," Max told him.

Duncan shook his head and followed Jamie into the exam room. The nurse took all of Jamie's measurements and left them to wait for the doctor. As soon as the door clicked shut, Jamie ripped into him.

"How could you do that? You humiliated me in front of all of those people in the waiting room, not to mention my boyfriend."

"Boyfriend?" His heart sank deeper than it already was. "He's your boyfriend now?"

"Yes, he is. Is that a problem?"

"No." *Yes!* He wanted to shout that word, but it wouldn't come.

"I don't know why you're being like this. You have a fiancée. Why can't I have some happiness too?"

He reached over and took her hand in his. "I want you to have all the happiness in this world, Jamie."

Her eyes met his, but before he could tell her about him and Dréa, the doctor walked into the room.

"How are we feeling today?" he asked.

"Feeling great," Jamie said.

"Eh," Duncan replied, knowing the question wasn't for him.

Jamie slipped her hand out of his grasp, which saddened him. He longed for that connection, any connection with her.

After all the routine questions and examination, the doctor said, "We're going to have you take the glucose test today, Jamie."

"I thought that was done a little later in pregnancy."

"Sometimes we do it sooner if there's a higher level of glucose in your urine, and that's what we've found."

"Should I be concerned?"

"Better to test you now to rule out gestational diabetes."

"Okay."

Duncan didn't like the sound of that, and Jamie began bouncing her knee and chewing on the corner of her lip.

When the doctor left, the nurse returned with a small bottle of orange liquid for Jamie to drink and informed her that she needed to go to the lab and have blood drawn one hour after drinking it. So, along with Max, they headed to the outpatient lab to wait. Together.

"How's everything with you, Duncan? We haven't talked much lately."

Duncan glanced at his cousin. "You've been busy." His gaze landed on Jamie.

"I'm sorry if you aren't happy Jamie and I are dating, but—"

"Yeah, I told you how I felt about that, but you aren't a very good listener."

Jamie's jaw dropped. "Duncan."

"He's my cousin, and you're carrying *my* baby."

"Shhh." Jamie glanced around the room. "Seriously? Could you embarrass me any more today?" She smiled politely at the people waiting nearby who were watching the three of them then turned to Duncan. "Max has been nothing but understanding about our past mistake."

Duncan took a deep breath in and looked her straight in the eye. "It wasn't a mistake."

Jamie's mouth fell open a little at his words. "I thought ..." Her lips pressed together, and he thought he saw tears in her eyes.

Was she happy that he'd said that? He pressed on. "I know it was wrong, the way it happened, but we're having this baby together, Jamie, and I can't seem to regret that."

He watched her until he got her attention again, wishing he could tell her how he really felt about her. He'd been so caught up in worrying about the kind of girl he thought he was supposed to marry, that he'd missed the one right in front of him.

The next hour was mostly quiet as they waited for Jamie's blood draw and parted ways. Max held the door of his car open for Jamie, then got in and drove off, taking Duncan's family away with him.

Chapter 39

"That was a little awkward, huh?" Max said as they drove toward Jamie's apartment.

"It was fine."

"Maybe we should've waited until after the baby's born to start dating."

"He isn't waiting until after the baby's born to get married, so we're not going to pause our life because he's uncomfortable."

He took her hand and squeezed.

She smiled, then watched out the window as they drove. Duncan was acting differently. The way he was looking at her, talking to her, touching her. He was less guarded than he'd been in recent weeks. And there was that moment in the doctor's office when it felt like he was going to tell her something, but they'd been interrupted.

Max pulled up to her place and left the engine running.

"Thanks for sticking around for my appointment today. I know you have to get back for work."

"I was happy to be there for you." He leaned over and pressed a quick kiss to her lips. "I'll call you tonight, okay?"

"Okay." She gave him a sweet smile then got out and waved goodbye as he drove away.

Jamie felt antsy and a little queasy as she went inside. She puttered around the house all afternoon and into the evening, straightening up her kitchen, putting dishes away, wiping the counter. It wasn't really dirty, but one of her pregnancy books said sometimes pregnant women had a desire to nest—to clean and prepare the home for the baby. It felt a little too soon for nesting, but it helped to distract her so she wouldn't think about the intensity in Duncan's eyes when he told her their night together wasn't a mistake.

He'd actually said those words.

All this time, she thought he regretted it. What had changed?

A knock pulled her from her thoughts, and she went to open the door. On the other side, she found Duncan taking up the entire space, one forearm against either side of the door frame.

"Duncan, what are you—"

Before she had a chance to finish her question, he stepped into her apartment, took her face in his hands, and pressed his lips against hers.

This had to be a dream. That's all she could think as his fingertips slid along the sides of her neck and into her hair, angling her head as he deepened the kiss. And she didn't fight him. She couldn't, even though her mind kept reminding her of two very important facts—she had a boyfriend, and he had a fiancée.

Her hands moved of their own accord, finding their way around his waist, gripping the back of his T-shirt. Her stomach flipped at the little growling sound he made when she brought herself as close to him as she could get.

She felt a fluttering in her belly, nothing like she had ever experienced with any guy she'd been with, and she realized it was the baby's movement. It came and went, and then it hit her hard. She pulled away from Duncan and dropped her hands to her belly.

He gripped her upper arms. "What is it?"

"The baby kicked. Hard."

Duncan's face lit up. "Are you serious?"

It kicked again. "Oh my gosh. That was really hard."

"What does it feel like?"

She took his hand and placed it on her belly, his throat moving as he swallowed. After the kiss they'd just shared, this touch felt intimate. He stared down at his hand, waiting, and then the baby kicked.

"Whoa!" Duncan's eyes shot to hers. "I felt that."

"You did?"

He laughed, and they both stood still, waiting for it to happen again.

"Come on, Coconut," Jamie urged. "Kick Daddy again."

When nothing happened, Duncan reached up with his free hand and touched her cheek.

"Duncan, what are you doing?" she whispered.

"I don't want you dating Max."

"You can't tell me what to do."

"It's not right. You're *my* family. Mine."

Her lips parted. She didn't know what to say to that, because it was what she wanted more than anything.

He rested his hands on her waist and leaned closer until their foreheads touched. "Jamie."

"Duncan, you can't do this to me. It's not fair."

"Break up with him."

"Why should I?"

"Because I don't want to share you and the baby with anyone."

She pulled back, her eyes narrowing. "But I have to share you with Dréa?"

He took her face in his hands once again. "Dréa and I broke up."

Her stomach somersaulted at his news, and goosebumps covered every inch of her body at the look he was giving her.

"I want *you*, Jamie. You and me and the baby. I want us to be a family."

This couldn't be happening. Could it? She felt suddenly lightheaded, and the room began to spin. She gripped his forearms just before everything went dark.

Chapter 40

Jamie's eyes opened to a dark room. She glanced around to get her bearings. There was an IV in her arm, the sound of beeping monitors, a dry erase board across the room with her name on it. In the chair to her left, Duncan was hunched over with a small blanket draped over half his body.

"Duncan," she whispered.

He stirred and jumped up from his seat, suddenly at her side. "Hey!" One hand smoothed over her head as he took her hand with his other. "You're awake."

"What happened?" she asked.

"You passed out."

Her hand shot to her belly. "The baby?"

"Safe and sound in there."

She let out a sigh of relief, tears prickling. "How long have I been here?"

"Overnight."

"Why did I pass out?" she asked.

"Your doctor said you were extremely dehydrated. You also failed the glucose test, which means you need to be tested further, so you may have gestational diabetes, which could've caused lightheadedness."

Immediately, she felt her heart rate rise at the thought of having to worry about that during pregnancy.

"It's okay." He squeezed her hand. "We'll get through this."

Her mind returned to her apartment, the moment before she'd blacked out. "Was I dreaming or did you tell me you're no longer getting married?"

"You weren't dreaming." His fingers softly brushed through her hair over and over.

"What happened?"

He shrugged his shoulders. "She dumped me."

"Why? I thought you two were so in love."

"Because she saw the truth before I did."

Jamie swallowed hard. "And what truth was that?"

His eyes met hers, and his fingers stopped moving. "That I'm in love with you."

She had imagined this differently. Not her in a hospital bed and him standing beside her, pushing her messy hair out of her face.

"Say something," he whispered.

The tears were back again, and she brushed them away. "Why am I crying so much lately? Maybe it's the pregnancy hormones."

"Maybe." He smiled sweetly.

The McGregor family chose that moment to enter the room, successfully interrupting a very important conversation.

"Jamie." Shannon was at her side, pushing Duncan out of the space, leaning in to hug her. "How are you feeling?"

"I don't know. I just woke up. I guess I was dehydrated, and I passed out. Duncan was with me when it happened."

"The baby?"

"The baby's fine."

Shannon's shoulders relaxed. "Thank God!"

The rest of the family took turns hugging her. Then Nana took her hand and Duncan's and squeezed. "God is watching over the three of you."

"Yes, he is," Duncan said.

Nana placed his hand atop Jamie's, and he gently took her hand in his, which sent chills up her arm. And when he smiled at her, an ache started deep inside her heart.

He and Dréa may have broken up, but the fact remained that he had blown her off because she wasn't good enough for him. He'd slept with her then went off to find the *right* kind of girl, and that still hurt.

And then there was Max. He was a good guy, and he had no problem with the girl she used to be. So for her, it wasn't as simple as breaking up with Max for Duncan, even though she wanted to be with him more than anything.

Before she could make any more life-altering decisions, they needed to talk. But right now, all she cared about was the safety of this child she was carrying inside her. That was the most important thing in her life at the moment.

"Let me help you." Duncan was at her bedside, crouched down, holding one of her socks in his hands.

She reached over and snatched it from him. "I am perfectly capable of dressing myself, Duncan." But it was too late. His hands were on her ankle, and she was sure he could see the goosebumps covering her skin at his touch.

He stared up at her and held his hand out until she caved and gave him the sock. He slipped it over her toes and tugged it unhurriedly over her foot, her ankle, her calf. His fingertips brushing against her skin warmed her all over. Especially when he finished and lingered there longer than necessary.

He held out his hand. "Other sock, please."

She swallowed hard and handed it over. "I'm not an invalid."

"What if you leaned over and got dizzy and passed out again? We don't know exactly what caused it. I'd rather help you than watch the color go out of your face again." His expression turned serious as he went silent for several long seconds. "Your body went completely limp in my arms. I thought I might lose you, Jamie. You *and* the baby."

"Duncan," she whispered.

He abandoned sock duty and wrapped his arms around behind her legs as he lay his head in her lap.

She ran her fingers through his hair, comforting him as best as she could. She couldn't imagine what that must've been like for him. "I'm okay, Duncan. I'm right here."

When he looked up at her, she was surprised to see tears in his eyes.

"Duncan." She gently touched his cheek, and his eyelids fell at her touch.

"Uh ... am I interrupting?"

Jamie glanced over her shoulder at Max, who stood in the doorway, staring at their interaction.

"No," Jamie replied, just as Duncan said, "Yes."

She looked down at him with her lips pressed together, giving him a warning glare.

Duncan smirked and finished helping with her sock then her shoes. He grabbed her bag, refusing to give it up when she reached for it. "I'll carry it out for you."

Jamie walked toward Max. "You didn't have to come all the way back today."

"When Shannon texted me this morning, I knew I had to come." He reached for her hand and wound his fingers through hers, guiding her out of the room and along the hallway.

She should've felt happy and comforted by the fact that Max was there, holding her hand, but she could feel Duncan's stare boring a hole in her back as they walked. She wanted to look back at him, but she forced herself to keep looking forward until they reached Max's car.

Max opened the passenger door for Jamie while Duncan opened a back door and placed her belongings on the seat.

"Thanks, Duncan," Jamie said over her shoulder.

He closed the back door and opened her passenger door a foot. "Can we talk later?"

"Of course." She was anxious to have a conversation with him since they kept getting interrupted.

"I'll call you."

"Okay."

"Are you sure you're okay?"

"Yes, stop fussing over me. I'm fine."

He frowned as Max got into the car.

"See ya, cuz," Max said.

"Get some rest, okay?" Duncan told Jamie.

He straightened and closed the door, his face no longer in her line of sight.

Jamie told herself not to look at Duncan as Max pulled out of the parking space, but she gave in at the last minute, and not surprisingly, he was staring at her through the windshield.

She gave him a little wave, and he held his hand up.

"I wish someone had called me sooner. I would've come back last night," Max told her.

"It's all right. I was in good hands." Now all she could think about were Duncan's hands on her.

"But you're really okay?"

"I have to go to my doctor if I feel the slightest bit off, but yeah, I'm fine. Severe dehydration, and I have to take another test because I failed the glucose test I took."

"I hope it's nothing serious. I don't want anything happening to you. I kinda like you."

She raised an eyebrow. "Is that so?"

"You know it is."

She smiled as she fought off the guilt about kissing Duncan last night.

By the time she arrived home, all she wanted was to sleep.

"Do you want me to stay?" Max said as Jamie lay down on her bed.

"I'm sorry I'm not better company. You drove all this way just to drive me home."

He leaned forward and placed a kiss on her forehead. "It was worth it."

She reached up and brushed a hair away from his brow. "You are the sweetest man, you know that?"

He gave her a sheepish grin. "I mean, I try."

She smiled up at him, then lowered her hand as she rolled onto her left side and snuggled into her pillow.

"I'm going to stay at Aunt Paulie's tonight. Can I see you tomorrow before I head back home?"

"You better."

"Okay. Get some rest."

She heard the faintest click as her door closed and then remembered nothing before the sound of her phone ringing who knows how many hours later. Her vision was blurry from sleep when she slapped her hand against it on her nightstand, answering before she had a chance to raise it to her ear.

"Hello? Hello?" Shannon's voice on the other end said.

"I'm here," she replied.

"Are you awake?"

Jamie pulled herself to sitting and leaned back against her pillows. "I am now."

"I'm so sorry. You need your rest. I'll call you later."

"Shannon, just tell me why you're calling."

Shannon cleared her throat. "I have some news."

"What news?" She had an idea she already knew.

"It's too good not to tell you in person. Can I come over?"

"I guess."

"On my way." Shannon hung up before Jamie had a chance to reply, and fifteen minutes later, she came knocking, carrying an armful of groceries.

"What's all this?"

"I brought healthy options. For you and the baby. I heard you might have gestational diabetes and these can only help."

"Did you empty your entire fridge before coming here?" Jamie watched in awe as Shannon pulled item after item from within the bags she brought.

"Pretty much."

"You know it hasn't been confirmed that that's what I have, right? I have to meet with my doctor in a couple days to take another test."

"Well, a little healthy eating can't hurt."

"True." She handed Shannon items from another bag, and Shannon went about putting them into the fridge and rearranging things for her. When she had finished, she turned and let out a deep breath. "Are you ready for my big news?"

"You and Micah picked a wedding date," Jamie guessed.

"Yes, we did, but that's not it."

"You picked a date? When?"

"June the tenth. The anniversary of our first date."

"Aww, that's so sweet."

"I know. I'm excited to start planning. I never would've imagined that God would bring him back into my life like this after all these years. I love him so much."

"Really? I couldn't tell." Jamie smirked.

Shannon's dreamy expression gave her away. "Anyway ... that wasn't it." She stepped forward and took hold of Jamie's hands.

Jamie was amused by the goofy look on her friend's face. "What is it?"

"Duncan and Dréa broke up!"

"Wow," Jamie replied with fake enthusiasm.

"Isn't this amazing?" She dropped Jamie's arms and clapped her hands together. "I mean, not that I didn't like her. She was a wonderful person ... but she wasn't you."

"Right."

"Why don't you sound more excited about this? Honestly, I thought this news might make you faint all over again, which is another reason I wanted to tell you in person."

"I already knew," Jamie admitted.

Shannon was silent for a beat, and her mouth fell open. "You *knew*? And you didn't tell me instantly?"

"He told me last night. And then I passed out."

This put Shannon into a fit of giggles. "So you did faint from this news."

"I'm glad you're so amused by this."

"So ..." Shannon stared silently, waiting for a response.

"So, what?"

"So, what did he say?"

"That it was because of me."

"I knew it!" Shannon pumped her fist in the air and began dancing around Jamie's kitchen.

"Your dance is a little premature, don't you think?"

She spun around, shimmying her hips back and forth. "Why would it be premature?"

"They *just* broke up, and I have a boyfriend."

"*Pfft!* You and Max have been dating for like a minute. You and Duncan ... you're having a baby together."

"So."

"It's *Duncan*, Jamie." She stopped dancing and gripped Jamie's shoulders. "*Duncan!*"

"Your point?"

"You want to be with him. And I know he loves you, Jamie. I just know it."

"I think he actually does." Jamie couldn't quite believe that herself. "But he hurt me. I wasn't good enough for him then, so why am I suddenly good enough for him now?"

"Because you've changed. Your faith has changed you. Duncan wanted someone who believes the way we do. That was why he couldn't be with you before."

"Well, it still hurts. It hurts that he blew me off. It hurts that he chose someone he thought was better than me. It hurts that he never tried to share his faith with me. And I'm not going to dump Max because Duncan is suddenly single."

"Isn't it better to end things now before you get too serious, rather than let him get more attached and hurt him more later?"

"Who says Max and I won't last?"

Shannon was silent again. "Come on, Jamie. Is Max who you really want to be with?"

"Maybe." She knew Shannon could see right through her.

"Okay, well, you keep telling yourself that. In the meantime, I'm going to pray for you, for all of you, that God would work everything out the way He wants. His plans are always best."

"Thank you."

"You're welcome." She glanced at the fridge. "Now, can I make you a nice healthy dinner?"

Jamie smiled at her health-conscious friend. "That would be amazing."

As Shannon prepared a delicious vegetable stir-fry, the girls chatted about their photography business and baby stuff. Shannon didn't press her about Duncan anymore that night, but he was stuck in Jamie's head. She couldn't shake the image of his eyes filled with tears at the hospital. And whenever she thought about the kiss they shared last night, her stomach did more flips than gymnast Simone Biles during her floor routine.

After sharing a nice dinner, Jamie hugged her friend at the door. "Thank you for everything, Shannon."

"Any time." Shannon glanced back over her shoulder as she walked out. "Think about what I said."

"I will." How could she not?

"Are you coming to the studio tomorrow?"

"I have to or I'll get behind on edits and album designs."

"You could work from home."

Jamie shook her head. "I need to get out of the apartment."

"Okay. See you tomorrow."

She returned to her bedroom once Shannon was gone and reclined against her headboard. She knew she shouldn't, but she kept replaying the kiss over and over in her mind. It wasn't just a fantasy. Duncan had kissed her again. Her mind replayed the conversation and stopped on the last thing he'd said to her that day.

I want us to be a family.

It was what she wanted more than anything, to be with him, to raise their baby together. It scared her that she might get everything she wanted so badly because it seemed too good to be true. She wanted to go to him right now and tell him she wanted him too. But they needed to have a serious talk before any of that could happen.

And she wasn't sure what to do about Max. He was the sweetest, kindest man, so willing to be there for her through her pregnancy with another man's child, and he'd never judged her, which was wonderful and refreshing.

But Duncan had. He had judged her based on her past and had gone looking for his future elsewhere instead of trying to help her change. He hadn't once asked her if she believed in Jesus or wanted to. If he had, maybe things would've been different from the start. Instead, he gave in to his attraction to her then found someone he saw as better. That wound still bled and wasn't easily overlooked.

Chapter 41

Duncan sat on the sun porch with a mug of steaming coffee, staring out at the back yard at nothing in particular. His mind was on Jamie, replaying the kiss they'd shared. He hadn't gone there with a plan to kiss her, but as soon as she opened the door, his longing for her had taken over. He needed her as close as he could get her, to feel her lips against his again after all those months. And it was so much better than he remembered.

But now things felt so up in the air. He'd told her how he felt. He'd put himself out there, and she hadn't responded as he'd hoped. He wanted her to dump his cousin and be with him. He wanted her to be his forever.

The quiet shuffle of Nana's slippers on the carpet caught his attention.

"Good morning, Nana."

"Morning, my dear boy." She stopped beside him and leaned down to kiss his cheek. "Did you sleep well?"

"Not really." He took a swig of the dark liquid.

"How is she?" Nana asked as she sat in her rocking chair.

"Who?" He played dumb.

"Jamie."

"Why don't you ask Max?" he snarled.

"You'll never win her with an attitude like that."

"What makes you think I want to win her?" He stared out into the yard again. Nana's silence drew his attention her way.

Her head was cocked to the side, and she stared at him disapprovingly.

"I'm sorry. You're right. I can't help it. It drives me crazy to see them together."

"Don't you think that's how she felt seeing you with Dréa?"

His head dropped forward. "I do now." He looked up at her. "I really blew it, didn't I?"

"An apology would go a long way."

"I told her I was sorry," he replied.

"For?"

"For blowing her off when I got to Denver."

"What else?"

His brow furrowed. "What do you mean?"

"Is that everything?"

"Yeah?"

Nana slowly rocked back and forth. "What about apologizing for taking her to bed?"

"Yeah." He thought about that for a moment. "Well, I guess I didn't apologize in so many words, but we talked about it, and we both took responsibility for that night."

"Okay, what about your engagement?"

"What about it?"

"Have you apologized for that?"

"To Dréa, you mean?"

"To Jamie."

He was confused. "Why would I apologize to Jamie?"

Nana sipped her tea as she rocked. "I'm going to let you think on that for a while. You get back to me when you figure it out."

"Nana, come on. Did she say something?"

"She didn't have to. I put myself in her shoes. Maybe you should try that."

Frustrated, Duncan stood and left the room, dumping the last third of his coffee down the drain and rinsing his cup, before heading to the bathroom to get cleaned up for the day. After a shower and a shave, he dressed and headed out with one destination in mind.

He'd spent every minute since he walked off that sun porch with thoughts of Jamie whirling around inside his head. He tried to do what his grandmother had encouraged him to, think about how Jamie must've felt when he left that morning, flew off to Denver, and never replied to a single one of her messages. But he'd already apologized for that. What else could there be?

She had liked him for a long time, just as he had liked her, he knew that much. If she had slept with him then blew him off and immediately started dating someone else, that would've hurt him for sure. Was that it? Was that what Nana meant? If so, he would make that right with her today. He didn't want anything unresolved between them.

And as far as Max, it was his own fault she was with him now, and if she decided to stay in that relationship, he would have to accept that. Though he was sure it would drive him mad to be around them.

Shannon had informed him that Jamie would be coming into the studio that day, so he headed straight there, hoping to steal her away to talk. He was disappointed to find Shannon alone at the studio when he arrived.

"Morning, D." Shannon strode across the room and welcomed him with a hug. "She's not here yet."

He attempted nonchalance. "What if I was here to see you?"

Shannon snorted. "Yeah, right."

He shrugged his shoulders. "Mom said you picked a wedding date."

Her face lit up. "June tenth."

"I thought you guys would run out and get married as fast as possible."

"We're doing this up right. I want the big wedding and all our family and friends and lots of flowers and music and amazing photos and—"

"I get it. I get it."

She laughed then sobered. "I spoke to Dréa."

His stomach dropped. "You did?"

"Yeah, I was the one who recommended she hire Maggie and Simon for wedding photography. She paid them a deposit, and she called me to ask if I thought she might be able to get a refund."

"Oh."

"Also … she asked how you were."

"What did you tell her?"

"I said you were sad but okay. I didn't want to tell her that you were madly in love with your baby mama." She grinned.

"Stop."

"I only speak the truth." She glanced toward the door then, and Duncan followed suit.

Standing outside the studio were Jamie and Max in an embrace. Max leaned in and kissed her cheek, and she waved as he walked away. Duncan's heart sank at the sight. He knew this wasn't going to turn out how he wanted, but he still needed to talk to her. He had to know where they stood once and for all. And then they could all move on.

"Hey." Jamie's voice was soft at the sight of him. "What are you doing here?"

"I came to make sure you were feeling okay today."

"I told you, I'm fine. You can stop worrying."

"Yeah, that's never going to happen."

The smile she gave him lit her up from within and gave him butterflies.

"Can we get a coffee and talk? I promise I won't take much time from your workday, but there are things that need to be said."

She pressed her lips together and nodded. "Let me put my stuff away."

Shannon gave him a thumbs-up as they walked out, and he held in a laugh.

Their walk to Starbucks was quiet yet comfortable with a little small talk along the way about the changing of the season and the cold snap that was to come that weekend.

Once inside, they sat together near the window. She was so beautiful with the sun shining through the glass behind her, her cheeks rosy and full from pregnancy, with a touch of color from swimming the other day.

"So … what did you want to talk about?" she asked, glancing sheepishly in his direction.

"I owe you an apology."

She looked at him expectantly.

"You know how sorry I am that I didn't call you after that night."

She nodded.

"I still feel really bad about that."

"It's fine, Duncan. Water under the bridge, as they say."

"Yes, but I never stopped to think about how hurt you must've been when I got engaged to Dréa so quickly."

"Well, it didn't feel good."

"I'm so sorry it all went down like that. I hope you can forgive me."

Disappointment crossed her face, and he reached across the table and took her hand.

"I want to be with you, Jamie. More than anything. Please, tell me we have a chance."

She stared down at her coffee cup before looking at him again, and he thought he saw sadness there. "Do you want to know what hurt the most, Duncan?" She glanced out the window. "I wasn't good enough for you, so you found someone who was."

"That's not—"

She slipped her hand from his grasp. "Don't deny it. I know you wanted someone who shared your faith, and I don't fault you for that. But I felt used, like all the other guys I had ever been with. And I never expected that from you. I never expected that night to happen in the first place, but I never thought you'd blow me off because I wasn't a Christian. I never thought you'd come home two months later with a fiancée, who was the epitome of the perfect Christian woman. I know that was the farthest thing from who I was and you wanted someone better, and it hurt that I wasn't enough for you. It still hurts."

"Jamie, I ..."

"And now, what, I'm supposed to drop Max and be with you, just like that? You think because your fiancée dumped you, I want to be your second choice?"

"That's not what this is."

"That's what it feels like. Max is a good man, and he has never judged me for my past. He accepted me and wanted to be part of my life, even though I'm having this baby. When I'm with him, I know I'm the one he wants to be with. But I've spent months sitting on the sidelines of Duncan and Dréa's great love story, and now I'm expected to just fall into your arms and pretend none of that ever happened?"

His mouth went dry, and he couldn't find the words to say.

After long moments of silence passed, she stood. "I need to get back."

He nodded, staring at the table in front of them.

She took a few steps then stopped. "Why didn't you ever share your faith with me, Duncan?"

He turned his head, their eyes meeting.

"We've known each other for four years. You could have at least invited me to church or something." She stood still as if awaiting his reply, and when he didn't speak, she turned on her heel and headed back to the studio.

His head fell forward into his hands as the door closed behind her and his hopes for a life with Jamie crumbled around him. He had hurt her more deeply than he'd known, and he didn't know what to do. She wasn't going to choose him. She was going to choose Max. And he didn't blame her.

"I'm sorry," he mumbled as a tear slipped down his cheek.

Chapter 42

"What are you doing?" Shannon marched across the kitchen and smacked Duncan across the back of the head.

"Hey!" he cried.

Mama and Nana both gasped.

"You've been moping around this place for the past five days."

"Mind your own business," he snapped.

"It's true," Nana said.

"You have," Mama added.

He gave them both a glare.

Shannon sat down across the table from him, and he could feel her stare, but avoided eye contact and poked at the grilled chicken Mama had made him for lunch.

"Fine. Don't talk to me. But you're making a big mistake."

"She made her choice. She doesn't want me. I'm letting her be happy with Max."

Shannon blew out a frustrated breath. "She doesn't really want Max, and she's not happy. She's been just about as mopey as you've been all week."

"Really?"

"Yes, but if you don't do something soon, I'm afraid you're going to lose your chance."

"What am I supposed to do?"

"Tell her how you feel."

"I did. I told her I wanted to be with her more than anything. But I hurt her. Deeply. I made her feel used, and she thinks I only chose her because Dréa ended things."

"Did you?"

"No! I love her. I love her so much." He raked his hands through his hair. "I can't sleep. I can't eat. I can't work. I'm going out of my mind over here."

When he looked at his sister, she was smiling ear to ear.

"Why are you smiling like that?"

"I wasn't a hundred percent sure this wasn't about Dréa, that maybe you were more hurt over losing her than you were letting on. But now I know I was right. You love Jamie, and that makes me so happy."

"Well, I'm glad you're happy because I'm not."

"So, get off your butt and do something about it." She stood and grabbed his arm. "Get up and go talk to her." She pulled until he was on his feet. "Tell her you're sorry." She turned him and pushed him toward the door.

"I apologized. What more can I say?"

"I don't know, but you have to find a way to make things right with her."

"What if it doesn't work? What if she still doesn't want to be with me?"

"If all else fails, grovel."

He laughed at his sister's pushiness and spun out of her grip, pulling her into a hug. "I love you, Shan."

"I love you too. And I want you to be happy. Both of you."

"I feel like I've already lost her. And I guess I have to be okay with that. For the baby."

Shannon gave him a tight squeeze before letting go. "Don't give up. Go talk to her."

"Okay. I will."

She looked up at him with a smile. "She's at the studio."

As Duncan approached the studio door, his palms sweated, nerves churned his stomach, and his heart raced in his chest. He'd spent the drive there thinking of all he wanted to say to her and how to show her he was serious about her, about them as a family.

She glanced up at the sound of the door chimes and stood. "Hi."

"Hi." He had a huge lump in his throat. "Can I talk to you?"

"Okay."

He felt a little lightheaded. "Can we take a walk? It's a nice day."

"All right." She grabbed her keys and went to the door, hanging a sign that read "Be Back Soon" and locking the door behind them.

They walked along in silence until Duncan reached his first destination—the baby boutique Jamie had stopped in front of the day she lost the coffee bet all those weeks ago.

"Let's go in." He motioned toward the door.

"What? We can't go in there. It's way too expensive. The only thing I can afford in there is a washcloth."

He chuckled. "Nothing's too expensive for our baby."

"This stuff is." Jamie motioned to her left then right as they entered the elegant store with high-end baby furniture and products throughout.

"Good morning," the saleswoman said.

"Good morning," Duncan replied.

"Hi." Jamie chewed her bottom lip.

"What can I help you with?" the woman asked.

"We would like to purchase *this*." Duncan pointed at the bassinet by the window.

Jamie's mouth fell open. "Duncan," she whispered.

"That one's beautiful. It's my favorite," the woman replied.

"I'm sorry," Jamie said. "He and I haven't had a chance to discuss this."

The woman looked back and forth between them.

"We'll take it." Duncan didn't hesitate.

The woman nodded and headed toward the rear of the shop.

"How did you know I liked that one?" Jamie asked.

"How do you think?"

Jamie rolled her eyes, and they both said "Shannon" at the same time and laughed.

He touched her arm. "I also saw you looking at it the first time we went to Starbucks together."

"Oh, right."

"I've been planning to buy it for you and the baby for a while now."

"You have?" A beautiful smile spread across her face.

Duncan stepped closer and took her face in his hands. "I would do anything to get you to smile at me like this."

She tilted her head to the side as a blush colored her cheeks.

"Your bassinet is ready to be loaded into your car," the saleswoman said.

"Great. Can I come back and pick it up later?" he asked.

"Of course." She smiled at them. "Is this your first child?"

"Yes," they both replied.

"What are you having?" she asked.

"We're having a—"

Duncan clamped his hand over Jamie's mouth before she got the word out. "We're waiting to find out."

"I see. Well, congratulations."

As they walked out, Jamie elbowed him in the ribs. "You know I wouldn't have told her, right?"

"It seemed like you were about to say it."

"I wouldn't do that to you."

They laughed, and it felt good, like they were back to normal.

He nodded eastward. "Come on. Let's go to the park."

They walked to the end of the street and settled in on a park bench facing the lake. Duncan lay his arm across the back of the bench, just out of reach of Jamie's shoulders, and looked over at her. His breath left his lungs at the beauty beside him.

The wind gently moved her hair as her full lips parted slightly and took in the fresh air around them. "I love it here," she said on an exhale.

"Me too." He fought himself from playing with a strand of her hair that had blown across his hand. Instead, he reached across her lap and took her hand in his. "There's so much I want to say. I hardly know where to start."

She squeezed his hand, which gave him the strength to continue.

"When I met Dréa, I was still so confused and feeling all kinds of shame and guilt about what had happened between us and how I had handled it. New relationships are fun and exciting, and that's all I was thinking about at the time. I was selfishly living in my own world, and I didn't consider how you might be feeling. And that makes me feel like the biggest loser on the planet. Especially after I learned about the baby, thinking about how you were alone and pregnant when you left town, and I didn't even know what you were going through."

"I should've told you," she said. "I shouldn't have taken off like that."

"You had every right. I was horrible to you. And worst of all, I didn't talk to God about any of this. I made myself believe Dréa was the one I was supposed to be with because I thought she was the right kind of girl. I thought God had brought her to me, but I never asked Him if He had. I fit her into this idea I had of the perfect wife. I made her into something she wasn't meant to be. I hurt her, and I hurt you, and I'm sorry for making such a mess of everything.

"But most of all, I'm sorry I made you feel used, Jamie. You have to know that is the last thing I ever wanted. That night with you was unexpected and ... amazing, but it went against all I knew to be right. I was brought up to believe you marry a good Christian woman, and even though what I felt for you was so strong, I thought it was wrong to want to be with an unbeliever. But I shouldn't have pulled away from you like that. I should have told you how much I cared about you. I should have done everything in my power to introduce you to Jesus rather than leave you by the wayside.

"I am so sorry, Jamie. So sorry. For everything."

A tear slid down her cheek. "Thank you. I really needed to hear that."

He let his arm surround her shoulders and brought their linked hands to his lips, pressing a soft kiss to the back of her hand. "I hope you can find it in your heart to forgive me."

"I do forgive you. And I want us to move forward and be the best parents we can be."

"Me too." He let go of her hand but kept his arm around her shoulders, savoring her warmth against his side. Oh, how he wanted to take her in his arms and kiss her, but he couldn't. "I want you to know I won't get in your way with Max. I'll be supportive instead of the jerk I've been lately. I just—"

"Duncan."

"No, I need to say this. As much as I want us to be together, I can't expect you to walk away from a good man like my cousin. He will treat you well, and he's a better man than I was to you."

Jamie's hand was suddenly over his mouth. "Will you stop talking, please."

His eyebrows lifted in amusement, and he nodded, his lips brushing against her palm.

She removed her hand and looked him in the eye. "I ended things with Max."

"You did?" His heart stuttered in his chest.

She nodded slowly, playing coy.

"What does this mean?" Could he dare to hope?

Jamie turned her body into his and rested her hand on his chest as she leaned closer. "I think you know what it means."

"I think I do, but I need you to say it."

"I don't want to be with Max. I want to be with you."

That was all he needed to hear before his lips were on hers, his arms around her, bringing her closer. Her fingers slid into his hair, her mouth responding to his. Was this really happening? It felt too good to be true.

"Get a room!" a passerby called out.

They pulled apart and laughed as Jamie rested her head against his shoulder.

It was a perfect moment. Jamie in his arms, the soft breeze off the lake, sitting in a place they both loved. He reached down and lifted her chin to bring her gaze to his.

"You *are* enough, Jamie Linde. More than enough. You are who I want to be with. You and our baby. You're everything."

She grinned up at him.

"I love you." Saying those words to Jamie came so naturally.

Another tear slid down her cheek. "I love you too."

His stomach flipped at her admission, and he brushed his thumb softly against her cheek, wiping away the wetness there. "Will you marry me?"

Her lips fell open. "What?"

"You heard me."

She sat up and stared at him, wide-eyed. "Are you serious right now?"

One side of his mouth lifted. "You're the one."

Her lips slowly spread into a smile. "Yes," she whispered. "Yes." A little louder. "YES!" She threw her arms around him and was in his lap in two seconds flat.

He wrapped his arms around her back and held her tightly against him, and they stayed in their embrace for long minutes, just holding each other.

"I can't believe this is happening," Jamie finally said.

Duncan pulled back. "Well, believe it." He brushed his lips against her cheek, along her jawline, and nipped at her ear, eliciting a shiver and a soft moan. He squeezed his arms tighter around her. "Mmm. Promise you'll make that sound every day for the rest of our lives."

She giggled as he nuzzled her neck.

"I say we go to the courthouse right now and get the marriage license," he whispered.

"Oh my gosh," she chuckled and pushed him away. "We got engaged like two seconds ago. We have to pick a date."

He kissed her neck. "As soon as possible."

Jamie laughed as she extracted herself from his arms and stood.

He pouted up at her.

She held out her hand to him. "Come on, Romeo. I can't leave the studio closed all day."

"Fine." He reluctantly stood and took her hands in his, leaning down to kiss her lips once more. "But I want us married before the baby comes."

Jamie was beaming. "So do I."

Chapter 43

The whole thing felt surreal. Jamie wasn't sure any of it was actually happening. Maybe it was all a dream brought on by her crazy pregnancy hormones. But when she squeezed, his hand was there within her grasp. And when she looked to her side, he was smiling down at her with love in his eyes.

They walked the street to the studio, unable to stop touching and kissing along the way. She loved the warmth and security of holding Duncan's hand, knowing they were together now. She gripped his arm with her other hand to bring herself closer and glanced up at him. The adoration she saw there made her heart flutter.

When they reached the studio, the sign in the window read "Open," which meant Shannon was back from her lunch.

Duncan stopped before the door and tapped his bottom lip with his index finger.

"What is this? Passage to get inside my own building?" Jamie asked.

"Absolutely."

She happily obliged, leaning in to kiss him.

Shannon stared at them dumbfounded when they entered hand in hand. "What is happening right now? Are you two …?"

"Getting married?" Duncan shrugged his shoulders. "Yeah, we are."

"What? You're engaged?" Shannon jumped up from her chair and raced across the room, throwing her arms around both of them. She abruptly pulled back, looking at her brother with one eyebrow raised. "Is this for real? Because you've been throwing a lot of marriage proposals around lately."

"Very funny." He gave her a friendly smack on the arm and looked at Jamie. "This is the only one that matters."

Shannon clasped her fingers. "I'm so happy I kicked your butt this morning."

"What's this?" Jamie asked.

"She may have given me a little nudge to come here and get my girl."

Jamie smiled at him—the man she loved, the father of her child, her future husband.

"I was actually sitting here at my desk praying for this very thing to happen," Shannon said.

Duncan smirked. "No, you weren't."

"I absolutely was. And that is the fastest any of my prayers have ever been answered."

They all laughed, and the two of them shared their story with Shannon.

"You got her the bassinet? That's so sweet, Duncan."

He grinned. "It was pretty sweet, wasn't it?"

Jamie slid her arms around his waist and snuggled into his side. "The sweetest."

He kissed the top of her head.

"I don't know if I can work today," Jamie said. "I'm too distracted."

"I'm glad you said that because we have some people to tell before the news starts spreading." Duncan eyed his sister.

Shannon gaped at him. "You think I'm not capable of keeping a secret? I'll have you know that I am the best secret-keeper on the planet. Have I told you if you're having a boy or a girl yet? No, I have not. And I promise I won't tell anyone. Well, except Micah. But I will let you tell the family."

"We would appreciate that," he replied.

Jamie finished a few last-minute tasks and gathered her things, while Duncan went to get his car and pick up the bassinet. When he returned, she joined him at his car and leaned back against the passenger door, blocking him from opening it for her.

"Thank you for the bassinet. It's beautiful." Jamie hoped her smile showed him how much she loved this gift. "I wonder if I'm the first woman to get a bassinet in place of an engagement ring."

Duncan groaned as he tilted his head back. "I'm sorry I don't have a ring yet. I didn't exactly plan to propose."

"I was teasing, Duncan."

"I planned to tell you how I felt and apologize, but to support your relationship with Max. I didn't expect you to be available, and I had to snatch you up before I lost you for good." He pressed his palms flat against the car, one on each side of her head, and leaned closer until his nose brushed hers. "And now you're mine. Forever." His warm breath softly caressed her mouth. "Engagement ring to come." He closed the distance, kissing her firmly, and a delicious shiver ran through her body. She was thoroughly enjoying having unlimited access to his lips.

"Duncan?" she whispered between kisses.

"Hmm?" He didn't stop.

"Can I please tell you what we're having?"

He pulled back abruptly. "What? No!"

"Why not? I want you to know. I want you to celebrate with me and shop with me for baby stuff, and I can't do that right now because if I buy a certain color then you'll know. I'm tired of buying neutrals. There are cute baby clothes that are one color or the other." She gave him her best pout, and he looked like he might actually cave. "Pleeease."

"Okay."

"Really?"

"But not yet," he quickly added.

Her brow furrowed. "When?"

"I'll tell you what. After we get married, you can tell me."

"Like a wedding present?"

"I don't want to know what I'm getting as a wedding present."

She nodded toward the back of his vehicle. "You gave me the bassinet."

"That was more for the baby."

"I'm fine with it being my wedding gift."

He smirked. "So, you get the expensive bassinet, and I get one word."

"But it's a really good word. You'll like it."

He grinned at her. "You want to say it so bad right now, don't you?"

"Yes!"

"Well, you can't. Not until we're husband and wife."

Jamie rolled her eyes. "Fine. And when will that be?"

"Tomorrow?" Duncan raised an eyebrow in question.

She ran her fingers up his chest and over his shoulders, burying them in the hair at the nape of his neck. "Not soon enough for me."

Duncan leaned his forehead against hers. "Me neither."

He wrapped her up in his arms and pulled her body flush against his. Just as he pressed his lips to hers, he jerked back. "Whoa! The baby kicked me!"

Jamie cracked up laughing. "I felt it. Coconut wants all the attention."

Duncan dropped to his knees in front of her and held his hands on her belly, waiting. He looked up at her when nothing happened. "Think it will happen again?"

"I don't—" *Kick!*

The two of them laughed together as the baby continued to kick.

Duncan pressed a soft kiss to her belly and whispered, "Daddy loves you, Coco."

Jamie snickered at that. "We're not naming the baby Coco. What if it's a boy?"

"A boy could be named Coco."

"I don't think so."

"*Is* it a boy?"

Jamie shrugged. "I'm not telling. We're not married yet."

He stood and wrapped his arms around her. "Now, where were we before we were so wonderfully interrupted?"

Jamie raised on her toes and brushed her lips against his. "Right about here."

Chapter 44

One month later, as the late afternoon sun bounced off the colorful fall leaves in Aunt Pauline's yard, Duncan stood under an arbor of flowers beneath one of the giant oak trees, waiting for his bride to emerge from the house. The last time Duncan had stood on this lawn before family and friends, he had been engaged to another, and now he was marrying the only woman he had ever really wanted.

It felt crazy how quickly everything came together. Some might say they were moving too fast, but they knew it was right. They had both known it from the night they spent together. It had just taken Duncan a little bit longer to figure it out and let God show him how wrong he had been.

The music shifted as first Sophia and then Shannon came out of the house. Beside Duncan stood his father—his best man—and Micah. Duncan watched his sisters walk the aisle, each of them reaching out and squeezing his arm as they moved into position.

Then the music changed again, and Jamie stepped from within.

She looked beautiful. Her hair was colored a soft shade of pink, and her dress was a pale blue with sheer sleeves over her shoulders and embroidery and beads covering every inch, but he only saw her eyes. Those beautiful brown eyes now looked at him with more love than he deserved.

The ceremony was brief, the vows short and sweet and not without a few tears.

"I now pronounce you husband and wife," the pastor declared. "You may kiss the bride."

"Gladly," Duncan said, hearing a few chuckles from their guests.

Jamie smiled at him, and he was struck by the happiness radiating from her. She was so beautiful, and she was all his. He took her in his arms and brought her close, kissing her for the first time as his wife.

The guests applauded, then whooped and cheered loudly when the kiss went on a little longer than was traditional.

Jamie pulled away first, smiling demurely, and he loved the soft, pink blush of her cheeks.

Duncan took her hand to head down the aisle, but she leaned close to his ear.

"Do you want to know what we're having?" she whispered.

His wide eyes darted to hers. "Now?"

"We're husband and wife."

A smile spread across his face. "Okay." For the past few weeks, he'd been looking forward to this with great anticipation.

Jamie gave him a coy smile. "Do you like my hair?"

His eyebrows pinched together. "You know I like whatever you do with your hair."

"Do you like the color?"

Her meaning became clear as she pointed to her newly pink hair.

His mouth dropped open. "A girl?" he whispered.

She nodded enthusiastically. "A girl."

He grabbed hold of her and hugged tightly before letting go to raise his arms in the air for all the guests to see. "We're having a girl!"

The yard filled with applause, and they received many congratulations as they moved down the aisle with their fingers wound together, greeting each of their guests with hugs and kisses as they started their life together.

Epilogue

Four years later

"Daddy, pwease tell me the story of you and Mommy again." Duncan tapped his daughter's little button nose. "Haven't you heard it too many times already?" he teased.

"No," she pouted.

"Okay, but then it's sleepy time."

That seemed to appease her.

"Once upon an April night, Mommy and Daddy fell in love, but we were very different people. Daddy believed in Jesus, but Mommy didn't, which made Daddy sad." He stuck out his lower lip, and she imitated him. "Then Mommy went away for a while to stay with Grandpa and Grandma Linde, and they told her all about Jesus, and she asked Him to come into her heart."

She clapped her hands and looked over at Jamie. "Yay, Mommy!"

Duncan clapped along and smiled at his wife before continuing. "Then Daddy and Mommy saw each other again, and we loved each other very much, so we got married, and God blessed us with a beautiful baby girl named Eloise."

"Just like Mommy," she said with a smile.

"That's right, like Mommy's middle name. And Eloise grew from a tiny baby into a sweet little girl ... who goes to bed when her parents tell her to." He tapped her nose again, and she giggled. "And we all lived happily ever after."

She clapped her tiny hands. "Again, again."

Jamie walked over from where she'd been standing in the doorway and knelt on the opposite side of the bed from Duncan. "Ellie, did you know you were also named after Daddy's grandma, Irene?"

She nodded. "Nana."

"That's right. Nana's name was Irene. That's where your middle name comes from. Do you remember Nana?"

Ellie shook her head.

"She was a very special lady, who lived to be one-hundred years old." Jamie smiled at Duncan.

Their daughter's eyes widened. "That's old."

They chuckled. "She had a good, long life and now she's with Jesus in Heaven."

"Can I see her someday in Heaven too?"

"Yes, you can." Jamie leaned close and brushed her nose back and forth against her daughter's then planted a soft kiss on the tip. "But right now, my sweet, you need to go to sleep."

"Nooo!"

"Yes," Jamie said.

Ellie immediately looked at her daddy. At nearly four, she was a master manipulator, and she knew how powerless Daddy was to her adorable pout.

"Bedtime, Eloise," Duncan said firmly. "The sooner you go to sleep, the sooner morning will get here. And you know what tomorrow is, don't you?"

"Fanksgiving at Nonni and Poppi's!" She bounced her arms up and down against the bed and kicked her little feet with excitement.

Duncan and Jamie chuckled.

"Thanksgiving, that's right," Duncan replied as he leaned in and kissed her forehead. "Sweet dreams, Ellie Bean."

Ellie closed her eyes and snuggled into her pillow as Jamie carefully tucked the blanket up under her arms and gently smoothed her perfect auburn curls back from her face.

They walked quietly to the door and closed it softly behind them.

Jamie headed toward their room, reaching back for her husband's hand. He tugged her back against him, resting his lips against the side of her neck.

"Don't you think it's about time for another one of those?"

"Soon." They'd been mentioning it more and more in the past few months, but Jamie wasn't sure she was quite ready yet. Ellie was a handful at times, and with the growth of the photography studio, it wasn't a decision to take lightly.

He squeezed her hips as he nipped at her ear. "We probably need some practice anyway."

She glanced back over her shoulder at him. "Is that so?"

"Absolutely. In fact, I think it's a priority."

Jamie laughed as she turned to face him, running the tips of her fingers along his jaw to his neck, then down over his broad chest, stopping just above his belly button.

His chest rose and fell, and the look in his eyes told her everything she needed to know.

"I love you," he whispered.

"I love you too." They leaned in at the same time, meeting in the middle in a slow, intoxicating kiss.

She pulled back for air and reached for his hand, her fingers winding with his. "Come on, baby, let's go fall in love all over again."

Acknowledgments

Thank you so much for reading Duncan and Jamie's story. So many of you have been waiting patiently for over a year for this, and it means so much to me that you've been so excited about this one.

This wasn't an easy book to write. The subject is one that can touch a nerve, but what I wanted most was to show one woman's perspective as she goes through the myriad of emotions surrounding this unexpected pregnancy, trying to figure out what to do that is best for her. And I pray I did her story justice.

Huge thanks go out to Anita and Rachel, my critique girls. They read through this only weeks before it was due because sickness put me behind schedule, and I could not have finished this book without them. Their input is always the best, and the book you've just read was made better because of them.

I am so blessed to have an awesome reader group on Facebook, A Work in Progress, who were super excited about this release, and my wonderful launch team, who help to spread the word about all my books.

And thanks to my husband for his support and love and encouragement. The editing schedule didn't go as planned this time around because of sickness and throwing my back out. I was in pain at times, and he shuffled his schedule to allow me time to work and time to heal. He's the best!

I'm excited to continue this series with Sophia's book next.
Stay tuned!

Happy reading, friends!
Krista

Made in the USA
Monee, IL
10 July 2020